THE LAUGHING LORD

"You are not made for subterfuge," Damien said. "Every feeling you have is reflected too clearly in those great, green eyes of yours."

Ariane had to compare herself to the victim of a cobra. The cobra did not attack its prey directly, but instead performed a mesmerizing dance. Like that prey, Ariane, her senses assaulted by the velvety warmth of Damien's eyes, had no thought of flight as he brought his lips down on hers.

His lips seared her, his touch lighting an irresistible fire within her. Only when he set her free did she see the triumphant smile on those lips and, as she fled, hear Damien's deep, amused chuckle.

She was merely a joke to him, was she? An amusing plaything? Well, she would see who would laugh last. . . .

Emma Lange is a graduate of the University of California at Berkeley, where she studied European history. She and her husband live in the Midwest and pursue, as they are able, interests in traveling and in sailing.

Emma Lange
Brighton Intrigue

A SIGNET BOOK

NEW AMERICAN LIBRARY

NAL BOOKS ARE AVAILABLE AT QUANTITY DISCOUNTS WHEN
USED TO PROMOTE PRODUCTS OR SERVICES. FOR INFORMATION
PLEASE WRITE TO PREMIUM MARKETING DIVISION, NEW AMERI-
CAN LIBRARY, 1633 BROADWAY, NEW YORK, NEW YORK 10019.

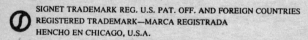

SIGNET TRADEMARK REG. U.S. PAT. OFF. AND FOREIGN COUNTRIES
REGISTERED TRADEMARK—MARCA REGISTRADA
HENCHO EN CHICAGO, U.S.A.

SIGNET, SIGNET CLASSIC, MENTOR, ONYX, PLUME,
MERIDIAN and NAL BOOKS are published by NAL PENGUIN
INC., 1633 Broadway, New York, New York 10019

First Printing, January, 1989

1 2 3 4 5 6 7 8 9

PRINTED IN THE UNITED STATES OF AMERICA

1

Mavis Barnes stared avidly across the smoky taproom, her hands on her ample hips. "You've the luck, 'Etty! Gettin' to wait on a fine-lookin' cove like 'im. One proper look from 'is black eyes, and I'd pay for 'is ale meself!"

"Forget 'is eyes, Mavis!" Her sister, Hetty, responded with a low, throaty laugh. "It's 'is breeches what caught my eye. Skintight they is, and I can tell you 'e don't need no paddin'."

"Here, Mavis, 'Etty! Get on with yer work. 'E's not interested in you gels."

"All right, all right, I'm goin'!" Mavis tossed her head. "But you can't blame a girl for lookin' at a gentleman what looks like that, John."

Shaking his head, John Morton, owner of the Mermaid tavern watched as Mavis, her hips swaying outrageously, made her way to a table suspiciously close to the gentleman in question, while Hetty, not to be undone, leaned so far forward to serve her next customer that her loose blouse came close to spilling its contents.

It did not surprise John that their efforts to attract the man's attention proved fruitless. Though dressed in a dark, plain jacket and breeches, it was obvious from the man's bearing that he was no rough workman and equally obvious—to John at least—that he would have little interest in the blousy barmaids of a simple fisherman's tavern.

What the gentleman was doing at the Mermaid at all was the question. Lynchurch was a remote fishing village in Kent. At the end of the road, it was rare for the 'Maid, as the locals called their only tavern, to be patronized by someone merely passing through. The only strangers were generally one or another species of law officers come to ferret out those whose cargoes consisted of more than fish.

But no revenue officer John had ever seen possessed the fine, honed lineaments and features this man did. Strikingly handsome, he had rendered Mavis and Hetty, girls who had had some experience of men, incapable of noticing anything but the cut of his breeches and his liquid black eyes.

John, not susceptible to the man's masculine charms, had been struck by the way those eyes, though veiled by half-closed lids, had kept a keen watch on the other patrons. He noted as well that, although the stranger lounged comfortably in his chair, he had chosen a seat in the corner and placed his back to the wall.

John's study of the stranger was interrupted when the door opened, letting in the tangy September breeze and a slender boy with a battered hat pulled low on his face. John cocked his broad head. Whatever did this mean? Here was another stranger.

But the two were not connected, John guessed as he watched the stranger's eyes flick disinterestedly over the lad. Certainly they were not of the same station. The boy's baggy and patched clothing attested to that.

Hiding a smile, John watched the boy saunter, or try to saunter, to the bar. He'd obviously not been in many a taproom, and John guessed he was in the Mermaid on a dare. He was likely one of Bessie Renfrew's nephews. John had heard she had three visiting, and had been challenged by his cousins to order an ale.

Unconsciously John winced. The lad had chosen to slide in beside Deke Mulligan, who, being in his cups, was in a fouler mood than usual.

"I'll 'ave an ale, sir," the boy said from beneath his hat. His gruff voice had a breathless quality that revealed him to be younger than John had at first guessed. Out of the corner of his eye, John watched the boy take a long draft of the bitter brew he'd ordered. When he coughed, John turned away to swallow his chuckle.

Having expected the boy to leave after he'd had his taste, John was surprised to find himself beckoned by the youngster.

"I don't see Jack Combs 'ere tonight, sir," the lad said in his gruff voice. "Do you expect him later?"

Several pairs of eyes swung around to fix on the lad, among them Deke Mulligan's small, red ones. Before John could forestall him, Deke demanded in a belligerent slur, "And who're you to be askin' after Jack?"

Though young, the boy did not lack for pride. "It's none of yer business who I am," he retorted unwisely.

Deke's eyes narrowed. "Is 'at so? Well, what if I make it my business?" he challenged, lifting his hand to cuff the boy.

"I wouldn't do that, if I were you." The words were said almost indifferently, but Deke's hand stopped short.

John looked in some surprise at the stranger. He'd have sworn the man was still in his seat only the instant before.

"The lad's too young to mean any trouble. He can come along with me, and no harm's done."

Deke did not look well-pleased to lose a whipping boy, but John was not surprised that he did no more than mutter his objection in an undertone. The stranger's height, now that he was standing, was impressive, and even Deke's bleary eyes could be counted on to see that his lean, sinewy body indicated a man able to acquit himself handily. John thought he would be very quick and very effective, if he had to be.

For his part, the boy jumped with surprise to find his arm in the stranger's authoritative grasp, but the man had him out the door before he could gather his wits to protest. It was not until the taproom door closed behind them that he cried fiercely, though still hoarsely, "Let me go!"

The lad wiggled frantically to free himself, but the stranger paid no heed as he marched him the few steps from the tavern to Lynchurch's only inn, through its low entry way, up its narrow stairs, and down a hallway to the last door.

"No! No!" the boy insisted, pushing mightily against the gentleman's unyielding arm.

His answer was to be thrust through the door.

As the gentleman closed it behind him with one hand, he

reached out casually with the other to tip the lad's battered hat from his head.

Two things happened simultaneously then. A wealth of crisp, black curls tumbled down to the lad's shoulders, and he, or she, as the young person was now revealed to be, exclaimed indignantly, "No! Don't!"

"Who are you?" the stranger demanded, unmoved. He was leaning against the door, his arms crossed over his chest, his black eyes expressionless. His seemingly negligent pose, as the girl saw at once, effectively eliminated any possibility of escape.

"You have no right to bring me here," she cried, furious beyond caution over the position in which she found herself. The moment she'd spoken, she knew she'd erred. The man's unwavering black eyes widened slightly, telling her he'd remarked her slip.

Thoroughly unsure of what to do or say now she had revealed too much, she sought refuge in the act of retrieving her hat.

His expression unreadable, the man watched the girl's clear brow furrow as she tried to think of a plausible explanation for why she, a girl of polite speech, had been caught frequenting a fisherman's tavern dressed as a boy.

As she was above-average height for a girl and slender, he'd not guessed her true gender until he'd observed in passing how nicely rounded was the seat of her pants. A quick scrutiny of her mouth, the only feature visible beneath her hat, had confirmed his suspicion. Her heart-shaped lips were entirely too soft to belong to a boy.

When the girl straightened, her hat in hand, she avoided the man's eyes. Trying to think what to do, she worried her generous lower lip with small white teeth.

Seeing the gesture, the man's eyes narrowed, and he studied her profile more closely. "Perhaps we should begin again," he said so suddenly she started and swung around. "My lodgings are humble, but I've some brandy. Sit down and I'll pour some."

"I beg your pardon," the girl exclaimed, clearly taken aback by the suggestion.

"You only drink ale?" The man smiled. Unaware she

did so, the girl blinked. His smile had been brief, a mere flashing of his strong white teeth, but it had transformed his hard, dangerous face into one which radiated an irresistible charm.

"No?" he continued smoothly when she said nothing. "Then, I shall have some while you make yourself comfortable."

He held out the room's only chair. It was clear from his tone that he expected obedience, but the girl hesitated as her glance slid to the door. To her dismay the key was no longer in the lock.

When she darted an anxious look at the stranger, he impassively patted his pocket and again gestured to the chair. Left with no choice, she sat down stiffly on the edge of it.

Her heart beating rapidly, she watched the man remove a bottle and glass from his portmanteau before he returned to sit on the end of his bed his knees only a few inches from hers.

The girl quelled a desire to push her chair back. He was extremely close, but there was no room behind her. She straightened her shoulders and with an effort dragged her gaze up to meet the man's. "I do appreciate the assistance you gave me with the man in the tavern. I really do, but I've family waiting for me and I really must be going. I only went to the 'Maid on a lark, you see, and now I realize how silly I was and have learned my lesson."

The man's mouth twitched, and despite her precarious situation, the girl's entire attention was caught by the lights dancing in his dark eyes. "A nice effort," he approved. "And I do hope you have learned your lesson. Masquerading as a boy in the 'Maid was a dangerously foolish thing to do, no matter your reasons."

The girl's thick lashes lifted, allowing the man to see clearly she had, as he had thought she would, eyes the color of emeralds. That she did not much care for being corrected, he could also see.

"I said I had learned my lesson," she told him, her pointed little chin lifting. "You don't need to belabor the issue. And now I wish you to unlock the door."

Once again the man's mouth quirked, this time in response to the girl's spirit. Most young girls of similar background would have reacted to finding themselves locked in a room with a stranger by swooning at the very least.

That she was a great deal more beautiful than most young girls of any background was true as well. A more speculative expression on his face, the man dispassionately inventoried her assets.

First, she carried herself exceedingly well. Her head held comfortably high on her slender neck, she looked every inch the lady, though she'd made not the least effort to pat her hair into place.

A glossy cloud of black curls, her hair contrasted dramatically with her creamy, rose-tinted complexion and made a glorious frame for her vivid face, each feature of which seemed perfectly formed.

The man knew ladies who had tried all their wiles to achieve the graceful arch that was natural to her eyebrows. No paints had been needed to make her slim nose appear nicely straight, nor did her soft pink mouth require creams to tint it so delectable a color. Still, it was her eyes, framed by thick, curly lashes, that held his attention. It was they that made her face come alive with their rich, pure color. Amazingly expressive, they revealed her feelings clearly, and at that moment were regarding him with an appealing mixture of dismay and defiance.

"I can't unlock the door just yet, I'm afraid," he replied to that look with a faint smile. "First you must tell me the real reason you went to the Mermaid this evening, and why you asked for Jack Combs. Did it have something to do with Colin Bennington by any chance?"

"However did you know?" she gasped incredulously.

"When your profile reminded me of his, I recalled that he told me once that he had a sister with his color hair but eyes as green as his are brown. You are his sister, are you not?"

The girl nodded slowly, her eyes now very wide. "How is it that you know Colin?" she asked. There was no mistaking the wariness in her tone, and the man mentally saluted her for it.

"I work for the same man as does Colin. I went to the 'Maid to see—as did you, I think—whether Jack Combs had returned from across the Channel; and if he had, why Colin did not come with him."

For a long moment the girl stared at him, her direct gaze searching him in a way he had seldom suffered. Understanding her reasons, however, the gentleman returned her gaze steadily. "Who are you?" she asked at last.

"Damien de Villars." He inclined his head. "Colin and I have worked together more than once. That is how I know that, like you, he frets his lip when he is thinking, and prefers a juicy squab to roast beef, rejects tea in favor of coffee, and continuing in the same perverse vein, abjures snuff, but will take tobacco in the form of vile-smelling cheroots."

"You do know him!" she cried, her green eyes lighting dramatically.

De Villars stared fascinated for the space of a heartbeat, and then, collecting himself, he replied, "And I, too, am concerned as to why he is so late returning. I would not be honest, however, if I did not add that the information he is seeking is vital to England's cause. I am concerned with it as much as with Colin."

Miss Bennington nodded slowly, as if that very admission made him more trustworthy in her eyes. "It is the sort of thing Colin would say. You've no idea why he is so late, then?"

"No," he replied grimly. "And Jack's not in the village to tell us." He frowned, thinking, then continued slowly, "It's possible his absence is a good sign. He may have gone to meet Colin, but I don't want to give you false hope, Miss Bennington."

Ariane accepted his assessment with a brave nod.

Damien de Villars gave her a smile for her courage, then asked how she'd come to know of Jack Combs.

"Colin let it slip once that Jack lent him his services occasionally. We live not very far from here, you see, and

11

he's known Jack since he was a lad. Because Jack's a smuggler, I knew no one would give Miss Ariane Bennington news of him, but I hoped they might be more open with an urchin lad.''

"An urchin lad they'd have recognized as Miss Ariane Bennington in another minute."

Ariane's slender nose elevated. "I did what I thought I had to!"

It was obvious that her companion did not think much of her reasoning, for his brow lifted in a most ironical way, but he did not test her further on the issue. "And how were you able to escape whoever your guardian is to come on this mission of yours?"

"I'm afraid Crissie has never been able to keep me from doing as I wanted," she admitted candidly. "She prophesied doom, of course, but there was nothing she could do, really. And truth to tell, she wanted news of Colin as much as I. After Papa's death two years ago and Maman's the year before that, we could neither of us stand to lose Colin."

"I see," Damien said, and Ariane recognized sincere sympathy in his dark eyes. Averting her glance quickly, she bit her lip to stem the fierce pain thoughts of her parents' deaths brought.

"It's time I saw you home. I imagine Miss . . . ?"

"Crisswell."

". . . Miss Crisswell must be worried half to death. Did you bring a horse?" When Ariane nodded, he continued. "Good, then I'll have mine saddled. No, don't protest, I could not possibly let you go alone at this time of night, however you're disguised. Besides, I've a proposition to put to you."

"To me?"

Seeing how incredulity warred with excitement in her expression, Damien's mouth curved. "To you, brat." He nodded. "Now, come along, before I think better of it."

He was already at the door, and Ariane, hat in hand, jumped up to go after him. She did not much care to be addressed as "brat," but she allowed fair-mindedly that a gentleman who appeared a decade older than her eighteen years might view her as a babe. Besides, it did not seem the time to let pride stand in her way. This altogether intriguing man said he had a proposition to put to her. To her!

2

The Willows, Ariane Bennington's home, proved to be a rambling structure, more comfortable than elegant; it lay some hour's ride from Lynchurch near the village of Appledyne.

A high hedge surrounded the house, marking it off from the surrounding fields, a small wooden gate in its center. This creaked mightily when Ariane pushed on it, and on the instant a small form catapulted from the door of the house to land directly at Ariane's feet.

"You're back, Rie," the form piped excitedly.

"In the flesh, as you see, Toby, love." Ariane laughed, giving the boy a quick hug.

"Crissie said you were sure to get into trouble, but I told her you wouldn't. Oh! Who's this?"

The little boy's eyes widened considerably when he espied the stranger standing behind his sister. Toby could be forgiven not noticing him sooner, for in the first place it was dark and, in the second, Damien had followed behind Ariane with a silent tread.

"Toby Bennington, may I present Damien de Villars?" Ariane said formally.

When Damien inclined his dark head, Toby, delighted to be treated in so adult a manner, overcame his desire to gawk and remembered his manners.

"Rie? Is that you?" called a woman from within the house.

"Yes, Crissie, safe and sound," Ariane called back as

she mounted the steps. Letting Toby precede her through the door, she glanced anxiously back at Damien. "You're still agreed not to say anything about Deke?" she whispered.

"As I said, infant, I don't foresee that it will be necessary to give her a full account of the trouble you nearly tumbled into. However, I cannot guarantee my silence. I may need to tell her in order to persuade her to my purposes."

Ariane's exasperated glare resolved itself into a smile when Crissie appeared. "Crissie, I've a guest." She turned to her governess-cum-companion. "Damien de Villars, I should like you to meet Miss Amanda Crisswell."

Miss Crisswell, a small, neatly dressed woman who, on account of her round spectacles, put Damien in mind of an owl, made an effort to smile politely, but her effort, as she took in the tall, dark stranger being thrust upon her, wavered most uncertainly.

"Mr. de Villars knows Colin," Ariane explained when the introductions were complete.

Immediately, Miss Crisswell's smile firmed, though it was Toby who spoke first.

"You do, really?" he cried eagerly.

"Yes, really," Damien assured him with a smile. "I've worked with Colin."

"Oh! Do tell us about it!"

When Miss Crisswell graciously seconded Toby's invitation, saying the tea tray was already prepared, Damien said he would be honored to oblige.

Ariane made to follow Damien and Toby into the parlor, until she became aware that Crissie was darting anxious, unhappy glances her way. "Now, Crissie, you will not insist that I change out of Jed's breeches, will you?" she asked, smiling a persuasive, sparkling smile that Damien thought had likely gotten her her way more than once. "I shall miss these stories about Colin if I leave, and, after all," she continued reasonably, "the damage has already been done. Mr. de Villars met me in the taproom dressed like this."

The reminder of where Ariane had been that night quite undid poor Miss Crisswell. As her hand fluttered to her throat, she looked apprehensively at Damien. "I hope, Mr. de Villars, that you understand why Ariane behaved as she did this evening. Truly, she believed it was the only way to learn her brother's whereabouts. I assure you her manners are, ah, impeccable most times, and I caution you not to form an impression of her based on the circumstances of your first meeting. If you find fault with anyone, it should be with me, for I know better than Rie the troubles she might have fallen into."

"Crissie!" Ariane frowned. "I shall not have you blaming yourself for anything. Mr. de Villars understands—I have explained it to him—that no one could have stopped me from going out tonight. You know very well that you tried in every way you could, short of locking me in my room." Darting a meaningful look Damien's way, Ariane added soothingly, "I am persuaded Mr. de Villars has no dreadful opinion of me, after all."

The impassive look Damien returned her made Ariane wonder if he would not give her away, which was as he intended, for he thought Ariane Bennington had had things her own way rather longer than was good for her. However, when he turned to Miss Crisswell, he had assumed in a sympathetic expression. It would be to no purpose if she were anxious over his opinion of her charge.

"Please don't fret yourself, Miss Crisswell," he spoke in a low, comfortable tone. "I do understand why Ariane chose to act so, shall we say, unconventionally. Her actions were foolish in the extreme, which I have already told her, but they have not compromised her in my eyes."

For his pains Damien received a stormy glare from Ariane. She took exception to having her brave adventure characterized so derogatorily, but Damien's attention remained upon Miss Crisswell. "Shall we put the matter behind us, ma'am? I should very much like to tell Toby about one of the best agents serving his country."

When Crissie, who did not seem able to look away from Damien's dark eyes, said, "Oh, yes, of course, we can go on very nicely indeed," Damien rewarded her with such a brilliant smile, she exclaimed, "Oh!" just beneath her breath.

Sipping her tea, Ariane listened as attentively as either Toby or Crissie to Damien, but she did take the time to remark to herself that he was kind to indulge them so. He could have brought her home, attended to the business he had yet to speak with Crissie about, and then left. Instead, seeing how anxious they all were about Colin, he told them one story after another of Colin's bravery and resourcefulness. It was, in the circumstances, the most reassuring thing he could have done.

Some half-hour later, when the tea and all Cook's special poppy-seed cakes were gone, and Damien had answered as many of Toby's questions as he was at liberty to do, he gravely, with due appreciation for the lad's dignity, asked him to leave the room. "I've something to ask of Miss Crisswell that is for her ears alone," he explained.

"But Rie gets to stay," Toby pointed out most unhappily.

"My request concerns your sister, Toby, and so, of course, she may be present."

Toby's lip jutted forward, but when Damien's eyebrow lifted, he thought better of protesting further.

Miss Crisswell beheld the boy's prompt departure with astonished eyes. Normally, it would have been a good half-hour's work to get him out, and even then he'd likely have hung by the door.

Sighing a little, Crissie returned her attention to their guest. He was looking at Ariane, his brow lifted as if in question, and she saw Ariane nod her head firmly.

It was then Crissie recalled the gentleman, who was also a stranger she reminded herself, had said he had some request to make of her that regarded Ariane.

"Before I begin, Miss Crisswell . . ." Crissie straightened nervously in her chair when Damien turned to her. Their accommodating guest was, she realized of a sudden, not a man she would care to cross. "I must ask for your assurance that what we say tonight will go no further than this parlor?''

Crissie's head bobbed, and he leaned forward, his dark countenance intent. ''For some time now, despite our concerted efforts, vital information concerning a myriad of things: the departure dates of supply ships, Wellesley's plans on the Peninsula, even the disposition of our shore defenses, has been reaching the French, enabling them to do crippling damage to our war effort.

''Colin was sent to France in the hope that he might come across information there that has eluded us on our side. Unaccountably, his return has been delayed, and our situation is no better than it was. Indeed, with an offensive being planned for the spring, one could argue that it is worse.

''It is time, long past in my opinion, to try a new tack, and as luck would have it, the man we suspect of betraying our troop movements has provided us a rare opportunity. He has sent the daughter, whom he normally leaves largely forgotten at his estate in Berkshire, down to Brighton.

''We are curious over this unprecedented action, but whether it has some relation to his spying or not, it does provide us the opportunity to establish an agent of ours as her friend. We do not believe the girl, herself, knows anything, but our agent will, through her, be able to keep a watch on her father when he joins her in Brighton.

''Perhaps you will have anticipated me.'' For the first time since he'd begun, de Villars' face relaxed in a brief smile. ''And if you have, you'll likely think me mad, but it is in this capacity that I should like to use Ariane. She is close to the girl's age, and being both young and at home in polite society, she is not likely to come under suspicion.''

3

Ariane was not at all surprised when Crissie gaped at Damien as if he had lost his senses. "But this is more outlandish than Rie hying off to the Mermaid in Jed Tregan's clothes!" she blurted. "How could I possibly consent to her involvement in such a scheme? Even if you could guarantee her safety, she could not simply go off with you, Mr. de Villars. We do not know you. Why, you might not even be married!"

"In fact, I am not married," he allowed without the least sign of discomfort. "However, I would not do Ariane such a bad turn as to compromise her. She will be staying with a very suitable companion, Solange Crécy, a Frenchwoman who was forced to flee France and now works for the War Office upon occasion.

"As to the danger involved, there is, of course, an element of it, but I shall be close by. I hope you will not be offended, Miss Crisswell, if I say I shall likely keep a stricter eye on Ariane than she has been accustomed to. She will not go out masquerading as a boy, I assure you."

Crissie flushed at that. What de Villars did not know, though he might suspect it, was that Ariane's trip to Lynchurch was by no means the only outrageous thing she had ever done. Why, only last week she'd taken her mare and gone quite alone for a bruising ride beneath the full moon simply "for the joy of it," as she'd told Crissie when Crissie had heard of it from Jed Tregan, their groom.

Even as an infant, Ariane had been full of life and strong-willed, and without her sweet mother's moderating influence or her father's stricter hand guiding her, she had grown, though she was a loving and loyal child, more than a trifle headstrong. With Colin so often away, Crissie found her increasingly impossible to control.

Mr. de Villars would not be so hard-put. There was little

question that, as he had said, he would be a stricter task-master than she. One only had to recall how neatly he'd handled Toby to be convinced of it.

Then, too, there was the matter of assisting one's country. Crissie's father, a captain in the army, had imbued her from early on with a sense of duty. Still, she hesitated. The stranger, who had appeared out of the night to propose taking Ariane away with him, claimed to have worked with Colin, but he'd offered no proof.

Seeing Crissie's indecision, Damien smiled wryly. "You'd like some credentials, I think, ma'am, and I cannot blame you. Perhaps it will help if I tell you that I am known to most people as the Marquess of Chatham. If you have not heard of me, Miss Crisswell, you will undoubtedly have heard of the Duke of Bourne, whose eldest son I am."

"You're a marquess?" Ariane exclaimed, more surprised than impressed.

Damien did not spare her a glance, but kept his eyes on Crissie, who was regarding him with all the awe lacking in Ariane's tone. "I will have my father send a sealed letter attesting to my character, if you request it," he told her without the least trace of rancor.

"The Marquess of Chatham!" Crissie managed to gasp at last. "But, but if you are Bourne's son and heir, how can it be you are involved in this sort of business?" was all she could think to say, for the idea of so lofty a nobleman stooping to the business of skulduggery eluded her comprehension.

Damien's white smile gleamed briefly. "I could say my involvement was for the good of England, but I would only be telling half the truth," he replied, a humorous glint lingering in his dark eyes. "I am sorry to say that until only a few years ago I did not lead the, ah, most upstanding life. Nothing I could be hanged for, but without a mother to gentle me—she was taken by fever when I was just coming of age—I grew dissolute enough that my father feared I would be dead before him unless I found some useful way to occupy my time. He might have suggested I return to care for our estates, but he knows I've never had much interest in farming, and that my brother, Lionel, does the job admirably without any interference from me. Luckily Father recalled an old friend at the War Office, thus saving me from the coils of idleness, while putting my modest talents to purposeful use.''

As Ariane listened to Damien explain his position to Crissie, it occurred to her that, though he may have renounced his wild ways, he had not forgotten how to charm the female of the species. Crissie was returning his gleaming smile as if she'd known him all her life.

''You are very persuasive, sir,'' Crissie admitted at last, shaking her head as she turned to Ariane. ''And I suppose I've little need to ask your opinion of Lord Chatham's request?''

The sparkle of Ariane's green eyes answered for her. ''There is nothing I should like to do more, Crissie,'' she exclaimed unnecessarily. ''It is quite possible that this spy may know where Colin is.''

''And your Aunt Chloe, Rie? She expects you in Bath this fall, you know.''

Ariane dismissed her aunt with a negligent wave of her hand. ''I shall tell her I am too concerned with Colin to come before Christmas. It is the truth, after all. I should not be able to abide looking for a husband, which is what she really intends, so long as I do not know if Colin lives or not.''

''We are agreed, then?'' Damien said when Crissie made no reply to Ariane.

Crissie looked from the nobleman's compelling eyes to Ariane, who sat watching her intently, and back again, before nodding. ''It would seem so.''

''I shall not forget this, ma'am,'' Damien told her quietly, his black eyes very warm. ''I do not take the trust you put in me lightly, and I promise I shall not betray it. Ariane shall be returned to you safely.''

Flustered at being regarded in such a way, Crissie actually experienced a sense of relief when Lord Chatham turned to Ariane. ''I shall return two days from now for you, infant. Pack only a few necessities, for we shall have to buy you new clothes if we are to present you to

Brighton, thin though society is there at the Season's end."

"I shall be ready," Ariane assured him, excited by the prospect before her and rather amazed that he had, in fact, brought Crissie around.

"Good." Damien nodded, then he added firmly, "And see, brat, that you don't fall into some scrape. No more gadding about the country at all hours of the day and night."

Her dignity offended, Ariane's soft lips tightened. "I gave you my assurance I would be ready."

Damien's mouth twitched, but he only said, "See that you are." Crissie he treated more grandly in farewell, kissing her hand as if she were a duchess and leaving her with a becoming pink tint in her cheeks.

"Well!" exclaimed Crissie when the door had closed behind him.

Oddly enough Ariane knew just what she meant, for the room seeemed unaccountably empty of a sudden.

"I do hope I've done the right thing," Crissie worried aloud.

"You have, Crissie," Ariane assured her quickly, guessing that without Damien's powerful presence all Crissie's second thoughts were rushing to the fore. "I shall help Lord Chatham capture his spy while he helps me to find Colin. And in the process"—an impish grin lit Ariane's young face—"I shall have an adventure, just as I have always wanted."

"I hope your adventure doesn't prove too much for you." Crissie looked so anxious, Ariane rushed to her side at once and begged her not to worry.

"I shall do very well. Lord Chatham will protect me. His voice alone can freeze a person."

Reaching out to stroke Ariane's tumbled curls, Crissie sighed. "I won't ask how you know that, though I can well believe it. Lord Chatham is a most authoritative man. But that is not what worries me, Rie. You know so little of the world. Oh, you have visited your aunt and cousins in Bath, but only infrequently, and now you are going off without any proper chaperonage at all."

Ariane did not misunderstand entirely. "You needn't

worry that Lord Chatham will try to take advantage of me, Crissie." She grinned. "I cannot think such a worldly gentleman would exert himself on my account. You must have heard the way he calls me brat! Too, he said he would not, and he does seem an honorable man."

Like Ariane, Crissie had sensed something fundamentally dependable in Lord Chatham's character. Had she not, she'd never have agreed to his scheme. It was, in fact, Ariane who concerned her. How could such a young, inexperienced girl remain unmoved by a man who was the stuff of any woman's fantasies, particularly when she would be in his company day after day?

"I hope that you will remember, my dear, that a man of the marquess's background is not free to marry as he might wish. He must consider his family's interests above his own, you know."

Ariane's eyes danced, and only Crissie's puckered expression kept her from laughing aloud. "I shall keep your wise words in mind, I promise," she said dutifully. Then, her lively spirits coming to the fore, she added, her mouth curving, "And if the marquess should take time from his spying to woo me, I shall repulse him firmly, saying that you told me he could only break my heart."

Despite herself, Crissie laughed, though she did ask one last time before they went up to bed, "Rie, you will have a care, won't you?"

In reply Ariane squeezed her hand affectionately, saying, "I will, I promise," and Crissie, as she kissed her good night, reflected that she would have to be content with that. The matter was out of her hands now, as, she admitted with a sigh, it likely had been from the first.

4

Y ou must know from Toby's boisterous welcome that Lord Chatham is here." Crissie entered Ariane's room, shaking her head. "I vow I thought the boy would knock his lordship down, his welcome was so violent."

When a young maid, laden with a stack of boxes, trailed in after her, Crissie smiled at Ariane's questioning look. "Lord Chatham has brought new clothes, and he wishes you to wear them today." She laughed, for she was eager to see what the boxes contained.

She was not disappointed. Her exclamations rivaled Ariane's as her charge withdrew an extremely modish, high-waisted silk carriage dress of impeccable cut from the first box. If Crissie remarked that its deep, pure green exactly matched Ariane's eyes, she did not let the fact concern her. The color of Rie's eyes was memorable, she knew.

Crissie was obliged to depart then, summoned by the sound of a loud thud emanating from the direction of the front parlor, leaving Ariane to marvel over the contents of the second and third boxes with the little maid, Betty. In one was a stylish sable-colored pelisse, and in the other was a pretty, high-crowned bonnet whose trim was the same rich tint as the pelisse.

They were the most fashionable garments Ariane had ever worn, and wanting to show off her finery as soon as possible, she quickly subdued her black curls with a ribbon tied in the back and rushed downstairs.

Bursting into the parlor, she twirled about so that her dress floated out around her. "Behold the new Miss Bennington—so tonnish a young lady not even exactly old Mrs. Briarwood would find fault with her! But"—her green eyes shining, she came to a breathless halt before

Damien—"however did you know my size so exactly, my lord? These clothes fit perfectly."

Crissie gave a little cough, though Ariane had not realized she had a cold, while Damien smiled innocently. "Merely a lucky guess, infant," he dismissed the matter with a light shrug. "And good day to you, too."

It was on the tip of Ariane's tongue to ask how he'd been able to guess so accurately, but the distinctly amused gleam in his eye made her think better of the question.

"Good day to you, sir." She retreated into a sparkling grin. "And please forgive my manners. My excuse is that I am overcome. Thank you very much. I have never owned such up-to-the-mark clothing before."

Thinking of the battles waged between Ariane and her aunt, Lady Grantham, over Ariane's generally haphazard approach to dress, Crissie stoutly reminded her that she had never cared before what mark her clothing achieved.

"Well, I was never going to Brighton before," Ariane responded reasonably, Lady Grantham far from her mind. Looking down once more at the lovely dress and the kid half-boots peeping out from beneath, she asked of no one in particular, "Am I not amazingly transformed?"

Damien regarded her bent head, a smile tugging at the corner of his mouth. "Considering that the last time I saw you, you were dressed in your groom's breeches, I should say that you do indeed look transformed—almost presentable, in fact."

Ariane's cheeks flushed with pleasure. "I do hope so," she cried sincerely, her response to his faint praise proving conclusively just how little she was accustomed to flattery.

Damien guessed that, in addition to the relative isolation in which Ariane lived in Appledyne, it was the extended periods of mourning required first for her mother and then for her father that had kept her from company and thus from hearing the compliments her beauty must inevitably elicit. But, whatever the reason, he was pleased. A beautiful, adventuresome innocent was exactly what he needed.

For his part, Toby was regarding his sister with astonishment. "Well, I think you look silly, Rie," he scoffed.

"You couldn't walk from here to the pond in those boots, and you could never fish in that dress."

Ariane took not the least offense. "But surely you see, Toby, that I must look like the other people in Brighton. Of course, if I were going fishing with you, I'd put on my, ah, well, my oldest dress," Ariane, studiously avoiding Crissie's eye, finished in something of a rush.

Damien caught her slip and, not wanting to waste his time on a discussion of Ariane's deplorable tendency to dress in male clothing when it suited her, rose to announce it was time they leave.

With Toby and his pet frog, whose temporary escape accounted for the thud Crissie had heard earlier, in the lead, the little party trooped out the door to Damien's sleek carriage. Remarking Crissie's doleful expression, Damien kept the leavetaking short, fearing, if he did not, that they would soon be awash in tears.

When Ariane had waved the Willows out of sight, Damien exhaled deeply. "You'll have to excuse me, brat." The corner of his mouth lifted briefly. "But I've not gotten much sleep arranging this business. Feast your eyes on the scenery, and I shall be with you when I am restored."

Without more ado, his feet resting casually on the seat opposite, Damien closed his eyes and to all appearances fell fast asleep. Ariane, oddly enough, did not take his desertion in bad grace. She had noticed a strained look around his eyes and could accept that he'd have had to lose more than a little sleep if he'd organized everything to his likely high standards in only two days' time.

They had changed horses once and the soft Kent countryside had become the harsher, more windswept landscape of Sussex, before Ariane, having had her fill of bucolic fields, turned her attention to her companion.

He was, even in sleep, the most striking man she'd ever, in her admittedly sheltered life, seen. His profile might not be chiseled to classical perfection, but it was quite well-molded enough to set Ariane's heart beating at a slightly faster pace.

His brow was wide below his thick, wavy, black hair. His eyebrows, which were the same color, were faintly arched, and she knew from experience, were amazingly expressive when he wished to emphasize a point. His nose was straight and could, perhaps, be called arrogant for the way his nostrils flared ever so slightly, while his firm mouth managed to convey a sensual nature, or so Ariane, who realized she was no authority, thought. A well-shaped chin with a small, intriguing cleft in the center, rounded out the picture of a face that, if the features were taken individually, was simply handsome, but in the final effect was something rather more powerful.

As Ariane's perusal continued downward, she had to smile. He was today a far cry from the stranger clad in rough workman's clothes whom she'd first met.

His coat of blue superfine was of the finest cut, hugging his lean torso so closely that Ariane spent a moment considering how he could have got it on at all. His neck-cloth was tied in a knot she thought Colin would have appreciated, intricate but not absurdly so, while his boots, she knew without doubt, Colin would have envied. They were of the finest make, and their polished gleam reflected the attention of an assiduous valet.

Quite suddenly Ariane's clothing did not seem so grand to her, or to put it more accurately, she felt extremely dubious that her new attire would possibly transform her into someone elegant enough to keep company with so polished a gentleman.

She knew the rudiments of polite behavior, of course, but she had very rarely been out in the sort of society someone of Lord Chatham's obvious elegance must inhabit.

"Not having second thoughts, are you, infant?"

Ariane jumped. She had been so engrossed in her thoughts, she'd not realized that Damien had awakened. He was, she saw after flicking him a quick glance, regarding her in a not unkindly way, so she decided that she might confide at least some of her doubts to him.

"I was wondering whether I could impress Sir Henry Mowbry as a proper friend for his daughter. I have never deliberately set out to please anyone before." It was not the whole truth, but it was as near as she could get in Damien's presence.

"You have never set out to displease, have you?" he asked reasonably.

"Well, no, of course not!"

"And were you heavily censored by your neighbors in Appledyne?" he continued.

"Goodness, no!" Ariane's brow lifted. "I've always been on the best of terms with our neighbors, even Mrs. Briarwood. She often deplored my dress, but she always welcomed me into her home."

"And did you visit Mrs. Briarwood often?"

"Not as often as I should have," Ariane admitted, abashed. "She's lonely, you see, for she's a widow with no children and possesses a rather sharp tongue. Still, she was kind enough to me. Her brother, a vicar in the north, regularly sent her books, which she was used to letting me borrow."

"And so you visited annually to return them?" Damien teased, though he was not at all certain why he pursued the topic of Mrs. Briarwood. Perhaps it was only to provoke Ariane into the sort of wide-eyed smile she was just giving him.

"You are gammoning me!" She laughed. "I went on Monday and Thursdays."

"Ah." Damien's tone indicated he understood completely, though, in truth, he had to strive for the effect. He had never before met a girl who visited sharp-tongued widows twice weekly because the old woman possessed a fine library. Nor, come to think of it, had he ever encountered a female who did not make the least complaint when he chose to sleep rather than to entertain her.

"I am sorry I awakened you," Ariane said then, her words causing Damien's gaze to sharpen. Now the sulking would commence, he thought.

Unaware of the train of her companion's thoughts, Ariane was equally unaware that she confounded him considerably when she remarked with every evidence of sincerity, "Frankly, you looked as if you needed sleep. It was just that I . . ." Realizing that she was about to betray all her fears, Ariane faltered. "Well, I, ah," she stumbled, flushing as Damien flicked his eyebrow impatiently. "I appreciate terribly that you would take the time to buy me these clothes. They are lovely, but . . . Well, I was just looking at you—that is what awakened you I imagine."

Her ingenuous remark caused Damien's mouth to curve, but Ariane did not notice, for her eyes were focused carefully on the toe of her new boot. "And I am afraid that I shall not look as if I belong alongside you."

His eyes half-veiled, Damien inspected his companion. Her wide, luminous eyes, turned to him now, betrayed not the least hint of coyness. Taking in the proud, graceful way she carried herself, her delicate bone structure, and the vivid expressiveness of her face, he wondered wryly if she'd ever used a pier glass.

Believing it would not much reassure her if he remarked on the assets she did not realize she possessed, however, he took another tack. "I shall be presenting you, Ariane, and I do not think I refine on the matter too greatly when I say my backing will be sufficient to assure you are accepted"—his smile flashed, making Ariane's breath come a fraction more quickly—"however you are dressed. But, if it is your clothes that worry you, I remind you that Mme Crécy will be there to make certain you're turned out acceptably. You've only to mind your manners and be guided by Solange and me. We are agreed that there will be no midnight rides or other tricks?"

Had Crissie been present, she'd have been stunned to see Ariane grin sheepishly. "I shall be the model of propriety," she promised sincerely, for she was aware that a very great deal depended upon her behavior.

Relieved by the reminder that she'd have Damien's cachet, which she knew instinctively he had not evaluated too highly, Ariane appeared satisfied, until a stray thought caused her to frown. "You said before that I was only half-presentable," she reminded him, her gaze so serious that he could scarcely keep from smiling.

Reaching out, he lifted a silky curl from her shoulder,

absently wrapping it round his finger. "I only meant that your hair looks a trifle schoolgirlish hanging down your back. It's an easily corrected problem," he finished, languidly relinquishing the dusky curl.

At Damien's touch, Ariane experienced a peculiar warmth that seemed to slow everything from the blood flowing in her veins to her thoughts, and left her momentarily unable to make any reply. Not that she'd have had much to say in any case. The cut of her hair seemed a very minor flaw.

"If there are any other hidden rough spots, the background I have thought of for you will explain them."

Curiosity over the role she was to play restored Ariane's equilibrium. Her reaction to so light a gesture, she would have to consider, she knew, but later, when the cause of it was not immediately beside her.

"Who am I to be, then?"

Damien responded to the sparkle in her eye with an amused half-smile. "No one terribly exotic, infant, only a distant relation of mine—the daughter of a cousin from Northumberland. Should anyone ask, we will say you have been sent to Brighton to separate you from a young man in whom you formed an unfortunate interest."

"What is the young man's name, and and why is he unsuitable? Is he a terrible rake, perhaps?"

Ariane's eyes lit with such unholy glee at the prospect that Damien laughed. "Such eagerness for a wastrel, infant. Still, if that is the sort of suitor you wish, then you may have him. Shall we call him Ian Mitchell? I'll find the name easy to recall, for one of my cousins did have to be separated from a man of that name."

When Ariane replied that the name suited her, Damien gave her such a playful smile her heart skipped a beat. "Your parents were wise to send you away from young Ian, Miss Bennington," he intoned with mock solemnity. "He'd have made you miserable inside a year."

Grinning hugely at his play, Ariane retorted, "And who would know better what a poor marriage partner a rake would be, I wonder?"

Damien bowed his head in defeat. "Truth from the mouth of a babe," he said so mournfully that Ariane laughed with delight.

Some hours later Damien admitted to a feeling very close to surprise. He had not expected that Ariane Bennington, a young girl with little experience of the world, would be capable of holding his interest for the majority of their ride.

Whoever had seen to her education had done a good deal more than simply send her off to her neighbor's library. In the first place she had read widely, in the second she had absorbed what she'd read, and third she'd actually reflected upon what she'd retained. The result was that his traveling companion could converse intelligently on subjects ranging from the war with Napoleon to how, exactly, to hold the reins of a mettlesome team, though the latter topic she knew more of than Damien thought she should.

Nor, if she had not previously considered a topic, was she the least reluctant to admit it. Mercifully, her questions were astute, if, he acknowledged with a faint smile, numerous. When he'd mentioned in passing that he had visited the Americas, he'd had to appease her curiosity for upward of an hour.

The devil of it was that he hadn't minded indulging her, her responses to his remarks were altogether too engaging to allow him to cut her off.

Too, Damien admitted, it did nothing to hinder Ariane's cause that he found the sparkle in her green eyes to be as lively as her mind. And the brightness of her smile something to be encouraged with an absurd remark such as that about her supposed suitor, the unsuitable Mr. Mitchell.

For her part, Ariane was not at all surprised to find Damien a keen observer who could express himself ably. That he treated her as an equal could not help but please her, and she enjoyed the remainder of her ride more than she could have thought possible.

As a consequence, though long, their journey passed quickly. And before she had the time to realize how tired she was, their carriage was rattling over Brighton's rough pavement.

5

Strangely enough Ariane had not thought to ask Damien about Solange Crécy, the Frenchwoman who would act as her companion. There had been too much else to speak of, it seemed. In consequence, as she rather stiffly mounted the steps of the elegant town house in which she would be staying, she found herself quite curious to see who awaited her.

She was not well-prepared. For no particular reason she had assumed that her companion would be older, but the woman who came, her generous mouth curved in a warm smile of welcome, into the hall to greet them was of an age with Damien.

Though not classically beautiful by any means, Mme Crécy made an attractive picture in her stylish, wine-colored gown, with her dark-brown hair pulled into a graceful chignon in the back.

Her figure was by no means youthful, but the humor lurking in her brown eyes certainly was, and seeing it, Ariane felt an immediate sympathy for the woman who was to be her companion.

"Damien! *Mon ami*, it is delightful to see you, as always," she said, extending a beringed hand for Damien to salute.

There was no mistaking the pleasure with which Damien regarded her, and Ariane experienced a moment's envy for the obvious friendship between them, but the feeling lasted only briefly. Almost immediately, Mme Crécy was smiling at her.

"Welcome, Ariane. I may call you that, no? And you will call me Solange, for we shall be quite good friends, I am most certain of it."

When Ariane had replied with her friendliest smile, Solange took her arm and led them into the drawing room.

Taking a seat with Ariane upon the couch, she left Damien to lean against the mantel and turned, her brown eyes twinkling merrily, to study Ariane. "*Alors, chérie*, you are more beautiful than Damien said you would be. It will be the greatest pleasure to dress you. And then, when we have done, we shall enjoy this business, for we shall have all the young men in Brighton making the clamor at our door."

Ariane blushed and, uncertain how to reply, instinctively looked to Damien.

His mouth curved wryly. "Did I forget to warn you, infant? Solange rattles on in this way a great deal of the time, but take heart, when she's not rattling, she's dressing someone. If you begin to feel like a stone before a sculptor, it won't be without reason. The compensation is that you'll have the most stylish clothes in England."

Feeling easier now her looks were not the subject of such fervent discussion, a feat she thought Damien had accomplished most deftly, Ariane laughed.

As did Solange even as she playfully waved Damien's words off, saying "Bah!" in the most dismissive way. Only a moment later, noting that Ariane was having difficulty keeping her eyes open, she threw up her hands dramatically. "But I am the imbecile," she cried. "Here I laugh and tease, and you are close to fainting with the fatigue. Forgive me, *chérie*. Come, I will show you to your room."

Grateful beyond words, for the journey had, at last, taken its toll, Ariane bid Damien good night and followed Solange to a room whose pretty chintz furniture she was too sleepy to appreciate. Suffering a maid's help changing into her nightdress, she was in the comfortable bed asleep almost before the door had closed.

When Solange returned to the salon, she saw that Damien had helped himself to brandy and removed to the couch. Her expression pensive, she went to the tray to pour herself a glass of sherry, but she did not join him on the couch. Instead, she walked slowly toward the fire, sipping her drink as she walked.

Because Damien made no attempt to intrude on her

thoughts, it was not until she turned about that she saw he was watching her, his gaze narrowed as if he'd guessed her thoughts and did not care for them. Taking a deep breath, Solange set her glass down upon an elegant little Adam table.

"The child is very innocent, *mon ami*," she said, holding his gaze, though it was not easy for one of her accommodating temperament.

Damien registered her subtle criticism with a brief flick of his brow. "Were she any less innocent she would not do."

"So it is Triens you are really after, then?"

Damien nodded. "Mowbry is only a pawn in this game. It is Triens who recruits these traitors and passes on their information, or I very much miss my guess.

"Maccauley has long suspected him, you know, and I do not believe it is coincidence that Mary Mowbry should be sent down to Brighton by her papa just when Triens takes up residence. Having his daughter here gives Mowbry an excellent excuse to conduct his business with Triens at any social event, and no one the wiser."

"And because Monsieur le Comte is a lover of *les jeune filles*, you think not only to use *la petite* to watch Mowbry, but to insinuate yourself into Triens' circle?"

Damien's black eyes gleamed. "Miss Bennington's fortuitous combination of innocence and spirited beauty will attract the count in the way a flower attracts the bees. But I shall not be the one to insinuate myself, as you put it. I have a suspicion I would put the always cautious Triens on his guard. It is you who will gain access to Triens' circle, Solange, as Ariane's companion. You will meet his friends, take note of his servants . . ." Damien shrugged as if to say the possibilities were endless.

"You are right, of course," Solange conceded, biting her lip. "It is an opportunity of the grandest, but, Damien, what of the child? She may well fall in love with Triens. What he lacks in youth, he makes up for in presence and style."

"Need I remind you, Solange"—Damien lifted cool eyes from his brandy glass—"that a great many people's lives hang on a successful conclusion to this matter?"

"*Mon ami*, you are very hard," Solange chided, though she did not dispute his assessment of the importance of their business. "Can you not tell her what you really intend? She could guard her affections, then."

Damien waved his hand impatiently. "She is not duplicitous enough to keep her knowledge secret, Solange," he replied curtly. "Those eyes would give her away the moment she met him. No, she must behave naturally, if she is to attract the canny Triens. My only concern is whether or not she can hold his interest until Mowbry arrives. That is when the real work will begin."

Damien finished off his brandy and rose, a faint smile curving his mouth as he eyed her creased brow. "Don't worry overmuch, Solange. The chit's got spirit. I'll say that for her. I doubt she'll fall head over heels for a man just because he's got address."

Having offered her that thin assurance, he waved good night and strolled out into the cool night, leaving Solange behind to shake her head and wonder if men knew anything at all. Did he not realize that older men, particularly ones who deliberately set out to charm, had the special sort of address to which young girls were particularly susceptible? *Eh, bien*, she threw up her hands. She would keep a sharp eye on the child and see to it that she did not lose her heart to the elegant Triens.

6

When Solange arrived at breakfast the next morning, she found Ariane there before her, looking entirely refreshed by her night's sleep.

"I slept very well, indeed," Ariane confirmed after

Solange had greeted her. "How could I not in such a lovely room?"

"I am glad you are pleased." Solange smiled warmly. "But tell me, *chérie*," she continued pleasantly as a footman poured her coffee, "Damien says your *maman* was *française*. How did she and your father chance to meet?"

"It was at a ball in Paris before the upheavals," Ariane told her, a particular warmth lighting her fine eyes. "Papa saw Maman across the room and was immediately *bouleversé*. Somehow he got himself introduced and then proceeded, as he put it, to lay siege." Ariane laughed. "He must have been persuasive, for, though Maman's parents objected to her marrying an Englishman whose only means of support was a rather limited inheritance, she insisted upon having him."

"I would venture that you are like your father," Solange remarked with a twinkle in her eye.

"Well, I do have his coloring," Ariane allowed in some surprise. "And, so Crissie says, his spirit. He settled considerably after their marriage, but he was never entirely subdued." Ariane smiled, thinking for a moment of her dashing father, but she did not let herself become lost in her memories. There was little contentment to be found there, she knew. After a moment, she said lightly, "Tell me, if you will, Solange, how it is you came to work with Damien."

"Ah, that." Solange good-humoredly shook her head. "I only do this work with him because he had the good sense not to fall in love with me." Startled by the forthright confidence, Ariane looked every bit as surprised as she was. "I have taken you aback, I see." Solange laughed, unabashed. "But, *voilà*, it is the truth. When I came to England, I had lost my husband of two years, my lands, and many in my family. I was very disconsolate, you understand, and when I met Damien, oh, I thought he was the answer. I made myself the cake over him." She grimaced so comically that Ariane could not help but laugh.

Solange nodded emphatically as she buttered her toast. "It is so," she assured Ariane. "But Damien had the sense I did not. He said we would not suit and, instead, offered me the opportunity to work with him." Looking up, Solange shrugged. "*Eh, bien*, he was right. I relish very much this helping to oust that *monstre*, Napoleon, for it was he who had my husband executed. And now I have met another man who suits me very well. We are to marry soon."

There was a pause after Ariane had extended her congratulations, before Solange, her expression warm but concerned, addressed her new friend. "And you, Ariane?" she began. "You will not make the same mistake of falling in love with Damien, as I? It is *tout à fait* easy to do, he is a man as few are."

Ariane did not contradict the sentiment. Though she had not gone out much in society, she knew full well that there could not be many men as powerfully attractive as Damien de Villars.

That he strongly affected her, in particular, she did not deny to herself. She was not so silly. But she had no intention of revealing that fact to Solange. Such a revelation could serve little purpose, for Solange would only tell her it was a dangerous sentiment, which Ariane, innocent though she might be, knew very well already.

Being young and in high spirits over her adventure, she simply did not want anyone, even someone as gracious as Mme Crécy, to cry doom over her. And anyway, she told herself, feeling an attraction to someone was certainly not the same as falling in love with that someone.

Not wanting to lie to Solange, however, Ariane shifted the subject slightly. "I do not think Damien is any more likely to want to mix business with pleasure now than in the past," she observed, her bright smile peeking out momentarily. "I think he would greet any interest on my part by saying most dismissively, 'Stow it, brat!' "

Solange laughed merrily, vastly reassured by Ariane's composure. It did not seem that she would have to worry overmuch about the child. The conclusion came as a relief, for it meant she could give her full attention to dressing

Ariane as she should be dressed, a task she anticipated with the greatest of relish.

By the end of her third day in Brighton, Ariane had come to the conclusion that there was less to recommend the life of a young lady of fashion than she had thought. First, in the mornings, she'd had to stand for hours upon end as the modiste measured her, draped her with an astounding array of materials, and pinned and pinned her; then, if that were not enough, in the afternoons, she was obliged to accompany Solange to a wearying number of shops to purchase the seemingly innumerable accessories that were absolutely—or so Solange said—necessary to complement the dresses the modiste had created. And now, when she'd have given a great deal for a romp across the fields on the back of her old mare, she'd had to agree to Solange's wish that she take a nap! They were going to the theater that night, their first outing into society, and her friend wished her to look her freshest.

Luckily Ariane's stamina was greater than Solange had imagined, for though reading was as close to a nap as she could come, she did look quite as fresh as a spring flower in the nile-green silk Solange had chosen for her. The color deepened the green of her eyes, while the loose-flowing cut of the high-waisted evening gown seemed to have been designed for Ariane's slightly taller-than-average, lithe, slender figure.

Solange herself came to supervise the dressing of Ariane's hair, and when the younger girl saw how her glossy curls cascaded from a psyche knot atop her head to fall in artfully arranged disarray onto the creamy skin of shoulder, she decided that Solange's artistry had transformed her even more greatly than Damien's clothes.

Before she left her room, the maid, as Solange had instructed her to do, fastened a lovely, thin diamond circlet around Ariane's throat and placed a pair of tiny eardrops on her ears. Ariane did not stop to admire the final effect. She might, indeed did, look the part of the new Miss Bennington, but there was enough of the old edition left that she could think of little beyond how much she longed to go for a gallop through the countryside.

"Damien, you are just the person I wanted to see," she cried happily when she found him waiting in the yellow salon. "Can you tell me if there is any way at all that I could rent a hack for a ride?"

"Good evening, infant," Damien drawled as he swept her with an amused regard that, unaccountably, persuaded Ariane that the tortuous hours she'd spent being turned out for the evening had been, after all, worth the trouble.

"It seems you still find the polite amenities irksome, my dear. Shall I demonstrate what is called for by saying that you look quite charming?" He bowed lazily, his smile flashing most disconcertingly. "You do—look quite charming, that is—infant. It would seem that you and Solange have had a most successful time at the modiste's."

Her heart racing ever so slightly, Ariane curtsied prettily as she should have done, and bid him good evening. "I stand corrected, sir," she said, her demure tone utterly belied by an impish grin. "And I thank you for your pretty flattery. It makes the hours I had to stand absolutely still lest I be jabbed with a pin almost worth the torture."

"Only almost?" Damien laughed. "I am put in my place! Normally I am told my good opinion is worth any price."

"Which only persuades me, my lord, that you are accustomed to keeping company with a very toadying sort of female," Ariane, her eyes sparkling, returned at once.

"Minx," Damien reproved, though the smile tugging at his lips made the reproof something less than harsh. Indeed, Ariane found she had to drop her gaze or risk a telling blush, so appealing was his expression.

"I take it you have a ride in mind as compensation for your torture at the hands of the modiste?" Damien asked after a moment.

At once Ariane's gaze returned to him. "It need not be a long one, my lord," she implored. "Only, I should dearly love to feel the wind in my face."

"Ah, so, if not long, your ride must at least be a romp, is that it?" Damien's smile flashed.

She grinned. "If it could be arranged."

Damien said he would see what he could do, and then

38

their talk turned to the evening ahead, for Solange, elegant in a watered-silk gown of celestial blue, joined them. "I am hopeful Mary Mowbry will be at the theater tonight," Damien began. "With company so thin this late in the Season, it stands to reason Lady Hester Stanhope, her companion, will turn to the opening of *The Tempest* for amusement."

When Ariane asked what he wished her to do, he frowned slightly. "I think it best for several reasons if Solange and I act as if we've an interest in each other. That will assure Lady Hester I've no interest in her charge, should she be foolish enough to worry that I might, and it will make you, brat, seem at loose ends. Hopefully, the seeming negligence of your companions will encourage Lady Hester to take you under her wing."

"Do you think I will like Miss Mowbry?" Ariane asked as they went out to Damien's carriage. Now that it came to the point, she was a little concerned that she might find it exceedingly difficult to feign amiability.

Damien, handing her into the carriage, merely shrugged. "I've never seen the chit. But you shouldn't find befriending her too difficult. She's a young woman like any other."

Though it was dark in the carriage, Solange could plainly see Ariane's mouth drop open as Damien casually revealed that he thought all young women indistinguishable. While her eyes twinkled at this further proof of Damien's masculine limitations, Solange took it upon herself to assure Ariane that Miss Mowbry's most salient characteristic was likely to be acute shyness.

"She has no brothers or sisters and has gone out but rarely in society, *chérie*. You will only have to offer her a sympathetic ear. She will be a lonely child, I think."

Ariane could see her point and, reassured, gave herself up to enjoying the evening. The only other instance of disagreement with Damien was when he insisted she take the best seat in their box, for she protested Solange deserved the honor of sitting in the very front.

Needless to say, Damien won the day, and Ariane, watching enthralled as the fanciful play unfolded before her, never noticed Solange lean toward Damien and whisper, "It is the count who looks so intently at *la petite*, is it not?"

Likewise she did not see Damien, his eyes narrowed like a hunter's, confirm Solange's guess with a quick nod.

The lobby at intermission was extremely crowded, provoking Ariane to murmur a question about some people's idea of "thin company," but Damien would not be baited and replied offhandedly, "They're mostly riffraff."

To Ariane's amusement the crowd made way for Damien without his having to make the least effort, but just as he came close to the windows, where two ladies were standing by themselves, he stumbled, as if he'd been pushed from behind, and inadvertently jostled the elder of the two women.

"I beg your pardon, ma'am," he said at once, before turning to glower at the man behind them, causing the poor fellow—poor because Ariane suspected he had never touched Damien—to take such a fright that he promptly took to his heels. "At least that is one less rascal to discommode us," Damien observed coolly, looking around once more at the woman.

She, a stout, elderly matron encased in a lavender gauze affair and turban to match, glanced up uncertainly at the elegant stranger looming over her. In a matter of seconds, however, her eyes widened dramatically.

"Why, Lord Chatham, I believe," she exclaimed breathlessly. "I was a friend of your mother's. I—"

"Of course, I recall," Damien interrupted smoothly. "Lady Hester Stanhope, isn't it?" An absurdly pleased smile appeared on the woman's heavily powdered face as she acknowledged her identity. "Please allow me to make known to you my young cousin, Ariane Bennington. She is Frederick's daughter. You may recall he married Elaine de Rochard."

"Ah, yes, indeed I do." Lady Hester nodded readily, though it was clear the memory was vague at best. "I see you've your coloring from the de Villars, my dear."

Ariane smiled politely as she executed a grateful curtsy.

Seeing how her black hair was almost exactly the same shade as Damien's, she realized Lady Hester had only stated the obvious, and she wondered if Damien had counted on the similarity of their coloring to confirm his story.

"And this," Damien continued, "is Madame Crécy. Her husband, before he was taken from us, was a friend of my father's. Now that Madame has sought refuge with us, we are doing our best to make her feel at home."

Damien lifted Solange's hand for a kiss. It was a gesture Lady Hester followed with such avid interest that Ariane found herself hard put not to laugh. Fortunately the good lady's manners soon asserted themselves, and tearing her rapt gaze from the woman she believed to be the notorious Lord Chatham's latest mistress, she presented the girl who had been standing quietly beside her.

Because she'd been attending to the interplay between Damien and Lady Hester, Ariane had not looked at her closely before. Now, noting Miss Mowbry's downcast eyes, Ariane realized she was as shy as Solange had predicted she would be.

When Mary finally lifted her eyes, Ariane saw that they were a soft brown and that they were gazing upon the three strangers before her with almost painful trepidation.

Ariane, her heart going out to Miss Mary Mowbry on the instant, greeted her with every ounce of warmth she possessed. It was enough. Mary smiled back, a brief, bright effort.

Damien, keeping with his plan, made the pleasantries exchanged short and persuaded Lady Hester to allow him and Solange to obtain refreshments for everyone. "It is quite a long play after all." He smiled charmingly.

Lady Hester, her eyes sparkling girlishly, nodded at once and Damien and Solange departed, leaving Ariane behind to set about the task of making friends. "Lady Hester, I am most pleased to have met you and Mary," she began with a sweet smile. "Damien and Solange—Madame Crécy—are, well, they are both delightful as you can see, but they've other, ah, things on their mind than the entertainment of a young cousin. I am not complaining, for they really have been kind. It is just that I am a little lonely for someone my own age."

"I do think it a trifle odd that you should be in their care," Lady Hester observed meaningfully.

"Oh, Damien wasn't supposed to stay after he brought me down," Ariane replied artlessly. "He intended to go back to town and leave me to provide Madame Crécy company. She is still recovering from the death of her husband, you know. But now that Damien has decided to stay on in Brighton, after all, I've been left with little to do."

"Well, you may come out with us, child," Lady Hester exclaimed, her kind offer causing Ariane to smile at how easily Damien's plan had succeeded. "Mary would be glad of company her age as well, wouldn't you, dear?"

"Yes, very much," Mary affirmed softly. Then obviously taking her courage in her hand, she asked with an anxious smile if Ariane would perhaps care to join them for tea the following day.

"I should be delighted," Ariane assured her. "Provided Solange agrees."

When she returned with Damien, Solange promptly gave her permission with the result that the little group of ladies, as they sipped their ratafia, wore pleased smiles.

Damien, who had thought Ariane's success with Miss Mowbry a foregone conclusion, alone did not smile. It was only when he saw, as he gazed casually out over the lobby, an elegantly dressed gentleman of forty and some years turn repeatedly to glance at Ariane's vivid face, that the faintest gleam of pleasure entered his eyes.

7

"Not another shop, Solange! Have pity! We've been to four already."

Solange took in Ariane's woebegone expression with a smile. "Don't despair, *chérie*. This one you will like."

Ariane remained dubious until Solange told her they were going to a bookseller's. "I hope to find there the latest fashion plates from Paris, *bien entendu*," she replied with a little laugh when Ariane asked what book interested her.

Still laughing over Solange's unabashed interest in fashion when they entered the shop, Ariane went to the desk to inquire of the proprietor if he had a book by the sea captain James Cook, for Colin had once highly recommended his account of his voyages. When he had brought it, she went to peer over her friend's shoulder.

"*Eh, bien*, Ariane. *Vois tu*!" Solange pointed to a particular plate. "*C'est magnifique, n'est ce pas?*"

Ariane was on the point of observing that, while the dress had style, it was also very revealing, when they were interrupted by a highly accented gentleman's voice.

"*Pardonnez-moi*, ladies." The man, a gentleman with thin, haughty, aristocratic features, made them both an elegant bow. In his middle forties, he was of medium height and trim figure, and though it was the middle of the day, he was dressed formally enough for a court appearance. Or so Ariane thought as she took in his black velvet coat, elaborately embroidered white satin waistcoat, and the extravagant fall of lace at both his throat and wrists.

"I could not help but hear that you were speaking *en français*," he said, smiling. The smile deepened the fine lines radiating out from the corner of his eyes and put a rather nice twinkle in his light-blue eyes. "I know it is presumptuous of me, but I am a french émigré who hoped

43

to meet fellow countrymen, or, as in this case country-women." His gaze widening to include Ariane, he added, "Surely only *la douce France* could produce such *belles fleurs.*"

He may have said flowers in the plural, but it was at Ariane he looked, and it was she who answered him.

"*Vous êtes tres gentil, monsieur,*" she said with a sparkling smile for his courtly appearance as much as his praise. "But I must disappoint you. Only Mme Crécy, here, deserves your kind words. My origins are entirely too mixed, I fear."

"*Voilà*, I am corrected, *mademoiselle.*" He smiled at her, and Ariane remarked once again how nicely his smile softened his severe features. "I had been told the English rose could be *très belle*, and now I see I was not misled." Once again he bowed to her with a flourish.

"But I forget myself, *madame*," he addressed Solange again. "Forgive me, please. Undone by such beauty, I have quite forgotten my manners. I am Louis Valence, Comte de Triens."

"The Comte de Triens," Solange repeated, frowning as if she sought to capture some elusive thought. "*Ah, oui!*" Her warm smile broke through. "We have mutual friends, I believe. You know Lord and Lady Carrington, do you not?"

"I do indeed," the count acknowledged. "I stayed with them when I first fled to England."

Solange extended her hand. "I am Madame Crécy. And, pray, allow me to present Arian Bennington, my companion while I am in Brighton learning once more to enjoy the pleasures of society."

At once the count turned to Ariane, his eyes betraying his admiration. "Permit me to say, Miss Bennington, that Mme Crécy has chosen her companion well. There is no *jeune fille* who could more eloquently demonstrate the pleasures to be derived from society."

Ariane tipped her head at that and gave the man a long look. His praise was so fulsome, she suspected him of teasing her. When his smile faltered under her direct gaze, however, she realized both that he had been sincere and that she was being rude.

"Forgive me," she apologized hastily. "I am a very silly girl, quite unaccustomed to such kind treatment." Her mouth curving sweetly, she added, "But you must leave off your praises, or you will render me unable to wear a single one of the bonnets I bought today."

Solange from her neutral vantage point watched amused as the assured, older man registered with a lift of his brow that he'd been reprimanded, albeit gently, by the young lady more than half his age. At once, he smoothly changed his course.

"It is I who should apologize, Miss Bennington," he protested earnestly. "For it is I who have let my tongue run away with me. Permit me to inquire, instead, what book it is you have chosen from Monsieur Arnold's vast collection?"

"Captain James Cook's account of his sea travels," Ariane replied, extending the leather-bound volume. "I hope to travel myself someday, but until then, I must make do with the experiences of others."

"You are an unusual *jeune fille,*" the Frenchman murmured, clearly surprised. "Most girls only want to marry and have families."

"I am not so exceptional, really, *monsieur*. The man I love is beyond my reach and so I dream other dreams."

Triens looked startled. "But you are young yet, *mademoiselle*. You will yet find a man to help you forget the first."

Ariane inclined her head, declining to argue the point. "Whatever may happen I doubt I will lose my interest in exotic places." She laughed.

"It is an interest we share, as it happens," the count revealed, looking quite pleased. "I have had the good fortune to travel extensively and to return with a collection of simple objects d'art. Perhaps you would care to see them sometime?"

"I should be delighted!"

"*Bien*!" Triens turned a persuasive smile upon Solange. "By chance on Thursday I am having a little dinner party. Perhaps you would care to come, *oui*? I should be pleased to show off my trifles, if it is convenient with you."

To Ariane's delight, for she was greatly curious to see

what such a man would have acquired, Solange did not hesitate to accept the invitation.

"I believe you have an admirer, my dear," Solange remarked with seeming casualness when the Frenchman had left them.

Ariane laughed at once. "Do you think so?" she asked, clearly pleased by the thought. "Myself, I thought him very polished," she added with a shrug. Looking closely at Solange, she realized her friend was regarding her intently and frowned back at her. "You are not afraid I shall be cozened by him, are you?"

"He is quite elegant," Solange pointed out.

"And old enough to be my father," Ariane declared roundly.

More heartened by Ariane's attitude than she could say, Solange laughed. "I worry too much, it seems," she said, shaking her head.

"I did like him, though," Ariane went on reflectively. "It isn't wrong to enjoy gallantry though it means nothing, is it?"

Her earnest question prompted Solange to give her a quick, vastly affectionate pat. "Not at all, *chérie*. Enjoy it with a whole heart. But what an actress you are!" she added as they gathered up their belongings. "I was very impressed with the sincerity of your tone when you said your true love was beyond your reach."

Ariane smiled her acceptance of the compliment, but swiftly turned the conversation to other things. It was not a matter she wished to consider too deeply. She was glad she had bethought herself of her role, but she was not so pleased that the image she had created of Ian Mitchell, based on an old friend of Colin's for whom she had had a schoolgirl crush, had not occurred to her at all in her time of need. When she had made mention of the true love she could never attain, the handsome, rakish face that had risen in her mind had been, disconcertingly, that of Damien de Villars.

"When you go to the Mowbrys' this afternoon," Solange's voice interrupted Ariane as she was telling herself that Damien's image had occurred to her simply because he was the only attractive man she had seen in several months, "you may say that Damien and I have gone out for a drive. It will make you seem the more neglected, *vrai*?"

They agreed that Ariane should forgo asking when Sir Henry Mowbry was expected, unless the question arose naturally in the course of conversation. As Solange said, "Make a friend of little Mary and the rest will follow."

When Ariane entered the Mowbry town house later that day, she thought to herself that she was looking forward very much to the task Solange and Damien had set her. She had had few friends her own age and sex—there were not many young ladies in Appledyne—and she'd always thought it would quite delightful to have someone with whom to share her thoughts.

Befriending Mary did not, at first, turn out to be so simple a matter as Ariane had thought it would be, however. The fault lay not with Mary but with Lady Hester, who, as soon as Ariane took her seat, turned the conversation to Damien.

After half an hour of answering questions about Damien, Solange, and again, Damien, Ariane's imagination was sorely taxed, and she was vastly grateful when Mary hesitantly suggested that she and Ariane go out for a walk up the Steyne. "You know how I have longed to do so," she begged.

Lady Hester, her curiosity satisfied for the moment, readily gave her permission. "You girls always seem to prefer the fresh air," she remarked, as if the desire to escape the confines of a stuffy parlor was something of a mystery to her.

When the two girls were safely outside the house, Mary turned to Ariane with apology writ large in her brown eyes. "I am most dreadfully sorry that Hester would quiz you in that way. Following the goings-on of others is the only way she has to enliven her life, I suppose. And, I am afraid, a man like your cousin is the sort of person who piques her interest the most."

Mary's normally pale cheeks were stained with her embarrassment, and Ariane immediately smiled to reassure her. "It does not signify in the least, I assure you. Please do not apologize over Lady Hester's interest in Damien. We are accustomed to it in the family." It was only a little lie, for Ariane thought that if she were in Damien's family, she would, indeed, have had to grow accustomed to the curiosity Damien piqued in others. "Let us speak of ourselves instead," Ariane continued as they strolled along ahead of Mary's maid. "I must say I was in alt to meet you, Mary. I haven't seen a person my age since I left home."

"And you are here to keep Madame Crécy company?" Mary asked softly.

"In part," Ariane agreed. She hated lying, but Damien had been so insistent that she tell everyone the story he'd concocted that she knew she must say that she'd been sent down to Brighton because her parents did not approve of Ian Mitchell's attentions to her. "They didn't know him, as I did," she concluded with a sniff.

Ariane was rather pleased with her performance until she saw that Mary stood regarding her with a still, anguished look. "What ever have said I to upset you, Mary?" she asked, greatly concerned. Mary shook her head, but Ariane could see there were tears in her eyes. "You must tell me," she insisted.

"It is only that your story resembles mine. I, I . . ." Mary stopped to dash a tear from her eye. "I, too, was in love with a boy of whom my father did not approve," she revealed in a low, strained voice. "When Father learned that I was meeting Richard, he became very angry and sent me away altogether."

Stricken that her playacting should have called up such unhappiness, Ariane took the girl's hand. "I am so sorry, Mary. Is it that your father has someone else in mind for you?"

Mary bit her lip. "He said he wishes me to marry a titled man of wealth."

"Did he have someone in particular in mind?" Ariane asked curiously.

Mary's thin shoulders lifted slightly. "I could not ask. My relations with my father are not close, you see." She gave Ariane such a tremulous look that all Ariane's considerable sympathies were immediately enlisted. "I know I should not be talking to you like this, but I've no one else. Lady Hester . . ." Mary shook her head as her voice trailed off.

"But, I am pleased to listen, Mary," Ariane hastened to assure her. "Where is Richard now?"

"In Berkshire, I suppose. I do not really know. Father forbade me to see him again."

"And you obeyed?" Ariane asked before she could curb herself.

But Mary did not take exception. "My father frightens me most dreadfully when he is very angry," she admitted in a whisper. "You seem much braver than I am."

Mary's fear of her father was almost palpable, and led Ariane to wonder if Sir Henry might not actually hit his daughter. The notion made her dismiss her own courage. "It is easy to be brave with only Crissie to scold me," she remarked candidly.

"Did you say a farewell to Mr. Mitchell?" Mary asked so sadly that Ariane cursed the role she was playing.

"You know, in truth, I realize now that I did not care so much for Ian as I thought," Ariane parried, getting as close to the truth as she could. "I am afraid my parents were right, at least as far as my feelings were concerned. But as to you, Mary, is there some way I might assist you? When do you expect your father to join you?"

"Not soon, though he has sent no specific word," Mary replied, her eyes darkening temporarily at the thought of her father. "Oh!" she cried suddenly, an excited gleam enlivening her eyes. "There is something you could do for me! I should like to send Richard a letter to explain where I am. There is nothing he can do, but . . ."

Mary's voice trailed away pathetically, and Ariane was moved to give her hand a quick, reassuring pat. "Of course I should be happy to send a letter off for you. You could bring it when you come for tea, which I hope you will do tomorrow."

Overjoyed, Mary squeezed Ariane's hand fervently and thanked her until Ariane thought she would blush. As she

49

remarked later to Solange, "Mary clung to me almost as if she were drowning. She seems deathly afraid of her father, and I felt like a beast turning her fears to my use."

Solange, however, would have none of it. "We have no idea what Sir Henry plans for her, *ma chère*. It may be that revealing him for what he is will be for the best. It would set Mary free to do as she wishes. If this Richard truly cares for her, it will not matter to him what her father's done."

"I do hope so," Ariane said with feeling. "She deserves some good fortune. I think she has not been well-used by Sir Henry. I may send the letter for her, then?"

But that Solange could not say. "We must ask Damien. He may think it will compromise your relations with the Mowbrys too greatly. If he does not come before the tea, you may take the letter to hold for his approval."

8

Damien came before tea. He came early the next morning when Ariane breakfasted alone.

She'd have given some glad cry of welcome when she looked up to see him stroll in for all the world as if he were expected, but her mouth full of ham, all she could do was bounce happily and look as pleased as she was.

Damien viewed her machinations with a hint of smile. "Good morning to you, as well, infant." He bowed off-handedly before taking a chair. "Early though it is, I rather thought you'd not be abed."

"I am relieved not to have dashed your expectations, sir." Ariane laughed, having swallowed her mouthful. "Should I find it significant that you are dressed for riding?" she added hopefully, just managing to suppress a sigh over how very handsome he looked in his riding clothes.

"Indeed you should. I've found a suitable hack for you."

"But that is wonderful," she cried, jumping up at once. "Why didn't you send word? I should have been dressed and ready."

"I have always been partial to Solange's coffee," Damien informed her even as he accepted a steaming cup from a footman who, it seemed, was acquainted with his partiality. "You have the fifteen minutes it will take me to savor it. If you have not returned by then, you will have to wait until tomorrow to ride."

Skipping at once toward the door, her swirling skirts revealing to the marquess's keen gaze a pair of neatly trimmed ankles, Ariane laughed. "What an odious man! You have arranged this affair exactly to suit yourself, I see."

"But of course," he replied composedly.

Her heart pounding as much from the effect Damien's gleaming eyes had upon her as from her hurry, Ariane quickly donned the striking dove-gray riding habit Solange had chosen for her, and grabbed her hat, adjusting it as she went. She would take no chance that Damien had only been teasing her. Just as he was finishing off his cup, she reentered the breakfast room.

"*Voilà*! I have done it," she announced triumphantly.

The habit was cut severely, its lines displaying her slender, feminine curves to a nicety, and her excitement had produced a brilliant sparkle in her eyes.

If Damien noticed how very fetching she looked, however, he said nothing. And Ariane could not have been aware that his hand hovered, arrested, for just the briefest moment over his cup when he first caught sight of her. In her desperate dash down the stairs, her hat had slipped, and exclaiming with annoyance, she was attempting to right it without benefit of a mirror.

"Allow me." Without waiting for permission, Damien came to settle the little hat at a rakish angle on her head, his long, lean fingers lightly grazing her chin as he tied the ribbons to his satisfaction.

Ariane stood straight before him, seemingly held spellbound by the white linen of his neckcloth. That she scarcely saw that piece of material was closer to the truth.

The mere thought that Damien was attending to her in such a personal way, not to mention the actual feel of his hands on her skin, however inadvertent his touch might be, had set her emotions in such a tumult that she was afraid she would act the veriest idiot and blush furiously, if she did not make the greatest effort to contain herself.

"Now, then." Damien stepped back to judge his work. "Superb effort, if I do say so. When my interest in government business wanes, perhaps I shall hire out as a lady's maid. I believe I have the knack."

"Not to mention the interest," Ariane was able to retort with a grin now that he was at some distance from her.

Damien laughed, even as he informed her she was being pert, and then told her to come along, they'd kept the horses waiting long enough.

Ariane immediately dismissed the large bay stallion as Damien's mount. The horse beside it was a dainty, spirited black mare. "She is mine?" Ariane asked, looking wonderingly at Damien.

He nodded in answer. "I thought your seat sufficient to merit something better than a hired hack."

"But she is beautiful," Ariane cried, flying down the steps. She was stroking the mare's silky nose when he joined her, and though her eyes were shining as if they'd been filled with sunlight, she said simply, "Thank you, Damien. I have never ridden a horse so fine."

He bowed. "My pleasure, infant."

After he'd tossed her lightly into the saddle, Damien mounted the bay and led the way through town. Within a quarter of an hour they had left the last buildings behind and were able to give the horses free rein. As if of one mind, they spurred their mounts, quickening the pace until the hedges seemed to fly by in a blur and Ariane's curls came loose from her hat.

"That was glorious!" She laughed, when, at last,

Damien slowed the pace. They'd reached the end of the lane he had chosen and were now upon a bare headland looking out to sea.

Damien acknowledged her remark on their hell-for-leather pace with a chuckle, but said nothing else as he dismounted. Before he could come to Ariane's assistance, she slipped down unaided. It had occurred to her as she rode from town that her reaction to Damien's lightest touch was quite out of all proportion to what it should be, and that, if she were to keep her interest in him under some control—she was not an utter fool, after all—then she should avoid having his hands on her even though his only intention was to assist her in the most acceptable of ways.

Studiously ignoring the arched brow with which he greeted her independent maneuver, she went to find a seat on the rocks overlooking the sea.

After attending to the horses, Damien joined her and mercifully said nothing about how ladies did not trip down from their horses' backs unassisted. Indeed, he said nothing at all, but simply sat down close by and joined her in watching the swell and roll of the sea as it came surging in to crash violently against the rocks below them.

They had sat in companionable silence for some time before Ariane sighed deeply. "I should dearly love to go to sea sometime," she exclaimed with a wealth of longing.

Damien nodded, as if he quite understood her desire, but made no reply. Lounging comfortably against a rock, he was watching a large yacht maneuver in the distance. "How was your tea with Miss Mowbry?"

Ariane made a face. "I didn't learn much of Sir Henry," she confessed. "I found it exceedingly difficult to escape Lady Hester's interest in your affairs. What a life you must live if even half the ladies in society are as hen-witted about you as she is."

"I contrive," Damien remarked dryly.

"Well, I didn't mean to tease you," Ariane hastened to assure him. "It is only that I thought it most annoying. In the end, it was Mary who got us out of the house so that we could have some conversation."

"And what did she say?" Damien asked.

"Amazingly she is in Brighton for much the same reason as I supposedly am. She was sent down from Berkshire because she'd formed a *tendre* for a young man her father considered unacceptable."

"Do you know his name?"

"Only that she called him Richard, but if you wish to know more, Mary is to bring me a letter addressed to him tomorrow."

"Why?" Damien inquired with such sharpness that Ariane experienced a sinking feeling.

"Sir Henry," she began, her chin lifting a fraction, "who by the way is not expected to arrive soon, whisked her from this young man's reach before Mary had a chance to explain where she was being taken or even why. She wishes to send him a letter with her explanations, but cannot post it herself for fear that Lady Hester or a servant will notice it. Seeing how undone she was—she was almost crying—I offered at once to assist her."

"Of course," was Damien's first and, to Ariane at least, excessively dry response. His second was to shake his head firmly. "You may not aid her in this, Ariane. I do not wish our already complicated intrigue to become more so with the addition of a thwarted lover. You do not know exactly why Mowbry chose Brighton as her place of exile, do you?"

Ariane frowned, then shook her head. "No. Mary only said that when he denied Richard, her father told her he intended her to marry titled wealth."

"Ah," Damien said, as if her statement meant something to him, but Ariane was too engrossed with Mary's plight to remark his tone.

"Please, Damien! Won't you reconsider?"

But though Ariane's expressive green eyes beseeched him eloquently, Damien did not soften. "No," he repeated firmly. "Sir Henry has doubtless left word with his staff to be on the lookout for Mary's swain. If he's spotted, it would be child's play for even Lady Hester to guess how he'd been summoned. She would then forbid further contact between you and her charge. If there is real feeling between the two, they can stand to wait the month or two it will take to see this business finished."

"But being left with no word at all is too great a test," Ariane protested. "She will lose him, and you cannot know how sad that would be, Damien. If you had seen the way she flinched when she spoke of her father, you'd be convinced, as I am, that he uses her ill. I felt the most fortunate of souls as we talked. I may have lost both my parents, but at least I was always secure in their affection."

Although Damien subjected Ariane to a prolonged look, he was not swayed. "There is much more at stake here than one girl's happiness. It is may sound dramatic, but I assure you it is fair to say that the fate of our nation hangs on this business. And if that is not enough, let me make clear that I mean a great many men's lives are at stake, including your own brother's."

Ariane bit her lip, shocked into silence. Of course she did not want to endanger Colin, but thinking of Mary . . . Her eyes clouded with distress; she looked away from Damien, giving him the last word, but clearly not happy to have done so.

Damien rose then and announced rather curtly that it was time they returned.

Her head drooping, Ariane followed after him. He'd gathered the horses' reins, but did not hold out the mare's when she approached. Instead, he lifted a dark curl from her cheek and efficiently tucked it into place beneath her hat. His action brought Ariane's head up.

To her surprise he was smiling, albeit wryly. "I owe Crissie an apology," he murmured enigmatically. "It would seem I did not fully comprehend what she was up against. Do you think, Ariane, that if I get word to this Richard that Mary is safe and will contact him with news of her whereabouts as soon as she is able, you could contrive to look a little less as if I have recently murdered your best friend?"

"Oh thank you, Damien!" Ariane only kept from embracing him by the greatest effort. "I am sorry to put you to such trouble when you've so many weightier matters on your mind, but if you can manage it, I would be most grateful.''

"You may save your expressions of that feeling for the time being, brat,'' he returned as he tossed her, without her leave, onto her mare. "I shall have to make certain first that nothing in Brighton is compromised by contacting the boy.''

Ariane said she understood, but it was clear to Damien from the way she was smiling that she fully expected him to manage somehow. What was not so clear, perhaps, was exactly why he sought to please her so, though he conceded the lugubrious expression she'd worn earlier had been most powerful.

"Did Solange tell you we met a French émigré, the Comte de Triens, at the booksellers?'' she inquired lightly when they had gone some little distance at a more decorous pace than that they'd maintained on their ride out.

"She did, actually. She also said you'd made quite an impression upon him.''

Ariane slanted Damien an annoyed glance, for he seemed singularly unmoved by her accomplishment. She had not wanted a great to-do; she wasn't in alt herself, but after all, the Frenchman was the first admirer she'd ever had.

"And what did you think of him?'' Damien asked after a moment.

Ariane had her share of pride. Not for anything would she have told him then, for his tone was impassive to the point of indifference, that she found the count's formal dress and elaborate addresses more amusing than heart-stirring.

"He was quite nice. Very elegant and extremely distinguished—just as you might imagine a French count would be,'' she said instead, truthfully enough.

After they'd negotiated their way past two farm carts driving in the middle of the lane, Damien turned to arch his brow at her. "You aren't going to be cozened by some sophisticate's polish, are you, brat?''

His tone was lazy enough, but his words cut and

Ariane's green eyes flashed angrily in response. "I cannot fathom," she snapped irately, "why it is that people feel it necessary to warn me about every man I encounter. I was scarcely born yesterday."

On the instant an amused gleam lit Damien's eye, though Ariane entirely missed the sight she secretly thought so appealing. Her chin dangerously elevated, she was pointedly looking anywhere but at her companion.

She simmered some minutes before Damien was able to sufficiently suppress his smile to make amends. In fact, the modest houses that lay on the edge of Brighton had come into view before he said, his tone beguilingly repentant, "Come forgive me, infant. Those of us who are, ah, more experienced are prone, I believe, to worry about those younger than ourselves."

Ariane did not deign to respond immediately, but she did peep at him out of the corner of her eye. When she realized that his tone was utterly belied by the laughter glinting in his black eyes, she quite lost her composure.

"Oh, you," she exclaimed, half-amused despite herself.

"I imagine it was Crissie who had a few words of wisdom to say about me?"

"And Solange," Ariane added, just to put him in his place.

"And Solange." He sounded surprised. "And what did you say to them?" he asked, seemingly as curious as he was amused.

Ariane shrugged as if the entire subject had become tedious. "Only that anyone could see you were a rake—you had as much as admitted it yourself—and that I am not so hen-witted as to be taken in by a rake."

Damien greeted her forcefully expressed assurance that she was entirely safe from him with a laugh, though, when he had sobered somewhat, he appeased her by saying, "Allow me to tender my apologies again. I had not realized how frequently a young lady must receive similar advice."

Ariane smiled quickly up at him, pleased that he should see how tiresome it was not to be thought to have any head at all on her shoulders. She very nearly ended up gaping at him stupidly, however, indeed likely did gape for a moment before she recalled herself, for she was not at all prepared for the tender smile warming Damien's eyes.

"You do understand, I hope, that it is only because we are exceedingly fond of you that we go to the trouble of offering our counsel?"

Quite lost, Ariane could only mumble rather incoherently, "Oh, yes, well, of course, yes," and pull her gaze away before she ended up seeming a complete fool.

9

So. Triens mentioned you in his note to Carrington." Damien's voice reflected his satisfaction with the news Solange had given him as they took a stroll along the sand.

"*Oui*," she said. "*Alors*, it was a most discreet inquiry, merely a remark that we had met. But so quickly sent off was it not, considering he has not written Lord Carrington in so long a time?"

Damien inclined his head, smiling, and Solange continued. "Equally as telling, I believe, is the scarcely subtle interrogation I endured last evening. *La petite* was not questioned at all, but I, the Frenchwoman, was asked extensively about . . . everything, where I lived, whom I knew, why I left, whom I still contacted . . ."

"And I am certain that you passed with flying colors, cleverly persuading Triens and his minion that you are an utterly innocent, rather giddy woman who poses no threat whatsoever to them. Was your questioner, by the by, a small man with sallow complexion and quick, nervous mannerisms?"

"You know him, then!"

Damien shook his head. "Only by repute. He was

mentioned in connection with some missing letters in Greenwich. Nothing was proven, but I do find it interesting that he should surface here with Triens."

Solange chuckled at Damien's ironic tone, but he was already asking what she'd learned about the count's yacht and its crew. "I watched her maneuver this morning. She's definitely seaworthy. Crossing the Channel would be child's play for her, though I do not imagine Triens risks using it to transport information. My guess is that he uses an unremarkable fishing scow for that purpose, and keeps the yacht at hand to transport him to safety, should he be threatened."

"And perhaps, as well, he uses it to keep an eye out for unusual ship movements. He told *la petite* that he was accustomed to taking it out frequently, and I can imagine no other reason. Seeing how eager she was to speak of his vessel—she is fascinated by the sea, the little one—he went on to reveal that his crew is entirely French, so that he may communicate easily in times of need, he told her when she was surprised."

There was a pause as Damien digested this. An acquaintance hailed him, but Damien frowned him off. "Triens is taken with Ariane, then?"

"He is not taken, no, not at all," Solange replied, her brown eyes twinkling. "He is, rather, infatuated! His eyes followed her all evening. It is as you had hoped."

"And Ariane? What was her response to having Triens at her feet?"

"Ah, such a lack of conceit she has!" Solange shook her head, amazed. "She is so unaware of her beauty, she has no understanding of its effect." Not waiting for Damien's response, Solange rushed off on her own train of thought. "She is so natural, so lovely a child! If I had her for a Season, *mon Dieu*, I could catch her a duke."

Damien did not disagree, but did give her a dry look. "We were speaking, I believe, of Ariane and the Comte de Triens, Solange."

Laughing, Solange bowed her head. "I like Ariane very well," she admitted by way of apology. "But as to Triens, she's no notion how great is his interest."

Ariane, had she been privy to the conversation, would have had to agree. She was aware that the count was certainly not averse to her, but she had no notion how difficult he had found it to keep his eyes from following her every move.

Happily occupied meeting the count's other guests, she had not spared her host an undue amount of consideration. All the particular attentions she was aware he paid her, such as the soft, tender way he'd kissed her hand in greeting, or the earnest manner in which he told her that he was obliged to her for gracing his affair, all these she dismissed as exaggerated politenesses in the Continental manner.

When she could not help but be aware that he singled her out, after dinner when he took all his guests to see the objets d'art he'd collected on his travels, she thought it was merely because he knew how particularly interested she was.

She vastly enjoyed the stories he had to tell—he had traveled widely for many years—and she found she very much liked his smile, particularly the way the creases around his eyes turned up. Able, therefore, to overlook his absurdly splendid white satin evening clothes, Ariane responded to the count as warmly and naturally as she would have with anyone to whom she took a liking.

"You find my collection interesting?" Triens asked, obviously pleased by the way her eyes had widened when she first entered his collection room.

"I should be foolish if I did not!" She sparkled at him. "I never imagined you would have so many beautiful things."

The count followed her gaze. "I have always been drawn to beauty, and at heart I am a collector. I find it impossible not to desire what pleases me."

"Do you have a particular favorite?" Ariane inquired, not aware that her companion was no longer looking at the objects he had collected.

"Indeed I do. Allow me to to show you." Extending his arm, he led her to a small statue in the center of the room. It was a beautiful likeness of a young girl—Chinese,

Ariane thought—preening before an invisible mirror.

"I am fascinated by this one, because the artist has captured that moment when a young woman first becomes aware that she is beautiful."

Ariane found the girl a little too aware, her smile a trifle too knowing, but she did think the statue a remarkable piece of work. "I feel almost as if I am trespassing, she seems so real."

The Comte de Triens smiled, pleased. "And you, Miss Bennington, do you have a favorite piece?" he asked.

"I have only had time to see a small portion of your collection, but I did find that garment, there, breathtaking. The weave is exquisite. I am not certain if it is red or gold or both, it shimmers so."

"It is an Indian garment called a sari," the count explained as they made their way toward the display Ariane had indicated. "The wearer winds it about her without the use of even one pin or tie."

"Not even a sash?"

Triens smiled at Ariane's startled expression. "Not even a sash," he affirmed. "But I assure you I never saw one in danger of falling off. Quite the contrary, actually, for Indian women move with remarkable sureness and grace."

The count remained with Ariane as long as he could politely do so. Her genuine interest would have been difficult to resist even had she not been such a delight to behold.

Watching him closely as they moved about the room together, Solange decided the young girl was still in no danger of forming a *tendre* for the count. As she reported to Damien, "Ariane is intrigued, *bien entendu*—Triens' experiences interest her—but it is not an affair of the heart."

Damien frowned, though why her words should cause him to do so Solange could not guess. "She is intrigued, though?"

Solange shrugged. *"Bien sûr.* He has traveled as she longs to do, and he is delighted to relate every adventure he has had. It is fortunate they share this interest in other lands. If you wish Triens to remain interested in her, he must believe she feels some enthusiasm for him. It would not be natural for him to pursue her if he felt she had no regard at all for him.''

When Damien made no response to this wisdom, Solange was forced to shrug again. ''*Eh, bien*, then, you may see for yourself if there is cause for worry. Triens is attending the Assembly at the Ship Inn this evening.''

''I shall come for you both at nine,'' Damien replied before turning their discussion to another matter.

Damien was good to his word. As the ormolu clock in the drawing room struck nine, Solange's butler opened the door to admit him. Ariane, who was waiting alone, began to smile, but her effort wavered as her gaze traveled the length of him. She had not been at all prepared for how very fine he would look in black satin evening clothes.

''I did not realize you could look so, so civilized,'' she rushed to say when she realized he had caught her staring at him.

The heightened gleam in Damien's eye left her certain she'd not hidden her admiration, a certainty confirmed when he said, without blinking an eye, ''Allow me to say, that you, too, look most tamed. That green is the height of refinement on you.''

It was impossible to resist him, and she grinned hugely. ''You are teasing me, sir, and so you must know I was overcome with how handsome you are in evening dress.''

''You did look a bit dazzled,'' he conceded, his smile flashing wickedly. ''But, alas, it seems my effect was not of long duration. Unless I miss my guess, you are casting about even now for your reticule, which can only mean that you are ready for other sights.''

''As, indeed, I am,'' Ariane informed him with a smile, having found the elusive reticule and having, not by chance, had the time to compose herself. ''If one handsome man is pleasant to behold, then I am assured that an assembly full of them will be wondrous.''

''Devil a bit!'' Damien laughed; then, seeing that Solange was in the hallway calling for their wraps, he extended his arm. "Come along, then, minx, and enjoy yourself, while I take the time to doubt the wisdom that advised me to take on your guardianship."

10

The Assembly Rooms at the Old Ship Inn were not so crowded as they might be in the early summer, but there were still enough young, unattached men present to promptly form an attentive court around Ariane after she entered.

Because she loved to dance, she responded to being led out for one dance after another with a sparkling smile, but their flattering addresses she dismissed out of hand. Many of her young partners found her apparent disregard for their praises odd, even a little unsettling, but few took exception. Indeed, the general opinion was summed up by one young buck when he remarked to his friend that Chatham's cousin was not only out of the common way, but seemed, as well, "a damned nice bit of fresh air."

Ariane, of course, knew nothing of the consensus. She only enjoyed herself and, from over her current partner's shoulder, observed the stir Damien created simply by being present.

She had known he must cut a dash in town—what rakish, handsome marquess would not? But she had not realized just what a figure of note he was until she saw that at any one moment almost half the ladies in the room could be observed eyeing him avidly over the tops of their fans.

In the tame company of the Assembly Rooms, his appearance was more compelling than ever. His severe, elegant clothing, its dark hue relieved only by the lace at his throat and a single, magnificent diamond pin, set him apart from the bright, gay colors affected by most of the other gentlemen. Beside them he seemed all the leaner, all the sharper, all the more dangerous, and all the more attractive.

And that, though he rarely unleashed his charm. For the most part, though polite enough, Damien maintained a decided air of reserve, observing those who scrambled to speak to him through cool, half-lidded eyes and according each of them only a few words.

Only twice did Ariane see his smile flash: once, when he was conversing with an older man who evidently knew him, and later when she saw him laugh wickedly at some sally an exceedingly voluptuous woman of about his age made.

Feeling her brow draw down in a frown, Ariane looked away at once. She was being absurd to watch Damien so, she knew, and deciding that what she needed was better company than that provided by her young partners, Ariane searched the room for Mary Mowbry. She found her sitting well back from the dance floor with Lady Hester and her friends.

"You have certainly been enjoying yourself, Ariane," Lady Hester observed with an indulgent smile after Ariane had bid her good evening. "I hope you will be able to persuade Mary to put herself forward a bit. It isn't natural for a young woman to wish to stay here with us."

As Ariane thought it rude to have made this speech in front of Mary, she made no reply, but asked if she could take Mary with her to procure a glass of punch. "I think I should like some intelligent company for a bit," she observed mildly but pointedly.

Mary smiled shyly when they were alone. "You needn't stand up for me that way. Lady Hester doesn't mean any harm, really, and she cannot know why I find the idea of dancing insupportable."

Knowing that Mary referred to Richard, Ariane asked curiously if Mary had known him all her life. "Did you grow up with him?"

"Oh, no," Mary replied swiftly, a warm gleam, which

Ariane found she envied slightly, entering her eye. "I knew him only a short while. Father allowed me to go from time to time to the Assemblies in Basingstoke, and it was there I met him. I was leaving the floor when I sensed someone watching me, and looked up to see a young man with the softest brown eyes in the world gazing at me. I am sure I blushed, and he grinned, and then—you will not credit it—he actually winked at me. I know it is an absurdly vulgar thing for him to have done, but I could not help but laugh. Somehow he contrived an introduction, and for several weeks afterward we met regularly there and in town, when I went to shop."

Mary's sigh spoke volumes about longing. "He often teased me unmercifully just to get a smile. But he defended me too, if anyone dared to make a critical remark, just as you did with Lady Hester." Mary laughed and glanced at her companion. "You won't countenance it, Ariane, but sometimes you remind me of Richard. I'm not certain why exactly." She paused to scrutinize her friend, but shook her head when the similarity eluded her. "It is something about your eyes, though they are not the same color at all. Perhaps it's the way your spirit shines through," she finished with a light chuckle for her fancy.

Ariane was just going to say Mary gave her altogether too much credit, when Mary, who had chanced to look over Ariane's shoulder, groaned. "It is a friend of my father's, a man I cannot much care for!" she whispered in response to Ariane's questioning look.

Glancing about, Ariane saw it was the Comte de Triens who approached. "Mademoiselle Bennington," he greeted her, bowing low over her hand. "May I say that the Assembly has never seemed quite so bright?"

"Only if you do not let anyone else hear you, my lord." Ariane laughed. "I am persuaded these lovely ladies would have just cause to take offense. You know Miss Mowbry, I believe?"

"Ah, but yes, of course. Good evening, *mademoiselle*. I did not realize you were acquainted with Mademoiselle Bennington."

When Mary seemed unable to do more than give a

strained smile in reply, Ariane explained that they had met at the theater. "We were literally thrown together by the crowd," she said with a smile, remembering the pushing that had gone on.

"This I can well believe." Triens laughed. "It is a charming theater, but so small. You should behold it when the Regent is present and all society with him," he said, shaking his head, his blue eyes twinkling warmly. "Rather than the Theater Royal, it could more correctly be named the Theater Crush, I believe."

Ariane was glad to see Mary smile, though, still, when the count left them, after having secured Ariane's hand for the next dance, she felt obliged to explain why she thought him interesting. "He has traveled a great deal, you see," she said earnestly. "And I suppose, too, that I find his old-fashioned air rather charming. Just look at those absurdly high heels he is wearing tonight. A powdered wig would not look out of place on him, I think."

Mary, smiling, agreed, and divulged that she had enjoyed him well enough that evening. A light blush tinting her cheek, she admitted, "Actually, I do believe it is the odious way my father toadies to the count that had put me off him. I've never even spoken to him at any length before."

Her dance with the count, Ariane found most enjoyable, more so, certainly, than her dances with the young men closer to her age, for he did not burden her with meaningless flattery. In reality, he scarcely had the time. As they danced a stately galliard, Ariane thought to ask if there were similar gatherings in the Orient, and the count replied that there was no need for them, that all marriages there were arranged. When he went on to say that the bride and groom generally did not even meet each other before their wedding day, Ariane proclaimed the custom barbaric.

"They might detest each other on sight," she pointed out with some heat, to which the count replied, smiling indulgently, that Eastern marriages did not seem to him any more unhappy than English ones.

Unconvinced, Ariane observed that the count had not made an arranged marriage and that she did not think he would care for a wife he did not choose. "What if she were dull?" she asked, as if dullness would be the very worst trait possible in a mate.

Triens laughed at that and allowed that he would not be happy with an insipid wife. "I should hope that, had my parents lived, they'd have had the good taste to choose a beautiful, spirited, and intelligent wife for me. I concede that I would be happy with nothing less."

As he lounged casually against a pillar, Damien attended absently to the conversation Lord and Lady Durham held with Solange. Had he been asked, he could have repeated little that had been said. He could, on the other hand, have detailed every move Ariane and her resplendent partner had made.

Solange, he saw after very little time, had not overstated the matter. Triens was indeed smitten with Ariane. He did not fawn over her, for he was too sophisticated to act the buffoon, but it was also true that he could not seem to pull his eyes from her face and that his smile seldom wavered. In the end, Damien decided that the older man seemed almost bemused, rather as if he himself were amazed by how affected he was.

At that moment Ariane laughed gaily at something the count said, bringing Damien's gaze flickering to her. She was radiant. Even from across the room he could see how her smile illuminated her face. And though he was too distant to discern it, he could easily enough imagine the sparkle that must be in her eye.

Briefly another couple interfered with his view. The girl, Miss Corliss, had been one of the reigning beauties of the previous London Season. Blond with brown eyes she, too, was smiling at her partner.

Damien mentally saluted Triens' taste. Feature for feature, Miss Corliss was as pleasingly constructed as Ariane. She only lacked, Damien thought, any sign of life.

Restlessly, he waited for Miss Corliss and her partner to move on. Over the years, he had seen so many of her kind, hothouse flowers groomed to catch titles, that it was difficult not to feel, at the very least, bored by her.

When Ariane and Triens returned to his view, Damien saw that Ariane was no longer smiling. Far from it. As the count spoke, she followed his words so intently that Damien was half surprised she remembered to dance.

A light pressure on his arm recalled Damien to the Durhams. After bidding them the most perfunctory of adieus, he returned his cool gaze to the dance floor.

"Am I not right about *monsieur*?" Solange asked when they were alone.

Damien did not look down, but did incline his head slightly. "He is as rapt as you said he would be," he agreed.

"You are not pleased," Solange observed, clearly surprised by Damien's closed expression.

"It is the extent of Ariane's interest that I question. She is hanging on his words as if they were made of gold."

Visibly relieved, Solange shrugged lightly. "Ah, well, the tales of his travels are like gold to her." As they watched, Ariane laughed again, and again her face seemed to come alive with some inner light.

Though Damien said nothing, his narrowed gaze gave eloquent voice to his thoughts, and Solange cast him a searching glance. "You make something of nothing," she assured him. "He is no more than a friend, an interesting friend, to be sure, but still, a friend. When she refers to him, she calls him quaint." Solange rolled her eyes playfully. "It is not the way a young girl describes a man for whom she has formed a *tendre*." Chuckling, she added, "Believe me, *mon ami*, I know. Am I not *française*?"

His frown lifting, Damien slanted Solange an amused look. "I beg pardon, my dear. I had forgotten your indisputable credentials."

"Believe me, then, when I say you would make the grand mistake if you make too much of Triens, Damien. I can see you wish to say something, but take care. You may well make him the forbidden fruit, if you do."

Although Damien assured Solange he would do nothing so foolish, he claimed Ariane's next dance. Not having bothered to sign her card, he was obliged to cut out the hapless young man who had, a simple matter. It took a single look and an "You don't mind do you, old man?" to convince the boy to relinquish Ariane's hand and even to smile doing it.

"Someone ought to have rapped your knuckles more often when you were young, Damien de Villars," Ariane remarked tartly as he led her onto the floor.

Damien's brow lifted. "And I suppose your impeccable manners are a result of your having suffered such discipline on a regular basis?"

She did not allow him such an easy victory. "As you can well imagine, I never once had my knuckles rapped," she conceded composedly. "But neither do I possess such address that I am able to get my way without having to give the least thought to others. Poor Mr. Wainton especially requested this waltz."

" 'Poor' Mr. Wainton's enthusiasm will only be whetted by a little difficulty, and when he does at last achieve his objective, you will thank me for having delayed the inevitable. He is an abominable dancer and will step on your toes the entire time."

"I do not believe you have ever seen Mr. Wainton dance even once, my lord," Ariane returned severely, though she could not suppress the curve of her mouth. "However, I suppose I cannot be too difficult on you, for I had not believed I would dance with you at all. You have been in astonishing demand since we arrived."

Damien gave her dry look. "It is amazing, is it not, how infallibly a title and some wealth draw attention."

The music started and Ariane went into his arms without replying. Surely he must know that the portly and chinless Lord Carstairs had a title and quite a bit of wealth, but was standing alone and had been for some time.

Damien was not portly. His body was lean, firm, and strong, and Ariane was intensely aware of all those qualities as she stood with her entire body only inches from his, his arms holding her to him. The place just above her waist where his hand touched her radiated with a warmth that seemed to pervade her.

"You have been no less sought-after than I, infant. Have you enjoyed yourself?"

His warm breath fanned her hair, rousing her only slowly from her bemusement. Lazily tilting her head back to reply, she almost forgot what she'd been going to say. He was so very close. She had never before noticed how soft the black of his eyes could seem . . .

"Yes, oh, yes, I have enjoyed myself," she cried hastily, drawing back as much as she could without seeming odd. "I enjoy dancing enormously."

When she said nothing more, Damien's brow quirked. "You've not enjoyed the compliments? I know you've received them, I heard that scamp Bosley positively gushing over you."

"Mosely," Ariane corrected with a smile. "But I can't recall what he said." Shaking her head, she confided candidly, "I find flattery sounds very much the same after a time. If I were to believe half what I've been told, I'd think my hair gleamed like a raven's wing, my eyes looked like emeralds, and my complexion was either as pure as snow or as fresh as a peach, you may take your pick."

When Damien laughed aloud, Ariane made a face. "Terrible stuff isn't it?" she asked, half-seriously. "I have a theory that every phrase comes from a single manual all young men in society are required to commit to memory. I wager that if I asked her, Miss Corliss would say she is told her eyes resemble amethysts, her hair gleams like the sun, and, ah"—Ariane craned to look over Damien's shoulder —"her complexion is like alabaster," she finished with a grin.

"I should curb the impulse to confirm that thought," Damien warned, his eyes dancing at the thought.

Ariane nodded absently, having gone on to another thought. "Of all my partners only the Comte de Triens had any real conversation."

There was a pause before Damien said evenly, "You must realize Triens has a good many years and as many flirtations over the boys who have partnered you tonight. Of course, he would be more adept at guessing how to please you."

70

"You are only trying to warn me off him again," Ariane retorted, not at all pleased with the thought that the count might be so calculating. "I tell you, he is not trying to . . ." Recollecting that she was on a crowded dance floor, Ariane snapped her mouth closed.

Damien laughed softly as her eyes flashed her frustration at him. "I am only telling you the truth. Believe me, I know."

It was as difficult to resist him as it was to deny he had more experience of the world. Still, with an effort, Ariane managed to keep herself from succumbing entirely. "Well, I find the count interesting," she repeated staunchly. "And enjoyable," she added for good measure.

Damien's response was a long, searching look.

A little bewildered by the intensity of his gaze, Ariane, nonetheless, returned it guilessly. She had nothing to hide in regard to the Comte de Triens.

"As long as relations between you remain only friendly, I've no objection," Damien allowed at last.

Ariane colored at the implication that she might allow more than friendly relations simply because the count's address was polished. "Thank you so very much, my lord," she retorted, exceedingly pleased with the irony she achieved.

If she'd thought to put Damien in his place, however, she failed, for he only flashed her a rakish grin. "Not at all, my infant. And now that we have that settled, shall we return to dancing?"

It was a purely rhetorical question which was just as well, for his smile had left her more than a little breathless. And without another thought for the Comte de Triens, Ariane realized ruefully when the heady dance was at last at an end.

11

Bonjour, chérie. I see you are to ride out with Damien this morning.''

"Solange!'' Ariane was too astonished by her companion's nearly unprecedented appearance at breakfast to reply to the obvious. "What can have taken you from your bed before noon?''

"Nothing dreadful.'' Solange smiled rather weakly. "I awoke with the *mal de tête*, that is all, and hoped some toast would help. Truly, it is nothing.''

Solange gave her order to the footman and did not ask if Ariane and Damien would be accompanied by a groom. When she had asked the question before, Ariane had answered simply, "There is no one who can keep pace with us.''

Solange had not insisted upon the matter. As cousins, it was perfectly acceptable for Damien and Ariane to ride out unescorted. And all Brighton accepted them as cousins.

Which was little wonder . . . Solange chuckled faintly to herself as she buttered her toast points. She had never thought to see the day Damien would behave so circumspectly toward a beautiful female, but he had, whether the three of them were alone or surrounded by potential gossips, behaved with Ariane exactly as the fond, occasionally indulgent, older cousin he was supposed to be.

If, on one or two occasions, she had caught something more than cousinly interest in Ariane's eye as she glanced at Damien, Solange did not refine on it over much. Those lapses had never occurred in public, and with a Gallic shrug she wondered what woman in normal health would not feel something more for Damien.

"Good Lord, Solange! Don't tell me the ceiling over your bed has fallen down.'' Damien, it seemed, was as surprised as Ariane by the sight of Solange at so early an hour.

Smiling only a little, for her head did ache, Solange made her explanation again, and then, lacking the spirit to participate much herself in the conversation, she watched as Damien greeted Ariane. As usual, there was nothing loverlike in his regard, though he was observing her with amusement.

"You can leave off drumming those fingers, brat." He eyed Ariane's agitated hand askance. "I shan't be hurried through my coffee regardless of the fact that I am late."

No, Solange thought, it was not a lover's speech, just as the pert grimace Ariane returned him would never be termed a lover's look. And certainly neither one reacted with anything close to undue interest when Solange, after apologizing because she did not think she would feel up to the rout they were scheduled to attend, extended Damien an invitation to supper and a quiet game of cards that evening.

When the two riders had left, Solange easily dismissed any thought of the relations between Ariane and Damien. As well-acquainted with Damien as she was, she knew he would never, under any circumstances, compromise a young lady under his protection.

But, if she had worried and if she had found a way to observe them unseen as they rode out together, she'd have found they behaved toward each other then in much the same way as they did when they were with her. The only difference in their behavior—and the difference would have surprised her, for Damien's relations with women were generally of a very different nature—was that, when they were alone together, there was between them a deep sense of companionship.

Following the pattern set on their first ride, they always galloped at a furious pace until they came to a headland, where they would rest before returning home. While Damien watched the sea and took note of which boats went where, Ariane watched the clouds floating overhead, or perhaps she too watched the sea.

Usually they talked, but only after a time. When Damien

remarked upon the ease between them, something he did less and less frequently, he conceded wryly that had not Ariane's ability to hold her tongue matched her ability to exercise it deftly, he'd not have kept her company so often. He could as easily have left her to ride with a groom and would have done so without a second thought had she been a chatterbox.

That particular morning there was no variation in their routine. They had been content with quiet for a very long time before Ariane lazily called Damien's name. Comfortably situated against a warm rock, her hat in her lap, she asked dreamily, her eyes occupied with observing a gull wheel and dip in the sky above her, "Did you see any Indian headdresses when you were in the Americas? I have read they wear the most remarkable ones, made entirely of feathers."

Damien left off his observation of a small scow beating its way into Triens' bay to glance at her. "Some may wear them,"—he shrugged—"but the only Indian headdress I saw was a beaver hat so fine it put mine quite in the shade."

"You are bamming me," she accused when she roused herself to see his eyes were gleaming in just the way they did when he wished to provoke her.

"I am not so ungentlemanly as to deliberately disappoint you, pet. He was quite civilized, I assure you, and had even attended some university or other."

"And you really saw no headdresses?"

"Not one," he assured her solemnly.

Accepting his assurance reluctantly, Ariane asked hopefully, "Well, you must have seen other examples of aboriginal craft and even returned with some."

"I'm afraid not." He shook his head, his expression amused. "I have no Indian war bonnets, pottery, peace pipes, or hatchets to show off to my friends."

"Do you have anything from the Americas?" she asked, clearly exasperated.

Damien laughed, his smile as always sending a thrill through her. "I did acquire a locket," he allowed innocently, "but I don't think . . ."

Whatever he had been going to say was lost when Ariane made a distinctly rude noise. "I did not mean some lover's token," she informed him shortly. Despite the wicked grin he threw her, she persevered loftily, "I meant any particularly fine examples of the arts."

"It wasn't a collector's voyage," he relented enough to say, reminding her that she had thought before he had gone on some assignment for the War Office. "Besides, I don't need to own every object of beauty I see," he observed turning around to watch the scow anchor beside Triens' yacht.

Ariane gave his back a sharp look. "If you are trying to lower the Comte de Triens in my estimation, you shan't succeed," she informed him briskly. "I find his collection most interesting. After all, I can scarcely appreciate your memories."

"No, I suppose you cannot," Damien allowed, looking back at her. "Though I can assure you, I do."

"Odious man!" Ariane looked away with an exaggerated sniff. "I see it is best you brought no mementos, or we should all be shocked."

"Don't try to cozen me, you insatiably curious child," Damien retorted, not the least taken in by her display of pique. "I know perfectly well by now that you would be particularly relentless if you thought I had something scandalous to show."

Her mouth curving, Ariane left off looking at the middle distance. "My education is so lacking that I confess I cannot even imagine what such a thing might be . . ."

Damien flicked the bridge of her slim nose with his finger. "Nor shall I be responsible for making you any the wiser, *chérie*."

On the ride home that bright morning Ariane could not deny her high spirits. She still had had no word from Colin, but she did not allow his continued absence to depress her. She was doing all she could to find him, and of a certainty, Colin would not have reproved her for thoroughly enjoying the business of spying.

She liked Mary Mowbry very much indeed and adored Solange, even going so far as to develop an interest in fashion to please that gracious lady. She attended the Assemblies, went to musicales and plays, and had at her disposal a truly well-stocked lending library.

Too, there was the man beside her. She cast a quick glance at Damien. It was little wonder that she was enjoying Brighton. She had Damien for a companion. And though she knew well enough she should question why the world seemed a more vivid place when he was present, she did not.

She did not care to. And, besides, there was little time for such reflection, for Damien was, very often, present. The only times when she could be absolutely certain he would be absent were when she was in company with the Comte de Triens, or when she was in Solange's drawing room during receiving hours. The first he would not explain, maintaining it was mere coincidence that he played least in sight when Triens approached. As for his absence every afternoon from three to five, he only said laconically that he did not come because he could not get a breath of fresh air then, there were so many of Ariane's admirers cluttering up the place.

Dinner that evening—*en famille*, as Damien dryly described it—was to Ariane a thoroughly welcome respite from the social rounds. Because there was no festivity to attend at a certain hour after dinner, the atmosphere was relaxed and warm. Had Solange been well, it would have been a perfect evening.

But Solange was not well, and after dinner she cried off from playing cards, though playing had been her suggestion, saying she would sit quietly on the couch with her needlework instead.

Ariane, observing her drawn expression, was not surprised when she gave up with that attempt at normalcy after a time. "You need not look so concerned, *petite*." Solange reassured Ariane, who could not help but be anxious, for she'd never seen her friend so pinched. "I have suffered this before. It passes with rest, but I do not like to take the laudanum and so resist. *Alors*, I shall trust you both to behave."

Ariane assured Solange she would follow her up to bed

shortly, while Damien merely wished her a healing rest.

When Solange had left, Damien and Ariane resumed their game of piquet in silence. The cards did not favor Ariane that night, and after some time of uninspired play, her eye chanced to fall upon the glass of brandy beside Damien's chair. "Damien?" she said then, eyeing its rich, intriguing amber color. When he answered with an absent murmur, she asked, "Whatever does brandy taste like?"

Damien, studying his hand, shrugged negligently. "Pleasant, I suppose. I drink enough of it."

Ariane lost the round, but did not seem to mind overmuch, for she was frowning at Damien's now depleted glass of brandy. It seemed absurd to her that she was forbidden even a taste of a drink that all the men of her acquaintance imbibed freely.

Looking up, she saw Damien was observing her with a faint smile. "Will you be desolate without a taste, brat?"

Ariane grinned. "Nothing so dramatic, but I should like to know what the attraction is."

To her delight, Damien was not reluctant to pour her a glass. "I promise not to tell Solange that you seized upon her absence to do something outrageous," he teased, handing her her drink.

"I am grateful, sir." Ariane sparkled back at him at once. "For, if you did, I should be obliged to inform her you were not least hesitant to abet me."

Damien only chuckled and watched fascinated as Ariane took a long swallow. "Ugh! I might as well be drinking fire."

"It is an acquired taste," Damien acknowledged, only just suppressing a laugh at the comical grimace contorting her face. "Too, it might help if you merely sipped it," he added mildly.

Game to the end, Ariane tried again and found he was right, though the taste was still too strong for her. "At least it doesn't burn so, however." She smiled and thanked him for his indulgence, then, rolling her eyes, confided artlessly, "The brandy is not exactly to my liking, but at least my curiosity is satisfied. A man like you can have no notion how difficult it is to be born female."

"I suppose not," Damien admitted with the ghost of a smile. "Enlighten me."

"Well." Ariane waved her nearly empty glass in the air. "We ladies are so carefully protected that we do not, most of us, even know exactly what it is we are being protected from." This observation made Damien chuckle, but Ariane scarcely paused to acknowledge his response.

"There is so little we are allowed to do. Or even to know! We may not, horror of horrors, go off alone in search of adventure. Nor, even if there is a need, may we speak too plainly, and of a certainty, we may not ask plain questions. The answers might shock us, I suppose. We may not ride out alone, walk alone, speak with too much animation, walk with too much animation." Ariane stopped, laughing. "There are rules circumscribing everything we do from the smallest action to the grandest. Oh, I am certain there is good reason for some of the hedging, but you must see how easy it is to feel stifled."

Damien made some indistinct, soothing sound and smothered a smile as he looked at Ariane. Having eschewed her shoes, she sat curled comfortably in her chair with her toes tucked beneath her. Her cheeks were flushed a rosy pink, and several tendrils of her black hair curled adorably but untidily around her face. Her head tipped to the side, she toyed absently with one of them, never thinking to return it or its fellows into place. It only took the brandy glass dangling from her slender hand to make Damien send up a prayer of thanks that no rule-makers were present.

Ariane did not notice his amusement. The cards in her lap quite forgotten, she gazed abstracted into the crackling fire. Damien had not long to wait to learn what preoccupied her so. After only a moment more, she peeped around at him, a grin tugging at her lips. "Damien," she exclaimed, leaning forward, her eyes sparkling with such mischief, Damien braced himself. "Do tell me what a rake's life is like."

Though he'd prepared himself, his brow shot up, giving Ariane notice that she'd succeeded in taking him aback.

"I mean, there must be so many amusements," she

clarified hastily. "And so much freedom! You must have attended a masque. Mary says they are reputed to be wicked affairs, but I've no idea why." Even had Damien had the least intention of enlightening her, she did not give him the opportunity. After taking another fortifying sip of brandy, she revealed, her brow knitting, "And Colin said—although not to me, I admit—that most gentlemen have mistresses. Why they should if they are married puzzles me a little." Ariane shrugged the perplexing thought aside, her thoughts traveling to yet another bit of information she'd heard Colin telling a friend. "He said the rakes in London will bet on anything, from which foot a certain horse will lift to whether it will rain the next day. Some men may even lose an entire fortune in one night, or so he said."

"Would you care for the life, infant?" Damien inquired when it seemed she had come to a stop.

At once Ariane grinned. "I think it would be terribly exciting to cut a dash and be a noted whipster . . . and be a devil with the ladies, of course," she added saucily.

Far from scandalized, Damien laughed aloud, his teeth flashing whitely in his dark face. Ariane laughed too, though she admitted after another drink of her brandy that she wouldn't like the gaming. "I should hate to lose even the smallest amount," she said, half-ashamed. "But I should like the dancing and the clothes. I am a deal fonder of nice clothes than I ever knew," she allowed so seriously that Damien chuckled, and she was forced to acknowledge the humor of her admission with a smile. "Though, for all that I should enjoy the city, I wouldn't forgo the country entirely. I should miss . . ."

"Horses?" Damien said with a smile.

Ariane nodded seriously. "Horses, and other things as well. I don't suppose one can enjoy the sharp air of autumn in the city, nor the color of the new leaves in spring, or . . . having the time to really converse, as you and I do. I like talking to you very much.

"Oh!" she cried, flushing with mortification as she realized what she'd said. "I am prosing on so! You must think me a perfect ninnyhammer." Casting an accusing look at the empty glass in her hand, she placed it a little unsteadily on the table beside her.

Uncomfortably aware that Damien had given her no reassuring rely, she peeked at him through her lashes. Her breath, in the next instant, came a good deal faster. Damien's black eyes seemed—and she had never seen them so before—as soft as the softest velvet. Without thinking, she lifted her head, an uncharacteristically shy, uncertain smile curving her lips.

No sooner had she looked at him than it was as if that melting look had never been. "I think it is time I left," Damien announced quietly, his eyes now veiled.

"I have made you angry." Whether she'd made a statement or asked a question was unclear, but the distress in her green eyes was not.

"Angry?" Damien asked with an irony she missed in her anxiety. "No, infant, I shouldn't say I am angry."

"But . . ." She made an ineffectual gesture toward the cards.

"You owe me fifteen thousand pounds as it is, sweeting. I don't think you can recoup your losses."

Looking up as he rose, Ariane searched his face for some clue as to how she had offended him so completely, for she must have offended him, she thought, or he would not be leaving so abruptly.

Her expression brought Damien to a halt beside her chair. "Believe me, you've not made me the least angry," he assured her softly.

She was not convinced, as her widened eyes showed, and Damien reached out with his thumb to smooth her brow. From there his fingers trailed lightly over her silky skin to her chin, stopping there. "Anger is not my feeling at all, *chérie*, believe me," he whispered, his warm breath fanning her cheek, before his lips brushed hers ever so lightly.

When the door closed behind him, Ariane was surprised to find she'd lifted her fingers to her lips. Gingerly she touched them, unable to believe Damien had really kissed her, there, on the mouth.

Unable to collect herself, she sat where she was until the

fire had nearly burned itself out. By then, the effect of the brandy having worn off somewhat, she had come to a more sober assessment of what had occurred.

At first she'd thought, perhaps, that his kiss, however fleeting, had meant he felt something more than affection for her. But as she made her way to bed, she acknowledged, sighing, that his butterfly kiss had likely been the merest commonplace. A farewell gesture, no more.

If her reaction to it had been intense out of all proportion—she'd felt dizzy just watching his mouth descend to hers—then it just proved what a silly, green chit she was.

At least she had, she allowed with a grimace, learned one valuable lesson that night: she would never, ever, drink brandy again.

12

Oh! What a joy it is to be out of town!"

Watching Ariane breathe deeply of the salt-tinged air, Solange smiled fondly. "You have been most patient, *ma chère*. Not once have you complained at not having your so-loved rides." Shaking her head, she added unhappily, "I could not know when I asked you to forgo them that Damien would be away so long."

Ariane looked up from watching the waves crash against the cliff below. "Have you heard from him, Solange?"

"*Non*." Solange shook her head. "There has been no word."

"Is it possible he has stayed away this month because of something to do with Colin, do you think?"

Solange's kind heart constricted before the fierce hope that flared in her young friend's eyes. In truth, she did not know why Damien had left at all, much less why he had not returned. At first she'd assumed Maccauley had summoned him, though he had not actually said so. Now, she was less certain. It was unusual for Damien to leave any project unattended for so long. True, Sir Henry had not come down from London as yet, but Triens was here.

Next she had wondered if something had not occurred between Ariane and Damien the night she had left them alone together due to her migraine. It was the next day he'd departed. But when Ariane had seemed as puzzled by the whole matter as she, she'd dismissed that notion as well.

Now, regarding Ariane with sympathetic eyes, she shook her head. "I do not know what keeps him," she said honestly. "But he will not forget Colin. You may be sure of it."

Misinterpreting Solange's frown, Ariane at once looked contrite. "I did not mean to press you, Solange. I know the wait has been difficult for you as well." Ariane turned to look out over the sea. "It is only that I feel so useless," she murmured half to herself. "I've learned nothing of value in all this time. Sometimes I wonder if Damien did not plan this scheme as an elaborate ruse to keep me away from whatever he is really doing."

"*Oh, non, ma pauvre*," Solange exclaimed. "You must not think it. We are the center of Damien's effort, I assure you."

Seeing the upset she had caused her friend, Ariane caught her hand and, giving it a squeeze, apologized so sweetly that Solange had to bite her tongue to keep from confiding that it was Ariane's friendship with the Comte de Triens around which everything revolved.

Because of it, Solange had free access to the count's circle and had been able to identify two of his associates and at least one of his servants as probable accomplices; had noted that a man with a relatively sensitive government position had left one of the count's dinner parties for a long tête-à-tête with his host; and could remark even now that the count's yacht had only just returned to the bay, its brief outing coinciding most amazingly with the departure of a large convoy of supply ships from Portsmouth.

But Ariane could only be told how effective she'd been at penetrating Sir Henry's household, which was, at least, the truth. Her relations with Mary Mowbry had blossomed into a true friendship, and Lady Hester was so taken by her that Ariane virtually had free run of the house.

If only she had not felt the prickings of her conscience as she watched Ariane's friendship with the count grow apace, Solange might not have looked so impatiently for Damien's return and an end to their business.

All the while Damien had been away, Ariane had not found anyone who interested her so much as the count did, and though she certainly had not come to love him, it was clear her affection for him had deepened considerably.

Perhaps they could manage to keep the truth from her in the end; Solange prayed that they might. It was not only that Ariane would be dismayed to learn her good friend was a spy. That would be a blow, but Solange, knowing her as well as she did, thought Ariane would be even more distraught to learn that her friendship with the man had been manipulated from the start by Damien. She would feel used, badly used, Solange feared.

Ariane saw the frown etching a line on Solange's brow, and believing it was her worries about Colin that had distressed her friend, she deliberately sought to lighten the mood.

"*Eh, bien.*" She shrugged, her imitation of Solange's gesture so exact that her companion could not keep from laughing with her. "Shall we rejoin the others? I think our luncheon will have been prepared by now. Not that we need hurry," she continued, her mouth lifting as she took Solange's arm. "If I know the count, we shall have enough food to satisfy three times our number."

The other guests were sheltering from the sea breeze behind a stand of trees an earlier owner of the estate had had the wisdom to plant, and when she rejoined them, Ariane saw with a smile that the arrangements the count had termed simple, were, in fact, sumptuous.

A table long enough to accommodate all twenty of his guests, and low enough to be reached while reclining upon a thick cushion, had been set as formally as if they were attending a banquet at Carlton House.

Upon it had been placed an astonishing variety of dishes. From where she stood Ariane saw three pâtés, sliced roast duck, prawns served cold and prawns served hot, breaded oysters, poached salmon, a ragout of vegetables, savoy cakes, lemon cakes, and raspberry ices.

Shaking her head, Ariane searched out her host, finding him quickly, for, dressed in a stiff brocade coat, the count stood out dramatically from the other men, most of whom were attired in mere superfine. He was seating Lady Hester, she saw, with the beginnings of a smile.

"I do declare even with this awning above us, I can feel the heat!" Ariane heard Mary's companion, who was never comfortable out of doors, fret. "They say too much heat will ruin the complexion, you know."

The count, ever diplomatic, soothed her, saying that her complexion was the milky color it should be. "The added light only allows us to admire it the more," he said politely.

"Do you think so, my lord?" Lady Hester cried hopefully. "I hadn't thought of that! Yes, thank you, perhaps I shall try a little of the duck, and the prawns as well."

The Comte de Triens served her himself, while his butler, Deparens, held the dish. For a moment Ariane was distracted by the sight of them together. She had not realized how much larger Deparens was than his master. His manner was so retiring that she had never noticed his height or the breadth of his shoulders.

Her attention was diverted from the butler when she encountered the count's gaze. He smiled, the creases around his blue eyes turning up, and when Lady Hester requested another pillow to support her back, he playfully rolled his eyes.

Smiling in response, Ariane immediately made her way toward him. Drawing Lady Hester's fire was the least she could do. After all, it was she who had mentioned with longing the picnics she and Toby had shared. And if her idea of a picnic and the count's differed vastly, that was not his fault. He had tried his best to provide what she wanted.

"May I sit beside you, Lady Hester?" Ariane inquired with a pretty smile after she had greeted her host.

"Oh, my child, I wish you to! Your good spirits will put me in just the right frame of mind to enjoy our outing. I confess if left to myself, I would likely never leave my drawing room."

"You are brave to have come along." Ariane patted her plump hand. "And wise, too, for I believe we all need a change from time to time, if only that we may know the better what it is we do like."

The count's blue eyes twinkled playfully at her for a moment before he suppressed his smile and looked to Lady Hester. "That such wisdom should coincide with such beauty is truly remarkable, do you not agree, *madame*?"

"You don't need to point out Ariane's good qualities to me, my lord," that lady replied staunchly. "I am ever so grateful to her for bringing Mary out of her shell."

"I did nothing for Mary, except to introduce her around," Ariane protested at once. "Mary's sweet temperament did the rest."

Instantly, Triens diverted Lady Hester to a consideration of which pâté she would like, and Ariane flashed him a grateful look. Lady Hester's remarks about Mary generally put her back up. Though Mary's companion often complained of Mary's shy nature, she had never once taken the trouble to inquire into the cause of it.

Looking around the party, Ariane saw Mary and Miss Corliss playing with a calico kitten. Mary was laughing, her eyes alight with wonder as the furry little creature cavorted at their ankles.

Only Ariane, of all those present, knew it was the first kitten Mary had ever had. Certainly her friend had not confided to Lady Hester that after her mother's death, her father, who had always been a remote figure in her life, had withdrawn almost totally from her, leaving her, his only child, in the care of indifferent servants. Without his supervision to spur them, they discharged their duties sullenly, denying even her simplest requests.

When Ariane learned they'd not allowed Mary a kitten, she had, within a day's time, found one for her, and then had persuaded Lady Hester to allow Mary to keep it.

In Ariane's opinion it was quite amazing that Mary was not more reticent than she was, and nothing short of miraculous that she was, in fact, the sweetest of persons. Had she been treated in the same manner, Ariane imagined she'd have become a hopelessly embittered recluse.

Indeed, Ariane's affection for Mary had grown to such an extent that she even regretted Mary's loyal attachment to Richard Rolfe. Were her friend not already in love, Ariane thought she'd have made the perfect match for Colin, her gentle wisdom the moderating influence his outrageous temperament needed.

If Colin was still alive, Ariane added before she could prevent herself. The thought made her clench her hands. She must not doubt it, she must trust Damien. He had said he would find Colin, and she must trust that he would.

It had been the day he left that he had promised so unequivocally. A wry smile touched her lips at the memory. Damien had not thought to see her that day. His surprise, when he saw her preparing to mount the steps just as he was leaving, had been apparent. He had recovered quickly, however.

And he smiled down at her in that way that made her heart beat erratically. "You must be reverting to your old ways, infant, if you and Mary were able to finish your shopping in so short a time. Solange said you left only half an hour ago."

"I've suffered no relapse. Lady Hester's head began to ache because it is so warm."

"More likely that good lady's head ached because there is so little in it," Damien observed, his dry response making Ariane laugh.

She'd felt awkward when she first caught sight of him standing there, his lean frame outlined in the doorway. All she could think of was that he had kissed her the night before, however briefly. Then, when she recalled how intensely she'd wished he would come back and kiss her again, her cheeks heated visibly.

His light remark about Lady Hester, however, restored them to something close to their usual footing. "Have you come to take Solange out for a drive?" she asked. It was the only reason she could think of for his being there at that hour.

To Ariane's surprise Damien shook his head. "Actually, you are just in time to wave me off," he informed her blandly, looking beyond her to the street. "They've just brought 'round my carriage."

"Off?"

"To London." Damien nodded.

As he started down the steps toward her, Ariane left off looking at him. Turning, she saw his chaise-and-four was indeed waiting.

She let out her breath sharply. "Is Brighton no longer intriguing enough?" she asked, her tone not as light as she'd wanted.

Finding it impossible to look at him, Ariane only heard the wry inflection in his voice as he replied, "I wouldn't say that, infant. As it happens, I've received a message requesting my presence in London."

She flicked him an appraising glance, but the sun was behind him, putting his face in the shade. Forced to rely on his tone, which was as cool as you please, she dismissed the highly appealing notion she had entertained momentarily; that his going had to do with their kiss. It seemed obvious he would laugh outright at such an inflated idea of her importance.

"Might the summons have to do with Colin?" she asked, taking hope as the thought occurred to her.

But Damien shook his head. "There was nothing said about Colin. But, Ariane"—his use of her name underscored the intent expression on his face—"whatever this may be about, I shall find Colin for you. I have given you my word that I will do so in return for the work you are doing for me. You must trust me on it."

"Of course," she replied without a moment's hesitation.

"Good, I shan't fail you," he said gravely, lifting her hand for a kiss. Absurdly she thought she could feel the warmth of his lips through her gloves. "And you," he went on, his mouth curving, "I trust to follow Solange's lead and to be such a model of decorum that Lady Hester remains enthralled."

Ariane smiled back. "I shall do my best," she assured him. Then, as much to keep him there with her as anything, she added pertly, "I shall even swear not to elope with the count before you return."

There was a flash of some emotion in his eyes before he gave her such a lazy smile she forgot everything but it. "See that you don't, infant," he drawled lightly, "I fear I should miss you, if you did."

And then he was gone, his carriage departing from her sight in the twinkling of an eye. Sometimes she wondered if he had ever been there, so long did it seem that he had been away.

But normally she was not so morose. Solange was too gay, and there were too many entertainments to attend. The count and Mary she particularly enjoyed, seeing one or the other or both every day. It was only occasionally now that her thoughts strayed to Colin . . . or to Damien.

13

That Damien could, in fact, entirely overtake her thoughts even when she was in company, Ariane had to admit with considerable chagrin, when she glanced up to see the Comte de Triens regarding her expectantly. It was obvious he was awaiting an answer to a question she had not heard, her mind having been attending to the Marquess of Chatham and not the flesh-and-blood company beside her.

"Ah, I think you are enjoying this day very much, are you not?" he asked fondly when Ariane admitted she had not heard his question. It was a very gracious thing to say in the circumstances, prompting her to give him her very best smile and reply that she was, indeed, very grateful for the outing he had given her.

When the count told her that he had merely asked if she would care to visit his yacht, Ariane positively beamed her reply. There was nothing, she said sincerely, that she would like more.

Accordingly, after luncheon, along with a group of eight other stalwart souls, including Solange, she donned a long cloak to keep the salt spray off her clothes and took her seat in the small launch that would ferry them out to the yacht.

The *Etoile du Jour*, for that was the name of his ship, had been built in Marseille, where, according to her host, the best French boat-builders resided. "They are masters with wood, as you shall see," he promised.

Once aboard, it was immediately apparent the count had spoken no more than the truth. Only the finest mahogany and teak had been used, and belowdeck, in the palatial salon, it had been carved in ornate and intricate designs.

In the master cabin, however, it was not the woodwork that drew Ariane's attention, but rather a painting of a very beautiful château. Placed by the painter on a picturesque hillside overlooking a river valley, its numerous turrets raised to a bright blue sky, it seemed a castle from a fairy tale. Behind her she heard one of the guests ask if the château was the count's home, and she was not surprised, somehow, when he admitted that it had, once, belonged to his family.

On the main deck again, the guests separated, trailing off to inspect whatever interested them the most. At the count's suggestion, Ariane accompanied him to the bow and stood for a moment pretending they were under sail.

The illusion was enjoyable, but she could not forget what she'd seen below. As revealed by the picture, the count's ancestral home was magnificent.

"I should find it difficult to be denied the ownership of so lovely a home, *monsieur*," she told him. "And yet you have never made the least complaint. I think you must be very brave."

"*Non.*" Triens shook his head, his voice low and vibrant. "There are things it is easier not to speak of, *ma chère*. The loss of my home is one."

"I am sorry," Ariane said simply.

The count inclined his head, accepting her sympathy, but making no reply.

Seeing how bleak his expression was, she said firmly after a moment, "But you must not despair! Napoleon will be defeated, and when he is, you shall return to your lovely château."

Triens' bitter laugh took her aback. "If the Bourbons are restored, I doubt I shall regain the Château Triens. I am not high enough in royalist circles. You see, I never had the opportunity to go to court and curry favor with that lot, for I was obliged to leave France altogether to seek the fortune I needed to fill my empty coffers." The count shook his head, his expression so withdrawn he seemed almost a different person. "Alas, my life has been a most unpleasant irony, *ma chère*, for, when I had lands and a château, I lacked the wealth to support them. But, when, after many years of struggle, I had gained the wealth I needed, I found I had lost my lands and even my château to the mobs. Now . . ." His shoulders lifted slightly as he looked over the sea toward his homeland. "Now, who knows what will happen."

Without thought Ariane reached out to cover his hand as he gripped the rail. "I think you very brave for going on with your life in the splendid way you do."

Though her companion gazed down at the slender hand that offered him comfort for a long moment, when he looked back at Ariane, he was again his usual polished, contained self. His mouth curved in a rueful smile, he said, "The sun Lady Hester complained about has turned me mawkish, I fear. Forgive me, please, for being tedious."

"But of course I do not find you tedious," Ariane chided, indignant at the thought. "We are friends, *monsieur*, or so I thought, and friends may hear troubles as well as triumphs."

The count smiled a real smile, one that turned up the lines around his eyes, and lifted her hand to his lips. "I forget to whom I speak, my dear Ariane. I may call you by your lovely name today? I should have known you would not be dismayed by my display of emotion. I wonder if you've any idea how rare you are, my dear?''

Ariane blushed before the warmth of his regard. "Please, sir, you will put me to shame," she begged.

"If you blush, *ma chère*," the count responded, still holding her hand in his, "it is only because you are not only beautiful and spirited, but also most amazingly modest. *Enfin*, you are perfection, Ariane."

Ariane was past blushing, and her eyes widened with alarm. The count, though he'd made his admiration for her clear from the beginning, had always been so composed when in her company that she'd come to think he regarded her rather like a favorite daughter.

That she had misjudged his feelings—and badly—she realized with considerable dismay. The light in his eyes was not the least paternal, and she was very much afraid he was about to say something irretrievable.

She could never love him as more than a friend. It simply was not possible. Other young women might do more than admire him, might even desire intimate contact with him, she knew, but not she. She could not lie to him if he were to say he wished her to be more than a friend.

Reading her open gaze easily, the count saw he'd gone too far. The realization did not make him reconsider his intention to make her his wife, an intention he'd formed some weeks ago, but he realized he must be patient still. She was not ready to receive his addresses and he did not wish to give her a disgust of him.

"I have made you uncomfortable, *chèrie*." He kissed her hand again and then released it, placing it carefully upon the rail. "I apologize for that, if not for the sentiments I have expressed. You will not hold a friend's admiration against him, I hope?"

His smile was so wistful that Ariane's heart went out to him. "There is nothing to apologize for, *monsieur*," she hastened to assure him. "It is only that . . ." She paused, uncertain how to phrase her remarks. "I am a green miss who knows little of admiration," she confessed at last with a quick smile. "Please, I would not like this to interfere with . . . my tour."

With a bow the count presented his arm. "Then, by all means, come with me, and I shall show you my very beautiful ship."

As the count explained the workings of the yacht, Ariane paid him close attention just as she would normally have done. There seemed little point in worrying just then about her relations with him. Later, she would seek Solange's advice. Older and infinitely wiser about the relations between men and women, Solange could tell her how she might both keep Triens as her friend and discourage any serious intentions he might have.

As if to prove that all was as it had always been between them, the count, after he had answered all the nautical questions Ariane thought she could plague him with, inquired curiously of her what costume she intended to wear to a fancy dress ball being held at the Castle Inn Assembly Rooms.

His interests in her costume did not surprise her, though it did make her smile. He had on more than one occasion made a suggestion as to what dress she might wear or what piece of jewelry would suit her. Though she had not always followed his advice, she had listened. Certainly she had never been offended. She knew very well the count's meticulous nature and how he must arrange everything about him to his satisfaction.

And as this was to be the final Assembly of the Season, a great deal had been made of the event. Many conversations during the past week, including several in which Ariane herself had been involved, had revolved around the costumes to be worn.

To Triens she confessed with a chuckle, "I am afraid Madame Crécy and I cannot come to an agreement. Her suggestion that I go dressed as a shepherdess—or a *jeune fille* with the sheep, as she says—does not find favor with me, while mine, that I dress as a pirate, nearly sent her into the boughs."

"As well it should!" The count laughed. "But a

shepherdess?" he asked rhetorically. "At least a dozen girls will be costumed in that insipid style."

"In truth Solange thinks fancy dress too silly to merit much thought." Ariane's eyes twinkled as she sought to excuse Solange's lapse. Normally the count praised Madame Crécy's taste, and Ariane did not wish her friend to fall entirely out of favor. "I believe she only made mention of a shepherdess's dress, because it was the first thing that came to her mind after I had made my suggestion."

"Anything but a pirate?" The count smiled. "But, wait," he exclaimed suddenly. "I have recalled a costume I own that would look very lovely on you, if you should care to wear it. It is the sari you admired."

"But I couldn't accept it, *monsieur!*" Ariane shook her head. "It is too precious."

"Of course you may wear it," the count said easily. "There is no reason you may not, for you will oblige me by not permitting our earlier discussion to influence you against me. I shall not make you a gift of the clothing, that would not be *convenable*, I understand. It is only a, ah, how do you say it? A loan! Yes, a loan, only, my dear. *Alors*, you will enjoy looking so exotic, I think."

He had guessed her feeling so accurately on all counts that Ariane laughed. It was, of course, their earlier discussion that had caused her to demur so hastily. To wear his costume when she did not want to encourage his expectations seemed foolish, indeed.

But the thought of wearing the beautiful, unusual garment was appealing. She would enjoy it, as he had said.

"*Alors*, we shall allow Madame Crécy to decide," he said, his blue eyes twinkling very nicely, and Ariane was not reluctant to accept the gallant compromise.

14

The light shed by the candles in the Castle Inn Assembly Rooms reflected off an improbable assortment of fanciful and luxurious costumes, but Evan Huntsleigh did not notice the effect. His rapt gaze remained upon his partner.

"I will admit, Miss Bennington, that I have never entertained the slightest interest in travel before tonight," he was telling Ariane, "but seeing how beautiful you look in that garment . . . I say, what did you call it?"

"A sari," Ariane supplied with a smile. Of all the young men who paid her court, Ariane liked Mr. Huntsleigh the best. Possessed of a shock of sandy-brown hair and a pair of guileless blue eyes, he was as sincere as his countenance was open.

"Well, stap me if I should mind visiting the country it comes from! Should the ladies there look even half so lovely as you, I would think I was in heaven."

Ariane, her eyes twinkling at such flattery, replied that she could never object to being an inspiration for travel.

She quietly studied her young partner's expression. If Mr. Huntsleigh harbored the slightest reservation about her costume, she knew he'd not be able to hide it. It gratified her to see unqualified approval reflected in his eyes.

After a lengthy discussion, during which Ariane had described fully her encounter with the count, Solange gave it as her opinion that nothing would be gained by refusing the count's gracious offer of the sari. "He seems to understand well enough your feelings, *ma petite*. And this material, it is extraordinary."

Having never seen anything half so fine as the shimmering silk—even to touch it was a pleasure—Ariane did not argue. When she wrapped the sari around her, however, and realized she could wear nothing but the thinnest chemise beneath it, she did wonder what Damien would think of it.

Solange, who had seen women go out in company after dampening their muslins, did not lift so much as a brow, and, reassured, Ariane went on to the Assembly, where her costume did create something of a sensation, but not a scandalous one, she thought.

Certainly the conservatively mannered Mr. Huntsleigh approved, she added to herself, smiling at that gentleman. Therefore she must be completely *convenable*.

The latest-comer to the Assembly Rooms, standing just inside the doorway, was not at all of like mind. The first costume to capture his attention when he entered had been the flame-colored silk that so gloriously displayed the lithe, slender figure it scarcely covered. He paused to enjoy how sensuously a woman who was not restricted by thick, cumbersome petticoats could move, and it took him a full minute to realize the object of his interest was none other than Ariane.

His brow drawn in a thunderous scowl, he turned abruptly in search of an explanation, not at all aware that he disappointed two ladies eagerly tripping forward to be the first to greet the incomparable Marquess of Chatham upon his return to Brighton.

Thoroughly taken aback when Damien made her only the briefest greeting before launching into a tirade on Ariene's costume—it was a scandalous rag that fit her indecently well—Solange said the first thing that came to her mind, and thereby effectively condemned Ariane in Damien's eyes.

"But, *chérie*," she protested a little fearfully, "it is not so transparent as that goddess's wrap Miss Hornsby wears there. And *la petite* did so want to wear it."

Too well Damien recalled how Ariane had charmed Miss Crisswell into overlooking the breeches she should have been reprimanded severely for wearing.

He'd thought Solange could resist her wiles better than Crissie, but apparently he'd been mistaken. Just as he'd been mistaken in believing that, in deference to him, Ariane would subdue any impulse to behave outrageously.

No sooner was his back turned, however, than she paraded herself before the world in next to nothing.

"And Triens, you cannot deny Ariane holds his interest as you wanted," Solange continued, making an uncertain gesture toward the count, who stood openly watching Ariane, rather, Damien thought sardonically, like a man dying of thirst might look at a cool glass of lemonade.

"I wanted him interested, yes, Solange, but not ready to devour her."

Solange shrank back slightly. When his temper was aroused, Damien could cause the staunchest soul to shrivel, and Solange had never been particularly staunch. "Surely it is not so bad . . ." She tried one last time to spare Ariane having to deal with Damien in this dangerous mood, but she did not succeed.

The music had ended and Damien was already moving to intercept Ariane and her dazzled partner as they made their way to the refreshment table. "It is so bad, if Ariane looks like a demirep," he said over his shoulder. "And don't try to fob me off by saying it's your responsibility, Solange. I've seen Ariane at work."

As that had been precisely what she had intended to say, Solange shut her mouth and watched helplessly as Damien bore down on her young friend, the tight set of his mouth boding very ill for Ariane.

Blissfully unaware of her impending doom, Ariane took Mr. Huntsleigh's arm as he made to lead her off the floor. She was listening closely to his account of a recent mill he'd ttended in order that she might send a detailed description to Toby, when Mr. Huntsleigh stumbled to a halt.

Glancing at him curiously, Ariane was surprised to see him looking over her shoulder with an expression that closely approached dismay.

"Ah, er, Lord Ch-Chatham."

Damien! Ariane swung about, her face alight with welcome.

"Damien!"

The sight of Damien standing with easy grace directly before her set her heart racing. It was a sensation she'd all but forgotten. Just as she'd nearly put from her mind how rakishly handsome he was.

Though he was not in fancy dress, he did not suffer by comparison with the elaborately garbed men around him. To the contrary, austerely clad in his customary black, Damien made them seem silly peacocks.

Her appreciative gaze having confirmed that it was indeed Damien before her, Ariane returned her gaze to his face, prepared to make him an extravagant welcome. Her words, when she took in the expression on his face, died unsaid.

"Infant," he drawled coolly, raking her costume with the coldest look she'd ever encountered.

Ariane's chin lifted, but Damien's attention was already turned to Evan.

"Your servant, Huntsleigh." He inclined his head imperiously.

It was to Evan Huntsleigh's credit that he did not slink away at once in deference to that plainly dismissive gesture. Instead, he glanced uncertainly at Ariane, evidently weighing whether or not he might say that she was to take refreshment with him. He did not linger over his decision. With Damien plainly breathing fire, he made her a stiff bow and made good his escape.

Ariane did not watch the young man's retreat. What exactly had put Damien in such a taking, she could not be certain, though she had the sinking feeling it was her costume that displeased him so. But whatever it was that had caused his eyes to narrow scornfully and his mouth to tighten furiously, she could see that there was no hope at all of reasoning with him. No coward, she decided she would emulate Mr. Huntsleigh's example and fade away until, hopefully, Damien was in a less fearsome mood.

Easily guessing her intent, Damien grasped her arm and virtually lifted her onto the dance floor. "I am due a welcoming dance, I believe."

Though a dangerous spark kindled in her eyes, Ariane did not have the opportunity to tell him what she thought of such summary treatment. He was again flicking her costume with a deadly gaze. It was a brief perusal, but when he had, once more, captured her gaze, Ariane's cheeks were flaming.

"And to think," he assaulted her before she had the time to regroup her forces, "that when I heard there was a costume ball, I actually feared you might appear as Jed Tregan. How unimaginative of me not to realize that you'd have grown beyond such simple immodesty as a pair of breeches."

The scathing set-down had the fortifying effect of igniting Ariane's not inconsiderable temper. Her eyes blazing, she put aside the thought she herself had questioned the propriety of her costume. However questionable it may have been, she was absolutely certain it was not so beyond the limit that she deserved such a cutting remark the first time Damien set eyes upon her after being away an entire month.

"I do beg pardon that my costume is not to your liking, my lord," she retorted, her quivering voice low in deference to their public position. "As you have been gone this month without sending the least word as to your whereabouts, I could scarcely ask for your opinion before wearing it. It was Solange, the person you told me to obey in all things while you jaunted off heaven knows where, upon whom I relied, and for your information, she did approve of it."

"It is only because Solange explained that fact to me that I have not taken you home already," Damien rejoined shortly as the music began.

When Damien moved to take her into his arms, Ariane stiffened. The thought of feeling him close to her while he bristled with contempt was insupportable.

Afraid of causing a spectacle, she hesitated too long. Damien's hand closed fast around her waist, leaving her with only sarcasm as a defense. "I cannot imagine why you would want to dance with someone as lost to propriety as I," she hissed.

"I rarely dance with anyone not lost to propriety," was the immediate, cool, clipped, infuriating reply.

Stiff, her movements mechanical, Ariane followed

Damien's lead in the dance, though she could not have identified the music.

It was Damien who held her attention. Over the course of the past month, she had imagined innumerable variations on the theme of his return, but never, not once, not even fleetingly, had she imagined he would be furiously angry with her. Biting her lip, she sought to stem the hot, disgraceful tears pricking at her lids.

Damien, for his part, welcomed the tension he felt in her body. It was her just desserts. His fury had actually increased when he'd taken her in his arms, for, feeling the warmth of her skin through the thin silk of her costume, he was forcefully reminded how little she wore beneath her dress. Ladies in their boudoirs were more heavily clothed, as he should know.

With the intention of informing her that they would leave immediately after the dance, if he had to drag her out himself, he glanced down at her.

But Ariane did not oblige him by returning his look. As she kept her head down, the only view she inadvertently afforded him was a glimpse of her mouth.

It would have surprised her greatly to know that so little was enough to pull the Marquess of Chatham up short. The realization that she was biting her lip so tensely that her jaw quivered made him feel, if for only an instant, an ogre. "You'll draw blood if you don't cease that," he snapped, annoyed.

Worse was yet to come. His voice had exploded so unexpectedly into the strained silence between them that Ariane's head jerked up.

The eyes that met his were brimming with tears. One thing Damien knew with certainty. Ariane would never deliberately resort to tears to get her way. She might smile, cajole, or even stamp her foot, but she would never cry unless she were well and truly hurt.

Not that the expression in her vivid eyes was one of defeat. Far from it, had her look been a fist, Damien judged he'd have been rocked on his heels.

But even as she looked daggers at him, her fiery glance was betrayed. With the abrupt movement of her head, a tear spilled to slide ignominiously down her cheek. Groaning furiously, Ariane looked away.

But Damien had seen, and before she could do so herself, he caught the drop with his finger. He was not a fanciful person, but her tear seemed to accuse him. Curbing Ariane's outrageous impulses was one thing, but hurting her so that she cried was quite another.

They continued to dance in tense silence as Damien contemplated the top of Ariane's glossy head and reminded himself she was the young girl who, if she'd known she should not wear her groom's tight-fitting breeches, had not had the least understanding why.

"I had not thought to make you cry when I first saw you," he said, truthfully, at last. The only sign that Ariane was aware he'd spoken was an involuntary tightening of her hand on his. "I plead fatigue," he continued undeterred. "I traveled all yesterday and today, then had to scour Brighton only to find you . . ." Damien smiled faintly as Ariane's chin lifted belligerently, though she still avoided looking at him. "Dressed in a fashion I, ah, would not have chosen myself."

Ariane glanced up quickly, uncertain if he was apologizing. As quickly, she looked away. Damien's smile lingered at the corners of his mouth, a too beguiling sight by far.

"Are you apologizing for being a perfect beast in regards to this costume? Or for not possessing the manners to inquire after my health as is customary when two reasonably friendly acquaintances are reunited after a prolonged absence? Or both?"

Damien's smile grew broader. He had, it seemed, almost forgotten what a spitfire she could be. "Both."

She was obliged to toss a glance at him then. Met with black eyes that gleamed beguilingly, she felt a decidedly treacherous warmth spread through her.

"Lady Hester found my gown acceptable enough that she told Mary I might set a new style," she challenged. Damien's mouth curved so that Ariane's heart seemed to turn over. "And," she continued firmly, "I have been the very model of decorum this entire month long. You've only to ask Lady Hester, if you doubt me. She thinks me quite charming.''

Damien could not prevent his mouth from quirking. "Was it very hard?"

With admirable resolution Ariane did not allow herself to glance at Damien's mouth. "I even gave up riding," she continued as if he'd not spoken, though in truth she was answering his question. "When Solange said she feared I would find it too tempting to ride away from a groom, I knew she was likely correct, and I did not want to chance seeming the hoyden."

She had, she saw with great pleasure, succeeded in rocking Damien. "You have not ridden at all?"

"Not once!" Ariane informed him righteously. "And," she added, returning to the bone of contention between them, for she simply could not allow his cutting remarks to pass unanswered, "I would have you know that whatever you may think of my costume, no one else this evening has condemned me. Far from it, everyone else has liked it very well indeed!"

A lazy smile curved Damien's fine mouth as he eyed the defiant sparkle in Ariane's green eyes and the rosy flags flying in her cheeks.

"I do not believe I said I did not like your costume, infant," he corrected her softly, his gaze drifting appreciatively downwards. "I merely said, correctly, that I thought it revealing. In the extreme."

"You are no gentleman, sir," she accused, his incisive look having made her feel as if she were standing before him entirely unclothed.

"If I have embarrassed you, I apologize," he replied unperturbed. "I simply wished to make a point."

"Which you did!" she admitted, her cheeks heating again as she met his amused gaze.

When he thought she had suffered enough, Damien pulled her closer. "I admit I have been away so long I had forgotten how unaware you are, brat, and I apologize for that." His quietly spoken, conciliatory words had the effect of making Ariane give a little sigh. Damien, hearing the contented sound, reflexively tightened his hold on her, bringing her nearer still. "I stand reminded that you likely had little idea how you would look to, ah, others. Cry truce?"

Ariane, though uncertain of his full meaning, did want to cry truce. "Oh, yes, Damien!" She pulled back to give him a tremulous smile. "I hate arguing with you."

He laughed at that. "You manage admirably, I must say. But we must have a way to celebrate our truce. Ah, yes, I have it. Did I mention that I arranged to have a small yacht brought down, or that I had thought to take it out tomorrow . . ."

"Oh, Damien!"

The near ecstasy of her exclamation, made him laugh again. "A sail would make up for everything?"

"Yes!" However, as an image of the boat appeared in her mind, Ariane's brilliant smiled dimmed. "I cannot believe I've waited so long to ask. Damien, have you any news of Colin?"

"I know nothing reliable." His hand tightened on hers, as her lashes fluttered down. "Don't despair, Ariane. Colin would be the first to tell you that as long as nothing definite is heard, there is still hope."

Ariane nodded, desperately trying to keep hold of the straw that grew weaker the longer she waited. She had counted more than she realized on Damien returning with good news.

Her disappointment was so great that, when Damien suggested that they leave the Assembly shortly afterward, she agreed without protest.

Solange may have realized that Damien's interest in an early departure had to do with Ariane's costume, but Ariane, her mind on her brother, had for the time being forgotten his displeasure with it.

She did not think again on Damien's reaction to her costume until she was in bed, unable to sleep. Then she had the unpleasant realization that Damien had made no mention of the count's having lent it to her. Instinctively she knew he would not be much pleased, and not wanting to suffer further rebuke, she made a mental note to ask

Solange not to volunteer the information. There seemed little point in his knowing, for, after all, the matter could not be undone.

15

It took only one look for Ariane to fall in love with Damien's sailboat. About one-third the size of the count's, it was a sleek, trim, utterly stout little craft, which she realized at once was only large enough for the two of them.

"She's not as grand as Triens', I imagine," Damien observed wryly as he helped Ariane aboard. Seeing her surprise, he said Solange had told him of their visit to the larger yacht.

"The *Etolle* is quite grand," Ariane agreed, feeling it would be disloyal of her to add that it was rather much for her tastes.

Taking a seat to the far side of the long, wooden tiller, she said to herself, "This is how it should be," as she took in how little fuss going out with just the two of them aboard would be.

When Damien chuckled, she realized she'd spoken aloud. "If not having a crew to do the work for us is as it should be, then you are in the right of it. Uncleat that line there and throw it ashore. Good. Now sit down and keep the tiller pointed toward the center while I raise the sails."

Delighted to be given a responsibility, Ariane playfully saluted him. "As you say, Captain!" She laughed, her show of obedience prompting Damien to remark that he might keep her on board, for she appeared to be altogether more tractable on the water.

As he made short work of the sails, Ariane was afforded the opportunity to note how easy he made the task seem.

His rippling muscles visible through the light jacket he wore, he sent the sails skyward, then came, graceful as a cat, to drop down beside her without a single misstep, though the craft rolled in the breeze.

With the same efficient ease, Damien steered them through Brighton's gaily painted fishing fleet. Above them all, the sky was clear but for a few clouds on the horizon made a delicate pink by the early-morning sun.

"The wind's fresh!" Damien's white smile reflected his satisfaction at finding the wind to his liking now that they'd left the shelter of Brighton's bay.

To Ariane he'd never been more handsome. His enthusiasm lit his strong, masculine features, making him seem almost boyish, an impression only heightened by the lock of black hair that had fallen onto his brow.

The lack of constraint between them was an enormous relief. She'd not been certain what to expect, but Damien had made no reference to their disagreement of the evening before.

Too, he seemed to have entirely forgotten the kiss he'd given her. And why not? Ariane asked herself. A month had passed since then, and she thought it all too likely that there had been more than a few more passionate kisses with far more experienced women in the interim.

Realizing if she kept on with those thoughts, she'd soon be too gloomy to match Damien's mood, she, in a symbolic gesture, tossed her hat onto a berth below. With it went her thoughts about Damien and his activities in London.

When she'd tied a scarf around her hair to keep it off of her face, Damien taught her how to steer the little craft, how to keep the sails filled with the wind, and for safety's sake, how to spill that wind. It took a little time for her to feel confident, but when she had gotten the hang of it, the wind seemed to quicken slightly, lifting the boat so that she skimmed in the most marvelous way over the waves.

"I never imagined it would be so wonderful," she cried, her eyes sparkling brightly as she turned to look at Damien.

With his arms draped over the railing and his legs

stretched comfortably before him, he observed her, his eyes gleaming with amusement.

"I am sailing properly, am I not?" she asked quickly.

"Without either hat or chaperon, I believe there are those who would say you are sailing most improperly." He grinned crookedly. "But as we have left their censorious eyes ashore, I am surprised to find you concerned with their opinion."

Ariane thought better of saying that he'd taught her well enough the night before to be concerned with the opinion of others. There was no point in spoiling their day by resurrecting their quarrel. "You know perfectly well what I meant," she admonished instead, before returning her attention to the sails.

He then pleased her enormously by saying, "You're a born sailor."

Evidently meaning what he said, Damien uncoiled himself and disappeared below, leaving Ariane alone on the deck. When he reappeared, he had a spyglass.

"Are you looking for anything in particular?" Ariane asked after he had turned his attention to the fishing fleet, which was now between them and the shore.

When Damien only made some noncommittal sound, she did not pursue the matter, having at that moment discovered that, when she had the boat on just the right course, the tiller actually hummed beneath her hand. It was a most rewarding feeling, and Ariane promptly gave herself up to it.

They had gone some way, both preoccupied with their own thoughts, when Ariane bethought herself of something she felt remiss at not having asked about before. "Damien, were you able to get word to Mary's young man while you were away?"

Damien did not answer immediately, but when he did, he informed her briefly that he had been unable to find Richard Rolfe.

Ariane frowned. "Did you try?"

Damien took the spyglass from his eye at that and arched his brow.

"I did not mean it the way it sounded," she apologized

hastily. "It is only that I am surprised. Mary said he'd gone into Berkshire to buy property, and I assumed he had done so."

"There was no trace of a Richard Rolfe in Berkshire," Damien told her unequivocally.

The news shocked her. "Do you think he was an adventurer, Damien?" she asked, disregarding the fact that he had gone back to watching the fishing fleet. "Perhaps Mary's father was right, and he was only interested in her estate, or what little of it remains."

"It's impossible to say without speaking to him," Damien replied indifferently. "Did Mary tell you that her father lost money on the Exchange?"

"Oh, drat!" Ariane exclaimed with such chagrin, Damien looked his surprise. "I thought I might have learned something you didn't know," she admitted glumly. "The state of Sir Henry's finances is the only thing of interest I have learned."

Damien eyed Ariane's dismal expression a moment. "And you are feeling useless?" he guessed. When she nodded, he did not, to her relief, laugh. Far from it, he looked sincerely sympathetic. "Waiting is the most difficult aspect of our business," he commiserated. "While we wait, all we can do is position ourselves to be in the correct place to bring our plans to a successful conclusion when something does occur. And that is precisely whta you've been doing, Ariane. When Mary's father does come down from London, you will be able to visit his household frequently."

It was amazing, the effect he had on her. Though Solange had said something similar, it was not until she heard Damien say it that she took heart. "I hope I hear something vital," she muttered.

At once Damien gave her a hard look. "You are not to take any undue chances in an excess of zeal, brat, do you understand?" When Ariane's yes seemed too perfunctory, he told her grimly, "My dear, the people with whom we are dealing would think nothing of murdering you and then dumping your lifeless body in the sea."

The gruesome warning brought Ariane's widened eyes

around to his. "Do you understand?" he demanded. This time Ariane nodded more firmly.

Apparently satisfied, Damien asked if Mary had given her a definite idea when Sir Henry was coming, to which Ariane replied that he was expected within the week.

After pondering her answer a moment, Damien looked back at her, the expression in his black eyes considerably softened. "We are nearly there. Can you hold on?"

Ariane had to pull her gaze from his before she could answer as steadily as she wanted. Busying herself with looking at the sails, she replied gruffly that of course she could hold out, she'd held on this long, hadn't she?

Smothering a smile at her thinly veiled indignation at having her stamina questioned, Damien went below to fetch the luncheon basket. It contained only some bread, two cheeses, apples, and a bottle of wine, all in all a far cry from the count's banquet, but it was, nonetheless, entirely adequate to Ariane's needs.

While she refreshed herself, Damien took the tiller and steered them closer to the shore. They were, she saw when she looked, at the mouth of the count's bay. Using the spyglass, she watched a group of men load several large boxes onto a launch for transport out to the yacht.

"It looks as if Triens' ship may sail soon," Damien observed.

Ariane nodded absently. "The count said he would be sailing to Scotland after his ball."

There was a moment's silence as Damien reminded himself that there had long been sympathy between the Scots and the French, and then he remarked aloud, "You are on a close footing with Triens, it would seem."

Perhaps it was his disparaging tone, or perhaps it was only that Ariane was sensitive over anything to do with the count, but she replied, "I am not!" with unwonted force.

Damien's eyebrow lifted, mocking her. "You dance with him twice at every Assembly, know his future plans, and not least, allow him to make you a gift of a rare piece of clothing, and you say you are not on a close footing?"

"He did not give me the sari," Ariane protested, even as she wondered when Solange had found the time to be so informative. "The count loaned it to me for one night only. There was nothing close-footed about it," she added, clearly nettled.

"Solange says you've expressed some concern about Triens' feelings toward you," Damien persisted coolly. "Allowing him to dress you, you are advised, is not the most infallible way to dampen a gentleman's ardor."

"He did not dress me," Ariane snapped.

"Particularly if he intends donating that sort of dress," Damien continued as if she'd not spoken. "Seeing your charms so silkily displayed is only likely to stimulate his enthusiasm."

"You are making it all seem so indecent, when it was not," Ariane cried, appalled at the picture he drew. "If I did leave off a few petticoats, I still revealed a great deal less than all those girls with their bosoms almost bursting out."

"All those girls are not trying, supposedly, to contain the man's interest," Damien returned coldly.

Frustrated, Ariane tossed her head angrily. "As my relations with the Comte de Triens have nothing whatsoever to do with you, my lord, you need not concern yourself with the distasteful matter any longer. I," she added defiantly, "can manage quite well by myself."

The sudden, arrested, distinctly dangerous gleam in Damien's eye made Ariane go still, her throat working as she stared at him.

"Can you?" he asked far too softly.

Had she been thinking, Ariane, by the simple expedient of disappearing into the cabin below, might have escaped until Damien's temper cooled somewhat. He could have not abandoned his place at the tiller to follow her.

She was not afforded the luxury of thinking, however. Before she could fully take in what was happening, he had cupped her chin in his large hand; then, swiftly, as she watched stunned, his mouth captured hers.

This kiss had no relation whatsoever to the light, butterfly kiss he'd bestowed upon her before. At first his touch was almost rough, for he was angry. But not for long. Ariane's lips were too soft and too sweet and too yielding.

As Damien's kiss deepened, his lips caressing her with a fierce possessiveness, a delicious warmth spiraled through Ariane. Without realizing what she did, she arched toward the source of such intense feeling and opened her mouth to him.

Completely overwhelmed, she never gave a thought to pushing Damien away. And certainly he did not pull back. It was the tiller that finally broke them apart. A sudden shift in the wind wrenched it from Damien's loose grasp and sent it banging hard against him. Startled, he released Ariane so abruptly she fell backward.

For the next two moments everything was chaos. The sails whipped about loudly, sounding like a pair of kettledrums played at different, alarming rhythms, while the boom snapped back and forth above them with loud, frightening cracks. Damien's hands were everywhere at once, pulling ropes, holding the tiller, and reaching out to keep Ariane down.

Almost as suddenly as it had begun, the mayhem ended. The sails, once more filled with wind, quieted, as did the stilled boom.

To Ariane the silence seemed as deafening as the noise had been. Her eyes flicked to Damien, then flicked away when she saw he was regarding her steadily.

She bit her lip in an effort to stifle a cry. He must think her a wanton! She had not made the least effort to evade him. Her cheeks stinging so they hurt, she lifted a trembling hand to cool them.

When Damien caught that hand, she jumped. "Look at me, Ariane," he commanded firmly.

Slowly, very slowly, she obeyed. "Oh." It was a small inarticulate sigh of relief. The oddly tender light in Damien's dark eyes was not what she'd expected.

"I think I had it in mind to teach you how easily these matters can get out of hand," he said, distractedly raking his hand through his thick hair. "I succeeded rather better than I intended." He smiled then, a chagrined, penitent, utterly charming smile that made Ariane's heart turn over. "I beg your pardon, Ariane."

He looked so sincerely rueful, she smiled. It was a tremulous effort, for she felt most unsteady and, too, not at all certain she wanted him to repent. She was going to say as much when her words were drowned by a sudden, violent clap of thunder.

Their attention dramatically redirected, they saw that the clouds that had been safely on the horizon when they'd started out were now racing to overtake them. Immediately Damien moved to adjust the sails with reassuring efficiency and ordered Ariane to go below. "You'll be dry there. Hand me the coat in the standing locker just to the right," he added when she had descended the steps.

Ariane found a heavy seaman's coat as well as a thick jacket. She handed out the coat and, clutching the jacket, tried to adjust to the increased roll of the boat. With the wind behind them, the little craft wallowed heavily from side to side, and though Damien yelled down to assure her everything was well in hand, Ariane realized with a lurch that for her stomach, at least, it was not.

She did try to stay, but in the end, the small, enclosed space was too much for her. Donning the jacket, she returned to the deck.

The wind struck her like a live, wild thing, whipping at her skirts and hurling the rain against her face. "Get back down there," Damien yelled, but Ariane, despite the raging elements, shook her head.

"It's unbearable!" she shouted back.

Damien, perhaps because he saw how green she looked, did not insist again. "You'll soon be soaked through," he warned, pulling her down to sit within the shelter of his body. Cold rain assaulted her head and dripped down to soak her front and back, but with Damien's warmth around her, the wet did not seem to matter. Feeling safe and protected in the circle of his arms, she peeked up at him.

And caught his eye. He grinned! Not, she understood at once, because of anything that had gone on between them earlier, but simply because he was exhilarated by the wind, which gusted lustily around them and hurled them home all the faster.

"This is a ride we're not likely to forget!" He laughed and she laughed with him, her eyes taking on an added sparkle when she felt him lightly kiss the top of her wet head as he returned to the challenge of holding his own against the elements.

16

The next morning Ariane awoke with a headache and a vague feeling of uneasiness. The headache was accounted for as soon as she recalled that Solange had insisted, when Ariane arrived home soaked and shivering, upon dosing her with laudanum and sending her to her bed.

The source of her uneasiness was not so easily discovered. Thanks to the laudanum, Ariane had only the haziest recollection of what had occurred before she fell asleep.

As she strained to remember, an image of Damien emerged in her mind, and she recalled that she had asked for him after Solange had put her to bed. Solange had been there too, of course, but then, could Solange have left?

Of course! Ariane's frown cleared suddenly. Mary had come to call, and Solange had gone down to explain why Ariane was not able to go out. What had Mary wanted? Ariane shook her head restlessly. She had no memory of what Solange had said about Mary.

Ariane closed her eyes and tried a trick Crissie used whenever she could not recall a word she needed. "Think of something else, and the word will come in a trice," her old governess had advised.

Ariane only had to think of Toby, from whom she'd received a hilarious letter two days earlier, before, of a sudden, a substantial portion the fog in her mind lifted.

Clearly, now, she remembered Damien standing by her bed, and she had insisted he sit down beside her. "Won't you hold me again?" she'd begged groggily.

"Solange's far enough up in the boughs now, brat," Damien had refused her with a crooked smile. "If she found me in your bed, she'd have my head. Don't forget that the French know a thing or two about taking heads." Lifting her hand, he'd kissed it. "That will have to do for now. Let your eyes close. Sleep off your chill. Yes, that's a good girl."

It was the last thing she remembered, but it was enough. Ariane's face flamed. The laudanum had addled her—she'd felt almost as cold in bed as she had in the storm—but that was little excuse for such brazen behavior.

Luckily it seemed Damien had understood she was not quite herself. She distinctly recalled his smile, and having been subjected to his glare, she knew the difference between Damien in a forgiving and unforgiving mood.

Of course, what rake would not have smiled? He must know he'd made another conquest! Unbidden a vivid recollection of their sail or, more precisely, of their kiss while sailing came to her. She'd not requested that, however much she'd responded. The kiss had been entirely his doing.

And how he had kissed her! Passionately, possessively even, if she were any judge. Almost at once Ariane admitted with a grimace that she was not. It had been her first real kiss, after all.

Still, it had not been a light, butterfly kiss. Of that she was a judge.

And why had he forgotten himself so? Had he been jealous, perhaps, it occurred to her for no good reason to wonder? Jealousy would explain why Damien had acted as he had as soon as mention of the Comte de Triens had been made. From the start, it seemed, Damien had reacted oddly to her friendship with the French nobleman.

The thought that Damien might be jealous of the count was so entrancing, she forgot her headache. If he were jealous, then it followed as day follows night that Damien must feel something more for her than mere affection.

For the first time that day Ariane's eyes began to sparkle. He must! She knew he did. Damien cared for her. And she, she admitted unreservedly, cared very much, very, very much for him. Of course, half the world—the female half that is—did as well, she acknowledged with a wry grimace. But in her case, her feelings stemmed from more than his looks. They were riveting, it was true, but Damien was a great deal more than his looks. He was someone whose spirit matched hers. She could talk to him about anything, ride with him, sail with him.

She loved him. And he loved her. How simple it all was, she thought, smiling blissfully.

"Ariane! *Chérie*! You are feeling better?"

Ariane smiled happily. She was at one with the world, and informed Solange she was feeling quite well, but for her head.

"That is good." Solange nodded. "I should make the minced meat of that Damien for not taking better care of you, but if there is no lasting harm, I shall not resort to such drastic measures."

Ariane laughed as she pushed back the bedclothes. It was on the tip of her tongue to say that Solange could not slaughter the man she loved, but Solange had begun to speak again and her words were so momentous, Ariane temporarily forgot Damien.

"We need you well, *chérie*," Solange was saying. "Sir Henry comes tomorrow. It is what Mary came to tell you. You remember that she came?" Without pausing to see Ariane nod or to notice her blush, Solange continued, "She was very distraught. I am not certain why—she does not know me well enough for confidences—but she is to come this morning. Are you recovered enough to see her?"

The moment she had awaited so long having finally arrived, Ariane had no intention of allowing a little personal discomfort to keep her from being on hand.

When Mary did arrive an hour later, Ariane had dressed, breakfasted, and banished the pain in her head by the efficacious expedient of ignoring it.

The moment she saw Mary's ashen face, Ariane realized

Solange had not exaggerated her friend's state of mind.

"Whatever is the matter, Mary?" she asked, taking the girl's cold hands in hers.

"Father's coming," she began, her eyes swimming with tears. "I know I should not feel so undone by my own parent's arrival, but . . ." Mary's lips trembled so, she could not go on.

Ariane patted her hand gently and said nothing until she thought Mary had regained some control. "But . . . ?" she prompted softly then.

Mary let out a deep, shaky breath. "I am afraid you will think me the greatest fool when I tell you," she admitted.

"Well, I think you are extremely foolish to think so," Ariane informed her, her judicious teasing making her friend give a watery smile.

"It is so very strange, you see," Mary began more calmly. "There is nothing to explain my feeling, but when I think of Father's arrival, I experience the awfulest dread. No matter how often I call myself a ninny, I cannot get it out of my mind that his coming will precipitate a catastrophe."

To say that Ariane felt like the veriest villain at that moment would not have been to exaggerate. Mary's trusting gaze cut her like a knife. If something truly dreadful did happen, she'd be nearly as responsible for it as Mary's father.

It was only the thought of Colin that kept Ariane from telling Mary everything. Damien had said absolute secrecy was necessary, and she could not risk Colin even for Mary's sake.

But she could tell Mary she did not think her foolish. "People have such presentiments all the time, you know. If anything should ever happen to Toby or Colin, I know I would feel it."

"Oh, I knew you would understand," Mary sighed, giving Ariane a grateful, if teary smile. "It is true that for most of my life I've not greeted news of a visit from Father with much pleasure, but I have never experienced this sense of dread before."

"Well, the first thing we must do is have tea," Ariane said, turning away to give Mary time to dry her eyes. "Then," she continued, handing Mary her cup, "we shall think what to do. Perhaps I could come to stay with you a day or two."

The hope that flared in Mary's eyes died almost immediately. "Father would think it extraordinarily odd that you would stay with us when you've your own home."

Ariane sipped her tea, frowning. "It would seem odd, I suppose," she allowed reluctantly. A silence fell then, each girl caught up in her own thoughts. Mary's considerations centered primarily on trying to discover what disaster it was she fered, while Ariane busied herself with inventing a plausible reason for moving into Sir Henry's house.

When she had thought of it, she put down her teacup with a decided clink. "I have it, Mary," she exclaimed. "Solange has been invited to a house party in Kent, but cannot go because she must stay with me. We could ask Lady Hester if I might stay with you for a few days, in order to allow Solange to escape her duties. Would Lady Hester oblige us then, do you think?"

Mary's relieved smile was a balm to Ariane's guilty feelings. "I think she might." She nodded. "She would be particularly pleased to do so if your cousin stayed in Brighton, but I suppose he plans to go to Kent with Madame Crécy?"

"No, no." Ariane shook her head firmly, for she knew full well Damien would not leave now that Sir Henry was returning. "The invitation came when Damien was away and does not include him. You think Lady Hester would be in alt receiving Damien, is that it?"

"I know she would be," Mary corrected, managing a wry smile. "Even now I can hear her regaling Lady Ogilvie with what the marquess said when he came to call."

Ariane laughed, satisfied. "I think it can all be easily arranged. You must go home and tell Lady Hester that Solange is off to Kent and that I must return home unless I can stay with you. You might say how sad I am to miss the count's ball, particularly as I had prevailed upon Damien to escort me. She won't be able to resist the idea that she may make her entrance on Damien's arm."

"And you think Madame Crécy really wishes to go to Kent?" Mary asked as if she could scarcely believe such a fortuitous coincidence.

Of course, Ariane had fabricated the story of a house party on the spur of the moment, but knowing that Damien would like above all things to have her in Sir Henry's house, she was able to reply with conviction that Solange really did want to go to Kent.

When Mary had departed, she went at once to the study, where the butler had informed her that Lord Chatham and Madame were awaiting her. She made no effort to prevent her eyes from going at once to Damien. He was smiling over something Solange had said when she entered, and thus she could not be certain that the warmth she detected in his dark eyes when he looked around at her was intended for her.

To her credit, she did not allow herself to be distracted by her uncertainty. Displaying a laudable degree of self-discipline, Ariane put aside her feelings for Damien to attend to the vastly important matter at hand.

"Excellent work, infant," Damien commended when she had finished describing her conversation with Mary, his praise bringing a light flush to her cheeks.

To Ariane's surprise, Solange was not so quick to agree to her plan. "But the finale is always *très dangereux*," she protested sternly. "I should be afraid for you, *chérie*, in Sir Henry's house all alone."

"But it is so much more than we had hoped for, Solange," Ariane returned eagerly. "I promise I shall be very careful. You may tell me now just what to do."

"You will only keep your eyes and ears open, and not chance getting caught," Damien said firmly before Solange could speak. "It is a subject on which we are already agreed, is it not?"

"Yes." Ariane looked from Damien to Solange without a hint of doubt or question.

Solange saw that clear, fearless gaze and sighed. "I would feel better if I did not know you so well, *petite*. You will try very hard not to give to me *la tristesse*, yes?"

Seeing how truly concerned Solange was, Ariane flew across the room to catch her hand. "Of course, my dear Solange, I shall not make you sad. I should feel the veriest ingrate if I did, for you have been the soul of kindness to me. I shall miss you sorely."

At once Solange gathered Ariane in her arms and kissed her on each cheek. When at last they separated, their eyes suspiciously moist, Damien informed them that if they were quite through being maudlin, he would take his leave.

As one, they turned to protest such a lowering term being applied to their leavetaking, but Damien only laughed and pointed out that he, for one, had never cried on taking leave of a friend. Declining to dignify such a reply with an answer, the ladies turned to shrug at each other, as if to say, Men, what do they know?

In the face of such unity in the female ranks, Damien could only beat a retreat, which he did, still laughing.

Ariane watched him go with regret. She would have liked to tell him what she'd discovered of her feelings, and too, she'd have liked very much to have her guess as to his confirmed. But at the moment there were more important matters afoot. When Sir Henry and his contact were captured, then they could take up the issue of their relations.

17

Sir Henry arrived in the afternoon. A heavy, florid man with a pair of small, hard, brown eyes, he ignored Mary altogether and interrupted Lady Hester's greeting in midsentence to demand rudely who in blazes Ariane was.

To her surprise Ariane had to brace herself against the

flat, cold look he turned upon her. She had not thought much about Mary's father, really, but when she had, she'd imagined he'd have some of Mary's softness and even assumed it was that trait, minus the starch of Mary's courage, that had allowed him to betray his country.

At once she saw she'd not been on the right track at all. Sir Henry's eyes revealed him to be a ruthless, brutal, even vindictive man as surely as the prominent broken veins in his face attested to his heavy drinking.

Understanding better now Mary's antipathy toward her father, Ariane shot her a supporting glance, but Mary did not see. Her eyes were downcast and she was so pale that Ariane feared she might faint.

Before she could move to comfort her friend with a light touch, Sir Henry's booming voice brought her attention swinging back to him.

"The Marquess of Chatham's cousin, eh?" he exclaimed with loud relish, having been appraised of her supposed connection with Damien by Lady Hester. "There ain't a more bang-up-to-the-mark fellow than old Bourne's son, and that's a fact!"

Recalling herself to her role, Ariane smiled charmingly, as if she agreed with Sir Henry's estimation of Damien. She did not speak, however. If she were to open her mouth, Ariane was very much afraid that her tone would clearly reveal the distaste she felt for her host.

When Damien arrived for the tea to which Lady Hester had invited him, Sir Henry's toadeating was so pronounced that Ariane could scarcely contain herself. Even before Damien came, Ariane, as she prepared to enter the salon, heard him angrily order Mary upstairs to change her dress. "That rag ain't fit to receive the heir to a dukedom, as you would know if you weren't such a worthless chit."

Mary had run from the room, and it was all that Ariane could do to convince her Sir Henry's opinion was unimportant. "Damien likes you very well, as you must know, because he talks to you, and he only talks to people he likes very well."

Smiling through her tears, Mary allowed herself to be

convinced, and they returned to the salon with Mary dressed in a becoming muslin that Ariane deliberately complimented within Sir Henry's hearing. When he made no remark whatsoever, Ariane realized that the absence of criticism was as close to a compliment as he would get with his daughter. For her, however, he let loose a gush of cloying praise.

When Damien's carriage arrived, Sir Henry, who had been pacing restlessly about the room drinking one brandy after another, was the first to realize it. At once he rushed into the hallway to welcome his illustrious guest personally.

"Look, ho! Chatham! Welcome to my humble abode!" His unpleasantly loud voice carried easily into the salon. "Might have known you'd have a diamond for a cousin, eh? So pleased to have such a little beauty with us."

Ariane waited with no little curiosity to see how Damien would respond to Sir Henry. Would Damien consider it necessary to humor the man he was trying to prove a spy, despite his repellent manner?

No, she saw at once, when the two men entered the room. Damien was today every inch the Marquess of Chatham, heir to the Duke of Bourne. Lifting his brow faintly, he regarded Sir Henry with a cool, disdainful expression, though he greeted Lady Hester and particularly Mary in a most charming manner.

It taught Ariane something of a lesson to see that Sir Henry was not in any way put off by Damien's condescension. Far from it, he seemed to accept it as his due and only smiled the more broadly in response. Ariane could scarcely keep her nose from wrinkling, as she watched Sir Henry's bulky form caper about the room securing Damien the best chair, the best claret, and the best plate of refreshments, though Damien behaved as if the honors done him were so much his due that they need not be acknowledged by even the slightest nod.

Mercifully he did not stay long, and when he'd left, Sir Henry adjourned to his study, taking with him the half-empty brandy decanter. Ariane remained with Lady Hester and Mary in the salon, and while Lady Hester rhapsodized over Damien, Ariane listened for the sound of a stranger's tread or voice.

She heard nothing suspicious that afternoon, nor did she hear anything more promising that evening when she went to her room to change for dinner. Most disappointing of all, she did not hear anything that night, when the ladies all retired to their rooms and left Sir Henry to yet more brandy.

Ariane kept a vigil until two in the morning, when she heard her host stumble his way to bed. The click of Sir Henry's latch was one of the most dismal sounds she'd ever heard.

Damien noted her subdued spirits when he came the next morning to take her for a ride. They had agreed that he should, as it would give them a time in which they could speak freely.

"You are looking in poor spirits," he said as soon as they were away from the house.

At once Ariane rounded on him. "I learned nothing," she cried irately, her eyes flashing. "Nothing! And there is precious little time now."

Biting her lip, Ariane looked away, trying to regain control of her emotions. Knowing that her lack of sleep had strained her almost as much as her failure, she was grateful that Damien made no effort to comfort her. Had he, she knew she'd have cried out her frustration, a stupid, missish reaction that would have shamed her.

It was only after their gallop that she could at last glance most ruefully at her companion. "I am sorry to have taken out my frustration on you, Damien," she apologized. "It's not your fault, after all, that Sir Henry was contacted by no one the whole of yesterday."

Damien regarded her gravely. "I did involve you in this business," he pointed out.

But Ariane, knowing where the responsibility for her involvement lay, shook her head. "No, you only extended the invitation, Damien. I said I would do it. And you never said we were guaranteed success," she added with a little sigh.

"All our planning and waiting may still come to naught," he concurred. Then, taking in Ariane's glum expression with a half-smile, he added, "However, if I had to lay a wager on it, I'd say we won't come up empty-handed. It might give you hope to know that as soon as particularly important information on troop movements came to Mowbry's attention, he left for Brighton."

"And you didn't tell me," Ariane cried, though her sparkling eyes proved she was not as angry at Damien's negligence as her words sounded. "Oh, Damien, do you think there will be a meeting tonight?"

In reply, Damien's broad shoulders lifted slightly. "I can only hope so. But, brat," he continued severely, "keep it firmly in that adventuresome mind of yours that all I wish from you is confirmation of a meeting. I want no heroics. Stay in your room with your eyes on your window. No more."

As Ariane waved Damien off after he'd returned her to Mowbry's, she took the time to congratulate herself on her restraint. Though her eyes had strayed more than once to his mouth, she'd succeeded at keeping most of her thoughts on her mission and away from him. It was not yet time to ask him to kiss her again, she told herself with a strained little giggle.

For the remainder of the day Ariane sat with an ear cocked, though the reward for her attentiveness was only the sound of Sir Henry's restless pacing. By the time she bid Mary good night, she was exhausted. Waiting was, she found, a wearying business.

She did not, however, look even once at her bed. After she'd changed into her nightclothes, she sat in the window seat, her eyes fixed on the mews behind the house, and willed some new, furtive sound to come to her ears. Once more, she heard nothing.

Though she did not think she'd closed her eyes, she must have dozed, because when she did, at last, hear something out of the ordinary, Ariane only realized it after the fact. And then she was not certain what she'd heard. Breathless, straining forward tensely, she waited, afraid it had only been her imagination playing tricks upon her.

But it had not. To her joy, she heard after only a few moments a muffled exclamation coming from the hallway below. Someone had stumbled into an object in the dark, but what concerned Ariane was that the voice was not one she recognized.

Before she was aware that she moved, Ariane was at the door of her room, listening with every fiber of her being. The sound was faint, but eventually she distinguished the click of a door closing.

Without giving Damien's insistence on caution even the courtesy of an argument, Ariane glided out the door and on noiseless, bare feet made her way to the stairs. Craning her neck to look down, she saw a thin shaft of light issuing from beneath the door of Sir Henry's study.

She would go to the middle of the steps, she decided. When the stranger came out, she would be able to see him from there, and yet, unless he looked up, he would not be able to see her on the darkened stairs. Recalling Damien's warnings now, particularly his grim description of her fate if she were caught, she shivered. But she did not pause.

Varying her rhythm as she knew to do from her clandestine adventures at home, Ariane arrived undetected at her destination. She did pause there, a moment perhaps, but the light from Sir Henry's study drew her on.

Clutching her wrapper as if it were armor, Ariane crept down the hall, thanking God that at least the house was relatively new and the floors did not yet creak. When she gained the door, she put her eye to the keyhole. To her dismay the key had been left in it, and she was denied any view of the room.

When she put her ear to the door, however, she met with greater success. A man was speaking. At first his words were an indistinguishable blur of sound, but when she shifted position, she found she could hear more clearly.

"I could not come then," he was protesting. "I had to be certain you're not being watched."

"You think I'm suspected?" That was Sir Henry's demanding voice.

When the other man spoke quickly to reassure him, Ariane realized she had heard his voice before. It was tantalizingly familiar, but though she racked her brain, she could not place it.

Biting her lip, keenly aware how exposed her position was—visible from both ends of the hall as well as the stairway—she pressed her ear more closely to the door.

The stranger was still speaking. "You can't be too careful. And you know how he demands the greatest caution."

"I know, I know," Sir Henry said, impatient now. "It's only that the information I've got must be sent off immediately. But, look here, man, I will only give it to him."

The other man said something Ariane couldn't distinguish. It must have been a protest, however, for Sir Henry's tone in reply was belligerent. "I've something to discuss with him that doesn't concern you," he fairly shouted. "If he wants the information I've got—and it is about the spring offensive—then he will have to see me to get it. We can meet at the ball without raising suspicion. It will not seem the least strange if we're absent at the same time, as you well know."

Ariane did not linger another moment. She could not know how much longer the man would remain, and there was no place for her to hide. She would simply have to hope that the stranger did not refuse Sir Henry again and that the meeting between Sir Henry and the man they had not named—the one who must head the spy ring—would take place as Sir Henry had suggested. As far as she knew, there was only one ball being held the next night: it was the Comte de Triens' final affair.

She was at the top of the stairs when Sir Henry's study door opened, but Ariane did not try to get a glimpse of the stranger. Prudence at last prevailed. The information she already had was so important, she could not risk being caught. In her room she waited until all was quiet to close her door, and even then she stayed pressed against it, her heart beating rapidly for several long, tense minutes.

When she did at last seek her bed, her sleep was fitful. As she half-listened for Sir Henry to stagger to bed, she tried to think who the stranger was, his voice familiar yet not familiar, but could not. Frustrated, she longed for the day and Damien to come.

18

You what?"

Ariane winced. "I know I took some risk," she conceded, trying for a light tone and failing. "But what I learned may well mean the end of this business. And, oh, please do not glower so! I did not come to harm."

Damien stared at her, his jaw clenching, as he considered what might have happened to her had she been found kneeling there at Mowbry's keyhole.

Her death, and anything else her captors might have done to her before dropping her lifeless body off a ship, would have been his responsibility. It was he who had insisted on using her over the objections of both Solange and Maccauley. The old master was one of the few men, other than his father, whose judgment Damien respected, but he'd wanted to take Triens so badly that he'd waved him off and persevered with his plan.

Aye, he was doubly damned, for not only had he not heeded their objections to using an amateur, he'd also known, none better, how brave she was, how young, and how very impetuous.

Darting him a nervous look, Ariane decided she would be best served if she looked away from his darkening expression before he daunted her entirely. For he must listen to her. He could not let her efforts go for naught, simply because he was angry with her.

"Damien . . ." She said his name tentatively. He did not turn, but neither did he silence her. "I am sorry to have disappointed you so, but please, you must listen."

And though he did not give her leave to do so, she told him all that she had heard as completely and carefully as possible.

There was silence when she had done, and then Damien asked curtly, "Was there any signal arranged between them?"

Ariane shook her head. "Not that I heard, but I did not stay after they had named the place they would meet."

"Caution, heaven be praised," Damien remarked so dryly she flushed.

"You've enough information, nonetheless?" she asked worriedly after a moment.

"Yes, though I am loathe to admit it, I've all the information I need."

Damien eyed the delighted smile with which she responded to his words coldly. "You broke your word to me, infant. I cannot like it."

Ariane's eyes widened briefly then fell. His tone was quiet, but it lashed her far more effectively than if he'd shouted. "You would do well to recall that your brother's very life depends on your actions." Though she shivered, he did not soften his tone. "Tonight you are to do nothing but dance. I want your word of honor that you will engage in no heroics, Ariane."

Chastened, for Damien seemed a stranger he was so cold, Ariane nodded meekly.

During the remainder of the day her resolution to keep well out of Damien's business did not waver. She did not want to suffer such a set-down again, nor, reminded of Colin, did she wish to risk threatening her brother's life.

Once she arrived at the ball, however, Ariane found it impossible to remain completely aloof. Simple curiosity, at the very least, kept her eyes upon Sir Henry from the moment he entered the ballroom.

She was careful to keep up a gay, carefree appearance, dancing and chatting as she normally would, for Damien's benefit as much as Sir Henry's, but whether he went to the punch bowl, stood talking to friends, strolled into the card room, or danced, she knew with a certainty where Mowbry was.

So great was her concentration upon Sir Henry that it was only when Lady Hester asked if she'd seen the marquess that Ariane realized she had not, in fact, seen Damien in some time. Over the shoulder of her next partner she idly scanned the crowd for his tall figure, but in vain.

His absence might have been of little moment, but when she resumed her watch on Sir Henry, she was just in time to see him slip quietly from the room.

As if she had absorbed a touch of Mary's prescience, Ariane knew, somehow, that the moment they'd been awaiting had arrived. Frantically she craned her head, looking for Damien. Again, to no avail. Something, Ariane could not help envisioning a particularly appealing brunette whom Damien had danced with earlier, had diverted him.

Abruptly, making some vague excuse to her bewildered partner, she left him standing on the dance floor and rushed from the ballroom. Reaching the hallway just in time to see her quarry disappear into another corridor, she followed quickly after him, holding her rustling silk skirt tightly, but when she peeped furtively around the corner, he was not in sight.

Though she knew little of the count's house, Ariane did know that behind the first of the three closed doors facing her was the room in which the count displayed his collection of objets d'art. She did not think anyone would use it as a meeting place—it was too public—but she recalled that another door led from it to the middle room. If the conspirators were there, she thought it just possible she would be able to overhear their conversation.

Quietly, hardly daring to breathe, she crept past a priceless display of Chinese vases and, reaching the door, knelt down, almost giggling aloud in her nervousness at the thought that listening at keyholes was becoming a habit.

With a heady rush of emotion she realized her prayers had been answered. As clearly as if she were in the room, she heard Sir Henry, his voice raised angrily say, "You promised, damn you! You promised me you would marry her. I want a title, man. Why else do you think I've done all this?"

"Why for the money, my dear Mowbry."

Had she been brutally slapped, Ariane could not have rocked back harder on her heels. The mocking reply had been made in an accented, unmistakable voice. It was the Comte de Triens Sir Henry had arranged to meet.

Shaking her head from side to side, she tried to deny the evidence of her own ears. It could not be.

And then she remembered the picture of his château. "I was never high in royalist circles . . ."

Of course. He'd thrown in his lot with Napoleon to retrieve his heritage. Little wonder he had seemed so strained that day. He must have known what she would think of him if she knew.

Did Damien suspect? The thought came unbidden. Perhaps it was the fear that she would fall in love with a dangerous spy that had made him so anxious over her relations with the count—not jealousy. But why had he risked that possibility? Why had he allowed her to make a friend of the man? Why had he not told her?

Ariane shook her head as if to clear her mind. Though it seemed as if the very ground beneath her had suddenly shifted, she must not collapse. There was still Colin to be thought of . . . and Mary. Though she was uncertain for the first time whether she truly cared to hear more, Ariane forced herself to return her ear to the door.

"It will not be my title that lifts you from obscurity, *mon ami*," Triens was saying. "I only promised to consider the marriage, but you must see how very little your wren and I care for each other—"

"Where do you think you'll get information as useful as mine, Triens?" Sir Henry blustered. "By God, I'd be a fool to continue risking my life now you've played this trick upon me."

Surprisingly the count did not seem much put out by the threat. "Do calm yourself, Mowbry," he advised silkily. "There's no use bringing in a stray passerby to see what it is upsets you so." There was the clink as of a glass being poured. After Sir Henry had had sufficient time to take his sustenance, the count resumed speaking, administering the coup de grace so deftly, Ariane felt chilled. "Now, then, my dear Sir Henry, as to your threat to end our, ah, relationship, I am afraid it carries very little weight at all. You see, I never work with anyone whom I believe has fallen under suspicion, and you, dear sir, I do believe, are suspected."

Sir Henry spluttered, choking on his brandy, but Triens scarcely paused. "Why else," he proceeded smoothly, "would an agent from the War Office have attempted to woo the sweet Miss Mary? Yes, Mowbry, I do know about Richard Rolfe."

Again Sir Henry made a choking sound, but Ariane scarcely heard his coughing.

Mary's Richard an agent! Could it be possible?

"I know as well," the count was speaking again, his voice demanding Ariane's attention, "that you have paid a certain Captain Hanks to make shark's bait out of the intrusive lad. Mowbry, Mowbry," he chided softly, "you are far too impetuous. Berkshire swarms with War Office agents now, you know. If they have not already discovered the late Mr. Rolfe's fate, they soon will, and with the assistance of a little gold, your servants—who are possessed of amazingly little loyalty, if I may digress to say so—will lay his death at your door. And so, I think, my dear Mowbry, you will spare me any further harpings on marriage. You will hand me the packet you possess in return, merely, for transportation out of England—and away from the hangman."

A pregnant silence fell, and Ariane imagined Sir Henry reaching frantically for another brandy. She'd not have refused one herself. There could be no doubting poor Richard Rolfe's fate. "Shark's bait," the count had said. It was terrifyingly similar to the fate Damien had warned her would be hers if she were caught out.

Her thoughts returned to Damien, she considered the implications of what Triens had said. If Richard were a confederate of Damien's, and it seemed he was, then Damien must have known about him from the beginning. While she had prattled on of Mary's one true love, he had been aware the man was a War Office agent.

Now, if Sir Henry's servants were as easily approached as the count had said, he must know as well Richard Rolfe's gruesome fate.

And he had said nothing to her.

Had he not trusted her to keep her knowledge from Mary, perhaps? Whatever the precise reason, it seemed there was only one conclusion to be drawn: Damien had not, in all, trusted her in the matter of Richard.

"We linger unduly, Mowbry." It was the count's voice, icy now, that interrupted Ariane's painful thoughts. "You cannot wish to be found with that document on your person. And if it helps to decide the issue, I agree to see that you are set up comfortably in the Indies. I daresay you'll not take living close to the source of rum particularly amiss," he added, dryly enough to cut.

Sir Henry made no response, but Ariane heard a chair creak, and in her mind's eye she could see him stand to withdraw the paper Triens wanted. The count must have taken it, for he said then, "I think it best if you leave now, my dear man. I'll send you word . . ."

"Ah, excuse me, gentlemen. I do apologize for interrupting, but I believe that parcel is, in fact, mine."

Damien! Where he had come from Ariane could not imagine, but that deep voice was unmistakably his.

"Chatham!" Sir Henry's harsh cry sounded loudly in Ariane's ears.

"Did it escape you that I work on occasion for Maccauley, Mowbry?" Damien replied, his tone as cool as you please.

"So it is you who have led the chase after me." Triens' quiet tone was in marked contrast to Sir Henry's. Apparently Damien inclined his head affirmatively, for the count then said—and Ariane could almost see his thin smile—"I confess I am not as surprised as my friend here seems to be. I had a premonition I should not invite you to this, or any other, gathering, but—"

"You could not forgo the lovely Miss Bennington," Damien finished, sounding for all the world as if he were enjoying their exchange. "Such a strong attachment is dangerous for a man in your profession, Triens."

"Ah, but you chose your bait well, did you not?" The Frenchman responded in the same seemingly amicable tone. "I was so entranced I never questioned the little one's background. Is she not even your cousin?"

"My cousins are all well beyond the age that interests you, *monsieur*. I confess that I had not expected her to charm you so completely," he continued, offhandedly clarifying whether he'd suspected the count all along and simply not trusted Ariane enough to tell her. "Still, I've no quarrel with my success. Now, gentlemen, shall we exit through the doors onto the terrace? My men are waiting."

"She won't know?"

"No."

There was no question to whom the two men she'd counted friends referred. It was she they intended to keep in ignorance, each for his own reasons. She felt betrayed by the count, but oddly she could, almost, forgive him. His interest in her had not been playacting. He loved her. Of course he would not want her to know what he was.

But she did not give the count much thought. It was not he who had engaged her deepest feelings. Damien had done that. And now she had learned that he had, as well, withheld his trust from her, that he had used her in a scheme without her knowledge or consent.

She had thought he might love her. Oh, folly! To him she was merely a well-wrapped piece of cheese.

Stifling a sob, she rose to flee, to place as much distance between herself and the marquess as possible. She would never see him again, she swore to herself.

It was a vow she was not destined to fulfill. When some sixth sense did at last warn her there was someone behind her, it was too late. Spinning about, she was caught by the count's butler, Deparens. Clamping a thick hand over her mouth before she could scream, he placed a knife at her throat with the other.

Far too late came the realization that it was Deparens who had met with Sir Henry the night before. Never having heard him say anything beyond the brief courtesies uttered by servants, she had not been able to identify the cool, businesslike tones of the stranger as his.

Quickly, before she could do more than lick her abused lips, Deparens removed his hand from her mouth and thrust her roughly before him into the count's study.

The three men to whose conversation she'd been listening were gathered near the window a few feet away,

Damien to one side of the other two, the lethal pistol in his hand trained on Triens.

All three spun about to see what had caused the disturbance at the door. The count's reaction was the most dramatic, for he sagged backward as if he'd been hit.

Damien's pistol did not so much as waver, nor did he, Ariane noted angrily, flick her the least glance. She could not forgive him the omission even when she realized that his narrowed gaze was fastened on Deparens' knife.

"Let her go, if you value your master's life, Deparens," Damien warned with what Ariane thought was a damning amount of calm.

But Deparens only stared at his master. In his turn, the count stared aghast at Ariane, seeming not even to have noticed how his servant threatened her.

"*Ma petite*," he began, his voice cracking, "I had hoped you would not have to know . . ." Distraught, he looked to Deparens to explain Ariane's appearance.

"She was listening at the door," he said.

The count spun to glare at Damien. "So! Your word is nothing, I see, *monsieur*. You had planned for her to know the truth."

"Tell your man to release her, Triens," Damien demanded again, his deadly gaze flicking only briefly from Deparens to the count as he ignored the count's outrage.

But Triens, infuriated, sought his revenge. "Alas, *chérie*." He gave Ariane a brief, sad smile. "You would have done best to encourage the offer I so desired to make. Unfortunately, you are at least a little in love with the marquess, are you not? I saw your interest, of course, but I dismissed it, for I thought you too closely related." He shook his head dismally. "He will not offer you marriage, you know, *ma belle*. He is betrothed and has been for some time."

It was absurd that Ariane should have felt any pain. She was already disillusioned with the man who'd taken her heart with such consummate ease. What did it matter, when he had teased her, indulged her, kissed her even, if all along he had been betrothed?

Absurd or not, her teeth clamping painfully upon her

soft lower lip, she looked to Damien. His implacable expression must have left her looking as stricken as she felt, for suddenly, irrevocably shattering the unbearable tension in the room, came Sir Henry's malicious laugh.

"Oh, that's rich," he gasped, wheezing loudly, "You little tart, you've played the whore for naught."

Later Ariane would recall that Damien's lips actually whitened, but at the time she only noticed that it was the count who whirled furiously upon his former confederate.

Ariane, however, needed no one to defend her from the likes of Sir Henry Mowbry. Despite Deparens' punishing grip, she drew herself up proudly. "I have played the whore for no one, Sir Henry," she informed him coolly. "I agreed to work for Lord Chatham in order to find my brother, Colin, who had been working with him."

The instantaneous change of expression on Sir Henry's face sent a shiver of dread down Ariane's spine. With complete certainty she knew she did not wish to hear what he would say next.

"Your brother," Sir Henry shouted, malevolent and gleeful all at once. "By George, I knew you reminded me of someone! It's the set of your features and the way you worry that luscious mouth, just as you're doing now. Rolfe, the deceased Rolfe, I should say, he was your brother!

"Oh, I do believe you are surprised, my dear. Didn't your master here tell you of his masquerade or of his unfortunate fate? Triens assures me that the War Office knows he's quite dead."

Had not Deparens been holding her, she'd have sunk to the floor. "Damien?" She turned her tortured gaze on him, begging him to deny Sir Henry.

He did not.

Seeing the flicker of sympathy in his eyes as they brushed hers, all the blood drained from her face. "You knew!" she accused, scarcely aware she spoke aloud.

"Triens!" Damien ground out, though Ariane did not hear him.

As if she were watching what occurred from a great

distance, she felt Deparens shake his head. His knife pricking at her throat, he jerked her backward into the collection room. She heard the door slam, heard Damien's voice shouting.

And then she was tossed aside like a rag doll. Landing in a heap upon the floor, she was vaguely aware she hurt, but she could not summon the will to care. She thought Deparens escaped through the French windows into the garden, but she was not certain.

There may have been shots, but as she picked herself up slowly from the floor, all she could seem to grasp was that Colin was dead. And Damien had known.

He may not have known from the very first where Colin was—he had gone to Lynchurch, after all—but at some point he had learned Colin was Mary's Richard. Then when he'd told her with such moving sympathy to keep her hopes up, he'd known full well that Colin was dead.

And he was the man she'd thought she loved. Stumbling to her feet, she clenched her fist so that her nails left marks in the palms of her hands. He had taken great care to make her love him. She saw that now. Because he'd not wanted her to question his slow progress tracing Colin, he'd distracted her with his charm.

Fool that she was, she'd fallen in as neatly as could be with his plans. She'd meant it when she said she trusted him. Trusting fool, unburdened by the knowledge of Colin's death, she'd laughed and played before the count, just as Damien had meant for her to do.

Crissie's words of warning returned to echo hollowly in her ear. "He must marry for his family, Rie. Don't forget it."

She had forgotten. More fool she.

"Miss Bennington? What on earth has happened? You look quite undone."

Stumbling to a halt, Ariane blinked and slowly recognized it was Evan Huntsleigh regarding her with such concern. She had made her way into the hall without being aware of it.

"Mr. Huntsleigh," she gasped, grasping his hand.

"Please, I must leave at once. Could you find Miss Mowbry and Lady Hester for me? I should be so grateful."

With a tact that Ariane would never forget, Mr. Huntsleigh did not ask again what was amiss. "I shall be happy to assist you," he said, and was rewarded for his gallantry with a semblance of a smile.

As he turned toward the ballroom, he only troubled her with one more question. "Shall I find Lord Chatham as well, Miss Bennington?" he asked.

Her answer was so fierce, Mr. Huntsleigh actually drew back. "No," Ariane cried, past caring what he made of her vehemence. "I never wish to see Lord Chatham again!"

19

Large, puffy clouds scudded softly across the sky, chased by a breeze that at last felt warm. It had been a long winter, and already that morning Bath's thoroughfares were crowded with people relishing their first taste of spring.

Only two of the pedestrians seemed oblivious to the benign change in the weather, their determined pace in distinct contrast to the leisurely stroll of the others.

For Crissie, at least, the pace was too great. When she stumbled over a cobblestone, she had to hold on to Ariane's arm to keep from falling.

"My pardon, Crissie," Ariane cried contritely as the older woman caught her breath. "My wits have gone begging. I was not even aware that I had you near a lather."

Crissie smiled at that, saying it was only the rough pavement that was to blame. When they resumed walking, they kept a more reasonable pace, and seeing that Ariane's expression was not so closed as it had been, Crissie ventured to ask, "Is your aunt insisting that you go to the Assembly, Rie?"

Ariane nodded grimly. "Yes. She's most adamant."

The hollow note in Ariane's tone elicited a sympathetic clucking from Crissie. "You must not take on so, my dear. Lady Grantham does not know the truth of the matter. She thinks you resist her out of stubbornness alone."

Ariane sighed. "I know Aunt Chloe only means well," she conceded. "And I am grateful she allowed me to remain at the Willows so long. But how can I possibly feel any enthusiasm for the social rounds?"

"Oh, my dear!" Crissie shook her head fretfully. Not for the first time she asked herself if she ought not to have allowed Ariane to announce Colin's death. Had she done so, the child might have observed her year of mourning and had the matter done with.

The answer to her question, as always, came quickly. How could they possibly pronounce Colin dead, when, still, they'd received no official word?

She had said as much before, but seeing Ariane's bleak expression, she knew she must try again. It would do Ariane no good at all to continue chafing over matters that were out of their control.

"Rie," she began uncertainly, "you must know that I understand how difficult this is for you. But you did agree that, until we received official notice about Colin, you would act as if Sir Henry had never said what he did to you. The only word we've had from the War Office was the one note from Lord Chatham, saying Colin's disappearance was yet under investigation."

No sooner had she mentioned Lord Chatham's name than Crissie wished she'd bitten her tongue. As usual, mention of him made Ariane's chin lift to a dangerous angle and, far worse, her cheeks pale.

The exact nature of the rift between Ariane and the marquess was unknown to Crissie. Ariane had only said that he'd withheld from her the news of Colin's death, an omission she had termed an unforgivable betrayal.

Privately Crissie thought Rie's description a bit strong. The marquess had not seemed the sort of man who would do such a thing unless he had very good reason.

However, on the one occasion when she'd tried to defend his lordship, Ariane's response had been such that she had not attempted to do so again. Even now Crissie shuddered to recall the way Ariane's eyes had flashed and the biting voice in which she'd commanded Crissie never, ever to say the man's name again. "You do not know him as I do, Crissie." Ariane had cried in such bitter tones Crissie's soft heart had hurt for her.

Shaking her head, Crissie dismissed her rambling thoughts. There was little use speculating over what had gone so wrong in Brighton. Instead, she must bend her thoughts to making this stay in Bath go well. Though she had not said so to Ariane, she thought it would be for the best if Ariane did go out in society. Not that she thought, as Lady Grantham did, that all of a young woman's problems could be solved by an advantageous match. It was merely that she believed the activity involved would be the perfect antidote for her young friend's depressed spirits.

"And," she continued, trying hard to ignore how very dark Ariane's eyes remained while Lord Chatham's name lingered in the air between them, "you know it was really on account of Toby that we decided to say Colin was abroad. You agreed that every feeling would be offended, if the child were made to mourn his brother unnecessarily."

Reminded of her duty toward her younger brother, Ariane's shoulders drooped fractionally. "You are right, as usual, Crissie," she conceded softly. "I should not carry on so over a decision already made." Catching how anxiously Crissie regarded her, Ariane took her arm. "I am a witch to make you worry so, my dear. I shall go to the Assembly just as I promised, and I shall be on my very best behavior. No one, I give you my assurance, will know how little I wish to be there."

Crissie's response, a pleased, most relieved smile, shamed Ariane. Though she had good cause for her moodiness, she was not proud to have been a trial to her old friend. She must cease, at least for the time being, mourning Colin. It was not fair to Crissie or to Toby to go back on her word now.

"I imagine," Crissie broke into Ariane's thoughts, "that in addition to your Aunt Chloe, Mr. Huntsleigh will be vastly pleased by your appearance at the Assembly."

Ariane summoned a smile and was relieved to see from the twinkle in Crissie's eye it was all the response she required. The coincidence of meeting Evan Huntsleigh on her second day in Bath had been so great she could scarcely contemplate it with equanimity even now.

She'd been at the lending library, scanning the poetry shelves while studiously avoiding those marked TRAVEL, for she could not bring herself to think of the sea, when she heard her name called.

The sudden appearance at her side of Evan Huntsleigh, his handsome, open face conjuring a host of unwelcome images, had left her speechless. She'd not seen him since that cataclysmic night in Brighton, nor, because she had not given him her direction, had she heard from him.

So delighted to see her that he did not note how pale she went, Mr. Huntsleigh immediately took her to task for rushing off from Brighton. "I vow it was as if you'd disappeared from the earth," he scolded.

Ariane excused herself by saying, truthfully, there had been an urgent matter on her mind, and then sincerely thanked him for his assistance in helping her to leave the Comte de Triens' house.

To Mr. Huntsleigh's announcement that the count had taken ill that night, she managed to ask in a nearly normal tone if he knew what the matter had been.

"No, not really." Mr. Huntsleigh shook his head. "Your cousin told us a doctor had been sent for, and we all left shortly thereafter."

The reminder that Mr. Huntsleigh thought the Marquess of Chatham her cousin felt something like a pail of icy water in the face. It had been six months since she had played at being a de Villars, and sometimes Ariane had difficulty believing she'd ever done so.

The matter took on some urgency when Ariane saw her real cousin, Dora, her Aunt Chloe's youngest daughter, approaching. With a deftness that Ariane sourly attributed to her time with Damien de Villars, she presented the young people to each other and quickly turned the conversation to Dora and her choice of books.

There was no difficulty saying later that she had met Mr. Huntsleigh in Brighton. Ariane already had told her aunt that Colin had taken her there for a visit before leaving on a journey whose itinerary she claimed he had left vague. It was a simple matter, then, to suggest that it was Colin who had introduced her to Mr. Huntsleigh.

Mr. Huntsleigh had come to call twice. He was as kind and admiring as he had been in Brighton, but Ariane responded only to the degree politeness demanded. She'd not soon, if ever, give her heart to another, she knew.

When Crissie called her name, Ariane realized with a start that while she'd been woolgathering, they'd reached their destination. After mounting the broad stairs of the large, old town house, she had only to knock once on its door before a young maid came to show them in. Having a female, not a stiff butler in the front hall, was an eccentricity of the owner of the house, Lady Adele Brompton. In her seventies and unmarried, Lady B, as she was called by her friends, saw no reason to discompose her spinster's sensibilities with a man's presence.

"They are forever wanting everything their way, don't you know," she'd explained to Ariane, who had agreed so wholeheartedly that Lady B had taken an instant liking to her.

The little maid preceded them without a word down a long, carpeted hallway. It was another of Lady B's peculiarities that she did not like the slightest noise to distress her, and so had had all her rooms carpeted.

As she had on each of her other visits, Ariane wondered how Mary Mowbry could endure the stillness. Perhaps it did, as she protested, suit her mood, but Ariane thought she'd have gone mad were she forced to live in such a tomblike atmosphere.

At last the maid showed them into the sun room, where

Lady B spent her afternoons swathed in blankets, listening to Mary read her improving tracts on Christian charity.

Seeing who was at the door, Lady B waved a thin, wrinkled hand in welcome. "Come in, come in, my dears," she called in her whispery voice. "It always does me good to look at your face, Ariane. You've such vitality, I feel years younger just being in your company."

Ariane smiled as she usually did when Lady B greeted her thus, and kissing her wizened cheek she teased, "I believe Aunt Chloe told me you were the last to leave Mrs. Darby's card party last evening, Lady B, which can only mean you are your own source of vitality unless Mrs. Darby supplied you some."

"Naughty girl!" Lady B chuckled. Mrs. Darby was notorious for her languid air and her constant complaints about her health. "I stayed late only because I was winning, and victory has ever been an inspiration for me."

Ariane laughed, and, she was pleased to see, so did Mary. Perhaps the combination of Lady B's twinkling eyes and the calm surroundings were indeed what her friend needed.

Still, Ariane cared too much for Mary not to ask outright how she was getting on. Seated in the bay window, watching her friend work a sampler with small, meticulous stitches, Ariane frowned anxiously. "You've no regrets about coming here, have you, Mary?"

Mary's needle paused as she glanced up with a reassuring smile. "You must not worry so about me, Rie," she chided softly. "I am perfectly well here. I like Lady B, and my duties help me occupy my time."

Ariane nodded her understanding, but nonetheless persisted with her thoughts. "The invitation to live with us at Aunt Chloe's is still open, should you change your mind. I miss you dreadfully, you know, and should be grateful for your company while I am put through this charade of a come-out."

Ariane's suggestion brought a firm response. "I would be the worst company possible for you, Rie." Mary shook her head. When Ariane made as if to protest, her friend forestalled her. "Please, Rie, I really would. I know it. It is not that I feel any blame for Father's disgrace. You successfully convinced me how foolish that was.'' Mary paused to give Ariane's hand a grateful squeeze. "I can never thank you enough for that. Your bracing counsel while I stayed at the Willows did me a world of good. You are like the sister I never had, as you know. Still, you must see that I am not yet ready to face the world. Inevitably there would be questions about Father, and I've not the strength to simply ignore them, as you would do. Perhaps in time . . . but not just yet. You understand?''

Ariane's smile was wry. "I do, and I promise I shall not again badger you bracingly or otherwise.''

"And you will thank your Aunt Chloe for finding me this position with Lady B? It suits me nicely, and she was kind to put herself out so for a stranger.''

"You are not a stranger, Mary,'' Ariane protested; then, seeing the determined look in Mary's eye, she shrugged. "If it pleases you, you will get your way,'' she relented.

When Mary went back to her needlework, the conversation turned to less weighty matters—to whit, the details of their lives. As they chatted about the habits of those with whom they'd recently come to live, Ariane thought how their relationship had changed since they'd met that long-ago night at the theater. It was natural that it had grown deeper, for they had suffered through much together.

Ariane had told Mary almost everything, from Richard Rolfe's true identity to her part in the unmasking of Sir Henry. She had hated having to reveal it, fearing Mary would think herself betrayed, but Mary would have none of it. In a firm voice, she had said, "In truth, Rie, you have shown me more affection in two months than my father did in twenty years. It is sad, perhaps, but no wonder, that I should be more relieved than anything else that his traitorous activities have been halted.''

Together at the Willows through the autumn and the winter, they had sustained each other. Their friendship had grown so that often one of them had only to begin a thought before the other knew what she would say. Sometimes, even, one would guess at the other's thoughts before she'd begun to speak aloud.

It was a result of that closeness that Mary could say with unerring accuracy, when their light chatter had come to an end, "You have had to bow to your aunt's wish that you go out in society, haven't you, Rie?"

"Yes, I am to go to the Assembly tomorrow."

"You must not feel so pulled. Colin would understand. You know that."

"And you do not despise me?" Ariane asked, her gaze searching Mary's.

"Of course I do not," Mary replied forcefully, though her gaze reflected her sympathy for Ariane's distress. "Oh, Rie! If only I could convince you of my belief that Colin is not dead, you would not suffer at all. I see that you will not be persuaded, as usual, but I do believe it to be true. And I shall continue to do so until Lord Chatham or someone else from the War Office tells us differently."

To Ariane's surprise, Mary had taken heart when she learned Colin had been sent to sea before being murdered. If no one had actually seen his body, then there was room for hope, she argued. When Ariane had asked how he could possibly escape from such a hopeless situation, Mary had lost heart until the possibility of a mutiny had occurred to her. Though Ariane protested that it was unlikely Colin could have fomented a rebellion, held captive belowdecks, Mary had waved aside her objection.

"I cannot say exactly how, but in some way or other, I am certain Colin found a way to escape death."

Ariane had let the matter drop there. She could not blame Mary for wanting to hold to hope. She tried to do the same, but failed miserably whenever she recalled Sir Henry's vindictive voice gloatingly informing her how he'd arranged Colin's death. It seemed impossible that such evil would not win the day.

And, too, she would recall every night when she lay in her bed with no activity to hold her memories at bay, how Damien had not denied the story.

At least he had not then before Sir Henry. Nor had she given him the chance to come to her in Brighton to do so.

Her emotions had been in such upheaval that night that even now she could not exactly remember how she had gotten Lady Hester and Mary away, except that Mr. Huntsleigh had assisted her. Once they had reached Sir Henry's town house, Ariane recalled, she had told them that Sir Henry was involved in some trouble that Lord Chatham was seeing to. She'd been proud of her discretion, for she had scarcely been able to think of anything save the truth.

She had left Lady Hester for Damien to handle. He was a master with women, after all, and even in her distress, Ariane admitted he would be the best one to decide what she should know. Mary, she took with her to the Willows when she left at dawn, having not slept at all. They were bound together in so many ways, Ariane never thought to do otherwise.

A fortnight later she had received an official-looking letter addressed to her. Though she had never seen his handwriting, she knew before she opened it that the bold, decisive hand was Damien's. Only Mary's concern that the letter might have some instruction for her had kept her from flinging it away as if it were a dangerous viper.

She need not have been so fearful. The terse message merely informed her in the most formal of terms that the War Office was investigating Sir Henry's explanation of Colin's fate, and that word would be sent to the Willows, when the investigation was completed. That was all, except for a scrawled set of initials at the bottom.

There was no grateful mention of her work, nor any explanation of why he'd acted as he had. Not that she'd have believed anything he might have said, of course. Still, that he did not even essay an excuse was further proof to her that Damien de Villars acted to suit his own ends without giving the least thought to the feelings of others.

There had been no word of any kind in the six months since. Likely, the Marquess of Chatham had forgotten all about her by now. Engrossed in another scheme that was ostensibly for the good of his country, but in reality was only to save him from boredom, he could not take the time to make her the explanations she deserved.

Scowling fiercely, Ariane wished she could tell him to his face what an uncaring cad he was. That she had missed the opportunity to do so by leaving Brighton so precipitately was the only regret she had.

20

Rie, but for those glowing green eyes you had from your mother, you are the feminine version of your father. And like him, I daresay you will break every available heart at the ball."

A sudden image of Damien de Villars, heartbroken, flashed through Ariane's mind, but she dismissed it as quickly as it appeared, and without any perceptible pause she smiled with great affection on her uncle. "You have ever spoiled me with your praise, Uncle Randall."

Randall Grantham fondly returned his niece's smile. "May I offer you a glass of ratafia, my dear? You've ample time for it. I am afraid the Grantham ladies are seldom prompt."

As she chatted easily with her uncle, Ariane silently commended her aunt for having shown the good sense to marry Sir Randall. From Crissie, Ariane knew her father's elder sister had been a much-sought-after beauty who might have had any one of a number of suitors. That she had chosen the staid Sir Randall, some years her senior and only a baronet, had greatly surprised her friends.

But time had vindicated Chloe Bennington. Sir Randall's affection for his wife had never wavered in all the years of their marriage, and whatever her whim, he was prepared with his sizable fortune to generously indulge it.

She herself was one of her aunt's projects. And though she'd have preferred to be sitting quietly at the Willows, Ariane mentally thanked her uncle for his unstinting generosity toward her. Never once had he made her feel the poor relation she in fact was.

The doors burst open suddenly, Dora Grantham having been too impatient to wait for a footman's dignified assistance. Skipping excitedly across the room, she clapped her hands when she saw her cousin. "Rie! You look so stylish," she exclaimed, transfixed by Ariane's pretty high-waisted gown of silver net.

Proving she had learned more than how to dress from Solange Crécy, Ariane merely laughed and dismissed the matter with a wave of her hand. "It is you who look pretty as a picture, Dora." She smiled. "I declare you will charm all the young men at first glance."

Dora did, indeed, look pretty with her glossy, dark hair, a shade browner in color than Ariane's, curled in fashionable sausage ringlets, and her hazel eyes shining brightly at the prospect of attending her first Assembly. Although her formal come-out would take place in the fall in London, Lady Grantham had decided she could make some appearances in Bath for the experience.

"Oh, do you really believe I shall charm anyone?" she cried, bounding down heavily beside Ariane. "What if I am left sitting all evening!"

As Ariane assured Dora there was no possibility of such a disaster occurring, she made a mental note to ask Evan Huntsleigh to lead her young cousin out. Young, handsome, and personable, he would appeal to Dora, she was certain.

Cheered by the sudden notion that Evan Huntsleigh might well find Dora a more comfortable young lady to be with than she, Ariane greeted her aunt and her elder cousin, Corinne, with a smile when they entered.

Corinne only smiled thinly in return. Although only a year separated the cousins, the two had never been good friends, Miss Grantham being the sort of prim, proper young woman who had always believed it her duty to report the mischief into which her more spirited cousin inevitably got.

Not unattractive, in a thin, haughty way, Corinne had received offers, and with her father's fortune at her disposal, she was free to choose whomever she liked. But neither the officer in the hussars nor the mere honorable, both of whom her mother had approved heartily, were acceptable. Corinne would have a title—or at least, the noblest of noble ancestry—or nothing.

While Sir Randall made his compliments to his daughters, Lady Grantham looked in surprise at her niece. "But where on earth did you come by such a splendid dress, Rie?" she asked in amazement. "I should never have thought silver would do so nicely on you, but it contrasts most pleasingly with your coloring. And that off-the-shoulder cut! Why, it is quite the latest thing. Surely there isn't a seamstress in Appledyne able to turn that sort of thing out?"

Ariane did not blink. She had known the question would arise, and she had prepared an answer to explain the clothes which Damien had paid for and which she had not left behind in Brighton. They were recompense, of a sort, for the work she'd done.

"Actually, it was the seamstress's sister, formerly a dressmaker in Brighton, who, forced to come to Appledyne for reasons of her health, made it and my other clothes as well. She's very capable, isn't she?"

Her aunt was satisfied, and as their wraps were brought, it once more occurred to Ariane to remark how effective a teacher of deception Damien de Villars had been.

They had no sooner than found their seats at the Assembly when Mr. Huntsleigh presented himself before them, and it did not escape Ariane that Dora blushed nicely as the young man addressed her.

Satisfied that there was some hope of establishing an interest between her young cousin and Mr. Huntsleigh, she was able, with a nod to Crissie, to give Mr. Huntsleigh a generous, if not brilliant smile.

Having a worthy project blunted the distress she felt at being one of the glittering, frivolous throng that night. Still grieving for Colin, she had precious little desire to laugh and be gay.

When Mr. Huntsleigh led her out, she waited a time, while he made most of the conversation, before beginning her campaign. "I hope I will not offend you, Mr. Huntsleigh, if I ask you for a great favor?" she asked lightly then.

Mr. Huntsleigh did not mind at all, and assured her so. "On the contrary, Miss Bennington. You must know I should be honored."

"I do not think it will be an onerous task." She smiled, liking him for his openness. "You see, it is Dora's first Assembly, and she is terribly afraid no one will ask her to dance. Will you, just to get her off to a good start?"

Seeing that he would please Ariane, Evan Huntsleigh promptly said he would be delighted to partner the younger Miss Grantham. "She won't have to worry about partners for long," he added, glancing across to see Dora, a charmingly wistful expression on her face, as she gazed at the dancers. "She's quite a pretty little thing, after all."

When he returned her to Lady Grantham, Mr. Huntsleigh suggested he fetch punch for everyone. "An Assembly is such thirsty work," he observed with a good-natured laugh before turning to Dora. "And after you've had refreshment, Miss Grantham, I hope you will honor me with a dance."

It amused Ariane in a deplorably spiteful way that Corinne turned around, thinking Mr. Huntsleigh had been addressing her. She'd not paid the least attention to him previously, scarcely even condescending to say good evening. That he lacked a title was bad enough in Corinne's eyes, but that the fortune he enjoyed had actually been amassed by his grandfather in trade put him quite beyond the pale.

Both Dora and Lady Grantham, Ariane was happy to note, had no such reservations, and remarked favorably on her friend, when he had gone. Wrinkling her thin nose, Corinne looked away, leaving the others to extol his considerable virtues unhindered.

They had been doing so for several minutes when Corinne, her gaze having just turned to the entrance, gave a little cry. "Why, look," she exclaimed with what for her was excitement. "There is Lady Helena Bandbrooke and her nephew, the marquess! Oh, and Miss Cecily Ashton, too.''

Dora was just confiding to Ariane that she thought Mr. Huntsleigh's blue eyes the color of the sky on a singularly bright day, and so Ariane did not look around. She knew too well that her elder cousin's obsession with titles was such that any nobleman, even if he were a toad of a person, was viewed with unlimited interest.

"And Mrs. Ashton, too," she absently heard her aunt observe. Something was said about Mrs. Ashton, and then Lady Grantham remarked chattily, "But you know the marquess is not Lady Helena's nephew, Corinne. Lord Chatham is actually her godson."

"Rie, are you quite well?" Dora asked anxiously. "You have gone so pale."

"Yes, yes, I am fine," Ariane said, though in truth she felt very hot of a sudden. Surely, in the name of heaven, she had heard her aunt wrong. It was not possible that Damien could be present in Bath on this particular evening, her first time out in society. Never once had he mentioned a connection in Bath.

Slowly, exercising great control, for she did not wish to call attention to her interest, Ariane turned to follow Corinne's rapt gaze. Three women, one considerably younger than the other two, stood on the dais before the door. But Ariane did not see them. Nor did she take any note of the several people who went to cluster around the latest arrivals as if they were people of unusual note.

Ariane's eyes fastened on the man. His back was to her, but she could see that he was tall and lean and wore his elegant evening clothes as if they were a second skin. His hair, as black as midnight, was brushed back close to his head. It was a style he could bear, for his head was well-shaped, as were his shoulders, his narrow waist, and his straight hips. He needed no padding—without a stitch on he'd have been as marvelous to behold as he was now, standing easily, but somehow alertly, in Bath's renowned Assembly Rooms.

Ariane closed her eyes. The room was spinning, but that

was not what made her squeeze her lids down tightly. It was impossible, however, to shut out the image of that compelling, sinewy figure.

She looked again, lifting her eyes quickly to have the matter done with, and stared, unprepared, directly into Damien de Villars' black eyes.

21

It was as if something invisible, but substantial nonetheless, crackled through the air between them. Sitting upright in her chair, Ariane actually wavered backward from the force of it.

How long their gazes remained locked Ariane did not know. She was not aware of time, of the music playing in the background, of the dancers, nor even of her cousins who sat beside her.

And then, without warning, Damien released her. Turning to attend to one of the ladies of his group, he left Ariane to stare at his well-remembered profile, her heart hammering as though she had run a great distance.

Inanely her first thought, when she recovered herself, blinking as someone might upon awakening from the throes of a strong dream, was that he had not regarded her half so intently when there had been a knife pricking the sensitive skin of her throat.

A bubble of half-hysterical laughter welled up in her throat, a reaction both to her memory of the scene in the count's study and to Damien's shatteringly unexpected appearance. Clenching her fist tightly, she controlled herself. She must think what she should do.

Almost immediately she dismissed the idea of leaving. Though the notion had an insidious attraction, she had only to remind herself, not of her aunt's probable reaction, but that leaving would be tantamount to flight.

Turning tail did not appeal. It was not she who had done so very much of which to be ashamed, after all.

Besides, a little voice in her mind whispered, what was she thinking of? Damien wasn't likely to acknowledge her. Why should he? They had not been friends, only "business" associates. On the instant she decided that neither would she acknowledge him.

By slow degrees she became aware again that she was in the midst of a ballroom crowded with people. She heard laughter, music, and by and by, her aunt speaking. Glancing around surreptitiously, Ariane saw no one looking at her strangely, or, indeed, looking at her all. It was then she realized how very short the duration of her silent exchange with Damien must have been. Her aunt was still speaking of Damien and the ladies with him.

"Mrs. Greene did tell me Lady Bandbrooke was having a house party, but she did not say how exalted the guests would be," Lady Grantham was remarking breezily to Corinne. "Lord Chatham is in the first stare of fashion, you know, as are Miss Ashton and her mother, of course."

"You must recall that I met Miss Ashton more than once last year in town," Corinne reminded her mother, half-affronted. Still regarding the little group whose members were finding seats not so very far from theirs, she added, not without a note of envy, "And I must say, she is quite as pretty now as she was then."

Glancing from beneath her lashes, Ariane considered the girl who could only be Miss Ashton. As Corinne had said, she was pretty. One noticed first her petite, perfectly proportioned figure and then the wealth of her very golden hair. Arranged in long, thick ringlets, it was the perfect frame for her lovely face.

"I was told that Miss Ashton and the marquees have an understanding. Did you not hear it as well, Corinne?"

So! Ariane's gaze veered back to the dainty beauty. She was not the sort of girl a man would kiss hotly while he was betrothed to another. She too closely resembled a fragile china figurine, was too much the model of a future marchioness.

While Ariane's gaze lingered on the pretty girl whom

Damien would marry, Corinne confirmed that she, too, had heard that there was an understanding between the Ashtons and de Villars. "It is regrettable that though Lionel de Villars looks a great deal like his elder brother, he lacks the marquess's air."

Lady Grantham agreed that Lionel was not so compelling a figure as his brother. "But, after all, there are few men who can rival Chatham," she pointed out reasonably. "And Lionel is said to possess a much steadier character. There are stories about Lord Chatham that it would not be fit to repeat in polite company."

"Oh, do tell, Mama," Dora implored, her eyes sparkling with curiosity.

Realizing belatedly the age of the many ears listening to her, Lady Grantham gave her youngest daughter a quelling look. "We are in polite company, Dora. Do, I beg you, strive not to look so eager. It is extremely vulgar."

Dora ignored her mother, whose bark was ever worse than her bite, and returned her fascinated gaze to the notorious marquess. "Oh!" she cried, suddenly shrinking behind her mother. "He is looking this way."

Though no one noticed, the announcement made Ariane's color come and go. Only by exerting every ounce of will she possessed did she not turn her head to look at him. Absolutely determined that she would not, she looked in quite the opposite direction.

Directly into Mr. Huntsleigh's nice blue eyes. She had forgotten him entirely.

If Ariane felt dizzy just thinking what he might say if he saw Damien, at least she did not have long to agonize. He was extending her glass to her, when his clear, open brow registered astonishment.

"You did not say your cousin, Lord Chatham, was in Bath, Miss Bennington."

What followed might have been amusing had Ariane been in the mood for amusement. Her aunt, looking from her to Mr. Huntsleigh and back again, cried, "Your cousin!"

The phrase was repeated in similarly astonished tones by first Corinne and then Dora. Only Sir Randall's voice was missing, but he had gone off earlier to chat with friends.

With eight pairs of expectant eyes upon her, Ariane's inventiveness deserted her when she needed it most. She tried, but nothing even remotely plausible occurred to her.

When it seemed the only solution was for her to sink quietly through the floor, she saw her aunt look up with a start, her much-celebrated Bennington brown eyes widening considerably.

"Lady Grantham, your servant," a cool, deep-timbered, dreadfully familiar voice said from behind Ariane.

At the sound she had never thought to hear again, Ariane's heart seemed to stop beating altogether.

"Good evening, Ariane," she thought she heard him say, but could not be certain, for there was a strange buzzing in her head.

When she noticed that her aunt was looking at her strangely, she realized, belatedly, that she must do something. For lack of anything more creative, she looked up.

The moment her gaze focused clearly upon Damien, all Ariane's confused, uncertain, half-expectant, half-fearful feelings crystallized.

He was laughing! Not outright, of course, but his eyes were gleaming, and she knew that look. Not the least repentant as she had every right to expect him to be, he was actually amused by her predicament. A predicament into which he had gotten her in the first place!

Bracing, fortifying anger swept her. Clinging to it, for it gave her direction, she inclined her head less than was strictly polite.

The icy reception did not daunt her nemesis a whit. Seeming to be completely at ease, he amicably bid Mr. Huntsleigh good evening, and then turned back to her aunt to explain, without the least difficulty, his supposed relationship to her.

"Ariane and I are related on her mother's side, ma'am. I suppose, you might say we've, ah, a connection through the French."

Ariane just did disguise her gasp as a cough. A connection through the French, indeed!

"But how did I not know of the connection?" was her aunt's logical query.

"It was only by merest chance that we discovered there was a link between us," Damien replied, his hand coming to rest upon the back of Ariane's chair, briefly touching her. "It was actually Colin and I who made the connection, you see. But there! I am certain you would find it tedious to hear the exact conversation. As to Ariane's saying nothing, I imagine it is because she is so reticent, don't you agree, my lady?"

Only Ariane seemed aware of the irony in the look Damien slanted her. Lady Grantham was so taken by the flashing smile Damien turned upon her that she nodded yes to his absurd characterization of Ariane.

Disgusted, Ariane wondered sourly where all her aunt's previous disapproval of the infamous marquess had gone. It seemed, she thought most unkindly, to have evaporated before Damien's smile like the mist before the sun.

Corinne and Dora had, of course, to be presented formally. When Damien asked Corinne for the honor of a dance, she fluttered her lashes and proffered her card with unseemly haste, or so Ariane thought.

For a spiteful moment she indulged herself with imagining what would happen if she sweetly asked Damien how his little betrothed viewed his dancing with anyone and everyone else, but she curbed herself. He was just then extending an invitation to Dora, his devastating smile making Ariane's younger cousin blush so prettily, Ariane could not find the heart to ruin her moment.

In the next instant, she wished she'd not been so forbearing. Damien, with an easy familiarity that in no way indicated he was asking the unthinkable of her, turned to request a dance—no, the very next dance—of her. "I hope I am not too late and your card is full?"

Ariane ignored his gleaming smile. "This is my first Assembly, my lord," she informed him stiffly. "I scarce know anyone in Bath."

That smile grew broader and more difficult to ignore. "Then, what luck for you that I've arrived, Rie."

There was no misreading the challenging glint in his

eyes. It incensed her almost as much as his use of her pet name. Color charged anew into her cheeks, but before she could inform him she was, and always would be, Miss Bennington to him, he forestalled her. "Ah, there's our music now. Shall we?"

There was nothing for it; her aunt would never forgive her if she made a scene. Gingerly, as if he were made of some dangerous substance she did not trust, she laid her fingers on his extended arm.

The contact was of the slightest, but still Ariane was affected strongly by it. Her fingers tingled so it felt as if some strange current passed between them. The notion was fanciful, perhaps, but undoubtedly the light touch brought back memories Ariane did not wish to recall.

With her gaze steadfastly averted from him, Ariane stumbled over Damien's foot when he stopped, prepared to take his place on the dance floor.

"If you lowered your chin a fraction, Rie, you might have some better idea where to put your feet."

He was grinning openly. She flashed him a speaking look, but made no other reply except to elevate her chin further. Looking directly into the broad expanse of his shoulder, she was prepared to ignore him the entire dance.

Damien, however, was not inclined to allow her that luxury. "Ariane, I must talk to you," he announced calmly, his tone implying there were no betrayals or betrothals between them.

If he had forgotten, Ariane had not. "I have nothing to say to you," she intoned glacially.

"I did not say I wished you to speak to me," Damien returned with infuriating composure. "I said I must speak with you, and I will!"

His arrogance earned him a furious look. "I do not know why you are here, my lord, nor why you have chosen to play the charming marquess with my aunt, but I wish you to leave me alone. I do not intend to listen to anything you have to say."

A momentary feeling of exaltation swept over her when she saw a muscle in Damien's jaw clench. He did not seem so amused now, she thought with unalloyed satisfaction.

It was a transitory feeling. Almost at once Damien turned the tables on her, coolly informing her that he would come the next day at four o'clock to take her for a drive. "Be ready," he commanded in a thoroughly uncompromising tone.

The totally irrelevant thought occurred to Ariane that if she did drive out with him, it would be the first time she had ever done so. He had used to come for her early in the morning with a fine horse. Biting her lip, she thrust the thought aside. She would not go, she began to say, but the music coming to an end prevented her.

Nor, as they left the floor, did she have the opportunity, for they met Mr. Huntsleigh leading Dora back to her mother. Evan looked almost as pleased with his companion as she did with him, and while the men exchanged polite remarks, Ariane smiled her congratulations at Dora, who grinned back most happily.

The moment she realized Damien was regarding her with quizzical amusement, Ariane sobered abruptly. While she was forced to suffer his company, she was determined not to behave with the least pleasantness.

She had ample opportunity to test her resolution on the issue, for Damien bedeviled her with his company a number of times that evening. Not only did he return to dance with both Corinne and Dora, but he also brought a glass of champagne for Lady Grantham.

It was then he met Sir Randall. From the dance floor, Ariane watched her aunt, beaming excitedly, make the introductions.

Not a great deal later, the Granthams left, but if Ariane thought their departure meant she'd no longer have to think of Damien, she was soon made aware how foolishly optimistic she'd been. Though her uncle spoke only a little of the marquess, her aunt and cousins all made up for his reticence. In the carriage going home and all the way upstairs to bed, they talked of no one else.

Corinne in particular babbled on about how divinely Chatham danced, what witty things he said, and how he'd asked to wait upon them the next afternoon.

It was a measure of the depth to which Ariane's spirits

had fallen that she again made not the least push to remind her cousin of Miss Ashton. Instead, as the others considered aloud what they should wear when he came, Ariane made plans not to be present at all.

If she did not wish to speak to Damien de Villars, then she need not. And let it be a lesson to him that he could not command her company against her will.

22

On the afternoon Damien was to come, Ariane accompanied Toby and a maid on their habitual outing for ices. She had made no mention to her brother of his hero's imminent arrival, for had she told him, he'd have remained at home and left her with no way to escape the house without having to ask for escort. And that would not have done, for then everyone would have realized what she was about.

Crissie took no notice of her departure, for she was napping upright in her chair, and Lady Grantham and Corinne were entirely too preoccupied with making certain that everything was arranged just so to think what Ariane was up to.

The only person Ariane had not accounted for was Dora, and that young lady, when she chanced upon Ariane dressed in her pelisse, displayed considerable surprise.

"You are not going out now, Rie?" asked Dora.

Ariane shrugged airly in reply. "Why, yes. I promised to take Toby for ices."

"But what of Lord Chatham?"

"We aren't very close, actually," Ariane responded.

Dora's eyes widened considerably as she addressed the only point that interested her. "But don't you want to become closer? He is so thrilling! When he smiled at me . . ." Dora rolled her eyes ecstatically, unable to put into words the raptures into which Damien's flashing smile had thrown her.

"I admit he is attractive," Ariane allowed thinly. "However, I cannot say I care for him."

"But he is your cousin! And, Rie, Mama will be furious!"

The threat of her aunt's possible displeasure was as nothing to Ariane's stubborn determination to evade Damien. "Don't worry," she assured her anxious cousin. "I shan't land too deeply in the suds. Aunt Chloe will be too pleased over having a marquess in the drawing room to be much concerned about my whereabouts."

Continuing along to Toby's room, Ariane did give some consideration to just how angry her aunt was likely to be. She even asked herself, for the first time, why she should not see Damien?

Immediately she asked herself why she should. If he wanted to give her news of Colin, he could send it by note, as he had done before. Unless he intended to apologize for the way he had used her—and apparently he had no such intention—they had nothing whatsoever to say to each other.

After a leisurely—Ariane made certain of it—visit to the tea room that dispensed their favorite ices, she was pleased to grant Toby's request: he wanted to feed the ducks in a small park that lay on their way home.

Before throwing out the last of his crumbs, Toby paused to exclaim with awe on a pair of matched blacks that had just raced around the corner.

As Ariane turned with idle interest to judge them for herself, they were pulled up sharply by the driver of the shiny curricle, and before she could register fully what was happening, Toby ran past her, shouting, "It's Lord Chatham!"

With a peculiar tightening in her throat, Ariane realized it was, indeed, Damian upon whom Toby was hurling himself with gleeful exuberance.

She could not hear Damien's reply to her brother's welcome, his voice was too low, but she could see his smile.

It was warm and amused without being the least mocking. The ache the sight of that smile caused in her chest made Ariane so angry her eyes flashed.

She met them with her chin elevated, determined not to allow Damien to browbeat her for not having obeyed his wishes. Her pose was brave, but also unnecessary. Damien's attention was all on Toby.

Belatedly Ariane realized that was because her brother was asking if Damien had had news of Colin. "It has been so long since we've heard from him," Toby added uncertainly.

Damien's gaze flicked to her. The contact was brief, but it was clear he was surprised. She tossed her head. How dare he be surprised! Of course she could not tell Toby, without some confirmation, what Sir Henry had said, no matter what she herself believed.

Realizing that Damien was about to reply to Toby, Ariane opened her mouth to speak, to prepare her little brother for what he must hear, but she was too late. Damien was already speaking, his words scattering all her thoughts, angry and otherwise, like so many leaves in the wind.

"We believe strongly—though we cannot be absolutely certain yet, Toby—that your brother was taken to the West Indies to be sold as a servant."

"To the West Indies?" Toby echoed shrilly.

Ariane heard her brother's high voice as if it came from a great distance. Dimly she thought Damien said every effort was being made to find Colin, but she could not have sworn to it, for the world had begun to spin in the most disconcerting way.

A strong hand took her arm, steadying her, and then gently lowered her to the bench behind her when her knees sagged. Though she realized it was Damien who assisted her, she could not regret the contact with him. Without it, she'd have sunk to the ground in a disgraceful heap.

A few minutes passed before a trace of color returned to her cheeks, but when it did, Damien addressed them both. "The captain to whom Colin was entrusted is known for pocketing money twice. Not only does he collect a fee by agreeing to dispose of a man, but he profits again by selling the supposedly dead man to anyone in the Indies who wants him. We have not as yet discovered Colin's exact whereabouts, but we do know for certain that a man fitting your brother's description was seen debarking from this captain's boat.''

When he fell silent, Ariane gazed mutely at him, searching his expression for the truth, unable to bear the thought of nurturing false hope. He was returning her look sternly, almost severely, but that could mean anything. She saw his jaw clench and wondered at it, and then Toby was jumping on the bench beside her asking if she were ill.

"You look so pale, Rie. You're not sick, are you? You can't be, now we know where Colin is."

"We don't know for certain where Colin is, Toby," Damien corrected swiftly, his eyes still upon Ariane. "I said only that we have good cause to believe he is in the West Indies. We've a man there now searching for him."

"He'll find Colin, I am certain of it," Toby exclaimed with youthful optimism. "And when he comes home, we won't have to stay at Aunt Chloe's! And I won't have to have a tutor! And Rie won't have to marry anyone!"

Watching Damien ruffle Toby's hair with a grin, Ariane nearly felt ashamed for having questioned, if only briefly, whether he had told them the truth. Whatever else he was, he was not such a villain as to raise Toby's hopes falsely. Sighing deeply, she relaxed back against the bench, feeling as if the greatest burden had been lifted from her shoulders. Colin was alive!

Tears welled up in her eyes, and when she sat up to wipe them away, she was in time to see Damien hand some halfpennies to Toby. At once her brother ran off in the direction of a man selling hot cross buns, with their maid trailing after him.

It was impossible not to remark on how neatly Damien had managed to get his time alone with her, but there was little time to spare for admiration. Aware that he stood above her, staring down at her, Ariane tried to think what she should say. She owed him thanks for the good news he had brought, but she couldn't help wondering how long he had known Colin very likely was alive.

It was little wonder then that it was Damien who spoke first, his voice sounding cool to her. "Had you not run away, I'd have told you some of that in Brighton and saved you at least a little worry."

Ariane swung about abruptly, the spurt of gratitude she had felt earlier quite forgotten. "I did not run away," she retorted hotly. "I left Brighton because my work for you was concluded. What you had to tell me, you might have included in the note you sent. There was space enough, certainly!

"Oh!" She threw up her hands distractedly. "I do not know why I am arguing with you. You are only trying to shift the fault to me. You had more than ample time to tell me everything you knew after you returned from London. Only you chose not to do so."

Faint white lines appeared around Damien's mouth, suggesting strongly that he kept his emotions in check with difficulty, but his voice, when he spoke, was controlled, betraying little, particularly not the guilt Ariane sought.

"Everything I knew was, in fact, very little, and most of that guesses." He defended himself curtly. "When I returned to Brighton after my trip to London, I had good reason to believe Colin had been killed, for I had learned by that time that he had, without consulting either Maccauley or myself, set off to become the mysterious Richard Rolfe in Berkshire. And I had learned as well that Mowbry had had him put aboard a boat with orders that he be tossed overboard at the captain's convenience. However, I had some hope, albeit little, that the captain would be the sort to pocket the blood money, use Colin as an unpaid deckhand on the crossing, and then sell him in the Indies. It has been done often enough before. I did not speak simply because I wished to confirm my theory before raising your hopes unduly."

Later, when she was in a more rational frame of mind, Ariane would be able to accept Damien's reasoning and even understand what he had left out: that he had not written her what he knew, because he did not think she would believe him. But at that moment all the grievances she had harbored against him for six months were too fresh in her mind to allow her to think clearly.

Her chin elevated, the unyielding gleam in her green eyes never wavering, her expression told Damien as clearly as words what she thought of his explanation. Not well-pleased with her stubbornness, he glared back at her, look for look, and they remained thus, conducting a battle of wills until suddenly Damien sighed and raked his hand through his hair.

"I did not come here to argue with you, Rie," he said, his tone undeniably rueful. "Though," he added, a stern light glinting now in his eye, "if I had, I would say a thing or two about your manners. I was not pleased to have to spend a half-hour at Grantham House for no reason."

"I did not agree to ride out with you. You only assumed I would obey your command!" Ariane sniffed, looking away.

Damien ignored her retort and without so much as a by-your-leave, dropped down beside her, stretching his arm along the back of the bench. From the corner of her eye Ariane saw that his strong, familiar hand was close enough that she might touch it with her cheek, if she were so inclined. She stiffened her spine on the instant.

"There are several things we must discuss in addition to Colin, Rie." Her eyes glared a protest at his uninvited familiarity, but Damien paid her no heed and went on without pause to say he must have Mary Mowbry's direction.

"As it turns out, a goodly portion of Sir Henry's moneys were actually Mary's," he explained when Ariane's brow lifted. "They were left her by a maternal uncle, though Mowbry seems to have concealed the fact from her, and they are not forfeit for his misdeeds as his own moneys are."

The news was so good and so unexpected that Ariane forgot herself and rounded on Damien with a little cry of pleasure. She had forgotten how close he was.

Immediately she edged away, putting as much distance

as the small bench would allow between them. Then and only then did she explain the circumstances behind Mary's employment with Lady Adele Brompton.

"Does Miss Mowbry know that Richard was in reality your brother?"

"Yes, I told her that much." Ariane nodded. "But, Damien," she continued anxiously, her grievances against him put aside for the moment, "I did not reveal to Mary the part her father played in Colin's disappearance."

"No, of course not." He nodded.

Relieved by his unspoken agreement to shield Mary, Ariane remarked on how welcome all Damien's news would be to her friend. "Though she maintains that being with Lady B suits her, she is only making the best of things, as always." Lost in her thoughts, Ariane shook her head. "That house is so maddeningly quiet," she murmured, half to herself, "I should have gone mad there after one night."

She turned then, intending to urge Damien to see Mary that very day, but her thought did not reach her tongue. When she found he was watching her, his eyes gleaming softly with something more than amusement, her heart seemed to turn over, and all she could summon was a whispered "Oh . . ."

How long she remained gazing silently at him, she was never certain. She only knew that she was returned to her senses by the sound of Toby's voice.

Damien was not so relieved as she at the sound of his piping chatter. Muttering an oath, he said urgently, "There is more I must say. I do not know if you are aware of it, but Deparens managed to escape that night."

Although his tone was neutral, Ariane winced. She knew very well who had provided the butler the opportunity to gain his freedom. Damien had more important matters on his mind at that moment than recriminations, however.

"We've had reliable word that he is now in the vicinity of Bath. We've no idea what he intends, but I must ask you not to go out alone, Rie. It seems unlikely that his arrival here is mere coincidence."

Aware that Toby was nearly upon them, Ariane found

herself nodding when Damien asked with unmistakable urgency, "Agreed?"

"I've all our buns, but yours, Rie," Toby announced with a flourish as he came bounding up to them.

Pulling her gaze from Damien, Ariane looked down at her brother's hand and saw there were two buns. "You've two left," she pointed out, resolving to put aside until later a thorough contemplation of Damien's warning.

"That is Lord Chatham's," Toby said, holding out Damien's for him to take. "And this is mine," he concluded, laying indisputable claim by taking a large bite. "I ate yours on the way, Rie, after I recalled that Aunt Chloe said you eat more than is proper."

Although Toby's teasing afforded Damien a laugh at her expense, Ariane was too amused by her brother's accurate imitation of her aunt's scandalized tone, to mind overmuch. Her eyes twinkling, she chucked her impish brother on the chin. "Alas, it seems my knight in shining armor has succumbed to the deadly sin of gluttony," she mourned.

Toby squeezed in between Damien and his sister and offered her a very small piece of the bun. "Well, since you put it that way, I shall let you have a bit." He laughed.

Ariane rolled her eyes. "A crumb I should say," she retorted, to Toby's amusement.

"I would be honored to share a portion of mine," Damien said, extending half of his to her. His strong smile was very engaging.

Sucking in her breath at the sight, Ariane shook her head and glanced away. How could she have allowed the atmosphere to become so dangerously amicable, she castigated herself. She ought not even to be smiling in Damien's presence!

When there was, at last, the opportunity to go, Toby having finished off Damien's indulgences, Ariane rose. Her brother looked as if he might protest having his chat with Damien cut short, but could not, when his hero also stood, dusting crumbs from his lap as he did so.

Ariane resolutely lifted her eyes from his extremely wellitting breeches and bid him good day in a civil, if not warm voice.

Toby, supplying the warmth, said he was out-of-reason glad the marquess had chanced upon them; then, at Damien's suggestion, he hurried off to the little lake to donate his remaining crumbs to his waterfowl friends. When Ariane turned to follow, Damien's hand on her shoulder detained her.

She might have told him he was being presumptuous, but that same hand had already moved to her cheek. His long fingers leaving a trail of warmth in their wake, he tucked an errent curl into place beneath her bonnet.

"Don't forget, infant," he reminded her softly, his dark eyes holding hers. "Take a companion any time you go out."

Ariane needed the several minutes it took her to catch Toby to compose herself. And even then the mere memory of Damien's light touch had the power to set her heart pounding violently. Her cheeks flushing, she swore angrily to herself. Devil it! It was not fair, not fair at all that the man could discompose her so.

23

It was not until the next day that Ariane had the opportunity to see Mary and share Damien's good news. When she had returned to Grantham House that afternoon, she had had to endure the peal her Aunt Chloe was determined to ring over her.

"I do wonder, Rie, if you can imagine my surprise when you were not here to greet the marquess, your own cousin?" Lady Grantham inquired unhappily when Ariane came to her in her room. "I declare I felt the veriest fool when Dora told us that you had taken Toby out for ice Ices! When we had a visitor. I did warn your father an mother countless times that allowing you to grow up u supervised as they did would come to no good end! An heaven knows, neither Colin nor Crissie have provide much restraint." Drawing herself up grandly, her au continued quite severely, "Well, you are now in my hom miss, and such disgraceful manners will not be allowe here. Do I make myself clear?"

Without the least resentment Ariane said that she unde stood very well and even went so far as to ask her aunt pardon for having discomfited her so.

If Lady Grantham noted that Ariane did not beg pardo for her actions, she did not make mention of it. She kne when she had won a victory, and that she had won one th afternoon, she was certain. She had never found her niec so amenable before.

Of course, she could not know that Ariane, even had sh wanted to, could not have defended herself. To have sai to her aunt that it did not matter that she had been impolit to Damien, because their relationship had never, from th moment she had first encountered him, conformed to th normal rules of society would only have provoked mor inquiry than Ariane cared to suffer.

Indeed, merely imagining her Aunt Chloe's reaction t the news that she had met Damien in a seaside taver where she'd gone dressed as a boy, had so debilitating a effect upon Ariane that she was forced to bow her head t hide her smile.

What her aunt said next, however, sobered her quickl enough. "Though Lady Bandbrooke cannot come—sh has twisted her ankle most painfully, it seems—th marquess, Mrs. Ashton, and Miss Ashton are coming t dinner on Thursday. There will be no rag manners then my girl. You will be here to do the polite as you ought.'

Ariane nodded, too taken up with marking a fresh grievance against Damien to do more. He'd made n mention of the invitation, though he had just received it True, he had had other, more pressing matters to discuss she conceded, but the suspicion that he had had the last laugh after all did not sit well with her.

Forbidding herself to think even once of the dinner, where she would be forced to sit in company with both Damien and his betrothed, Ariane went early the next morning to see Mary.

She had forgotten Lady B's rigid schedule, however, and was obliged to wait some little time before she could have her friend to herself. First they had to escort Lady Brompton to the Pump Room, which she had been visiting on Wednesday mornings since before Ariane was born. Only after the older lady was at last ensconced in a comfortable chair, a glass of the restorative waters at her elbow, was Mary released, and then it was to do her errands.

"Oh, Rie, I thought we should never get her settled! Thank heaven Crissie was willing to stay! I thought I should die if I could not talk to you."

Thus did the normally quiet, shy, reserved Mary turn to Ariane the moment the imposing door of the Pump Room had closed behind them.

"I see the marquess called upon you." Ariane laughed.

"And such news he brought," Mary cried, embracing Ariane tightly in her joy. Though they neither one could speak for some time, the tears brimming in their eyes communicated eloquently just how glad they both were.

When they had wiped their eyes and were walking once more arm in arm, Mary confided with a chuckle, "And to think I was actually dismayed to see Lord Chatham at first. I have never felt very comfortable in his presence, you know. He is so . . . compelling." Laughing, she shook her head. "I am persuaded you will not understand my mutterings at all, Rie, for the marquess never seemed to disconcert you in the least."

In fact, Ariane understood quite well what her friend meant, but not wishing to enter into a discussion of Damien's disturbing attributes, she simply gave a faint shrug and said, "I believe I do understand, my dear. Was he very different yesterday?"

Mary nodded. "He was the most charming, kind man I have ever met, excepting Colin, of course."

It occurred to Ariane that Damien had set out the day before to charm the world. Certainly everyone at Grantham House, from Toby to Corinne, had been extolling his address without pause. And now Mary . . . Well, she would not let the majority sway her, Ariane swore.

"You know how uncertain I have been about my future," Mary was bubbling happily on, oblivious to Ariane's brief scowl. "I do like Lady B very much, but the prospect of being a companion the rest of my life was not particularly inspiring. But now, I needn't worry. Whatever happens, according to Lord Chatham, I have the funds to support myself in some comfort."

They had come to the milliner's shop where Mary was to collect a lace cap Lady Brompton had ordered, but she was too filled with her thoughts to stop talking. Her eyes shining with admiration, she informed Ariane that she believed Damien responsible for her good fortune. "Though the marquess would take no credit, I believe it is due to him that my moneys were separated from Father's. I am certain that it would take someone with his influence to see the matter through to such a conclusion."

While Mary carried out her commission in the milliner's, Ariane considered what she'd said, and decided she was most likely right. Without a determined push, the courts would not have been inclined to look out for a traitor's daughter.

"Lord Chatham also brought news of my father," Mary confided in a much-subdued tone as soon as they had left the shop. She paused so long Ariane was not certain she would continue, and when she did, her voice was close to a whisper. "He, he is not to be hanged," she confided through stiff lips.

Seeing Mary would cry if she said anything, Ariane contented herself with giving her friend's arm a squeeze. After taking a deep breath, Mary admitted, "I know he has done the most terrible things and has never been a real father to me, but still, he is my parent and I am glad for the leniency."

"Of course you are," Ariane soothed her quietly. Recalling the malevolent look with which Sir Henry had told her he'd had her brother killed, she herself experienced a spurt of anger that the villainous man should not have to suffer the direst consequences, but the feeling only lasted a moment. Confinement was terrible enough—and there was Mary to think of.

"You have saved the best until last, have you not?" Ariane asked lightly, hoping to turn Mary's thoughts away from her father.

Her ploy was successful, for Mary's eyes immediately took on a sparkle. "I have indeed," she agreed, a teasing smile brightening her sweet face. "And as this is likely one of the few opportunities I ever shall have to say, 'I told you so,' I am going to avail myself of it." When Ariane grimaced playfully, Mary laughed and once more clasped her friend's arm. "I believe I could almost burst with happiness. I am certain Colin is alive, though Lord Chatham did caution me not to get my hopes too high. He said anything might happen to a man in the West Indies, but I know Colin is safe!

"Lord Chatham said it was the very worst luck that Colin was not traced sooner," Mary went on, shaking her head. "In the normal run of things, there would have been an agent working with him who'd have reported his disappearance when it occurred. But no one at the War Office knew he had gone to Berkshire. Lord Chatham said they know now that when Colin failed to learn anything of interest in France, being your brother—those are Lord Chatham's very words—he took it upon himself to hie off on a new scheme before apprising anyone of that fact. When Colin returns, I do believe Lord Chatham will give him a piece of his mind for acting so hastily, and I cannot blame him. Still, it seems Colin did try to send word of his plans. He instructed a sea captain of his acquaintance to hand-deliver a letter. Unfortunately the man is a smuggler, and when the revenuers tried to board his boat, he put back out to sea, failing to return until long after Colin had been found out by the count's men.

"As you may imagine, tracing Colin's cold trail took considerable time, and it is only in this last week that Lord Chatham received the news that a man answering Colin's description had been sold by an unscrupulous captain."

There was silence, and when Mary continued speaking, her voice was suddenly very small. "Rie, do you think Colin was only feigning an interest in me? He needed an entry into my father's house—"

"No, I most certainly do not," Ariane leapt to say with complete conviction. "Colin could have found any number of simpler ways to gather information on your father. He might even have been hired on as a groom—he's that good with horses. He formed an interest in you, my dear Mary, because you are the sweetest, gentlest person imaginable and the perfect girl for him."

Few people could withstand Ariane at her most certain, which she was in this instance, and certainly one of those people was not Mary, who in any case wished very much to believe what her friend had said. The shine restored to her soft eyes, Mary laughed. "I shall have to believe you, Rie, for when you get the glint in your eye, I know you would scold me severely if I did not."

The matter settled to their mutual satisfaction, they entered the shop where Mary bought the threads and needles with which she did her needlework. The interlude gave Ariane, who had not the slightest interest in such things, the time to consider what Mary had told her of Colin's disappearance.

She shook her head at the thought that if only Jack Combs had been in the Maid that night, she'd never have had to go to Brighton. He'd have told her Colin was on some new mission in Berkshire, and she'd have returned home, unscathed by adventure.

With some justice she could say that she'd gone because she had been chafing to escape from her placid existence at the Willows. But that, too, was only a very small part of the truth.

The greatest part of the truth was that she had gone

simply because it was Damien who had asked her to go. She could admit it now. He had had only to crook his finger and she'd found reasons aplenty to rush off blithely into waters that were, though she'd been too green to know it, well beyond her depth.

But Damien had known how deep they were! And he had deliberately kept his knowledge from her.

"Rie, you are not still thinking Colin has suffered some deadly accident, are you?" Not party to Ariane's thoughts, Mary put the only interpretation on her friend's darkened expression that she could. They were once more walking down the street, and looking anxiously at Ariane, Mary strove to reassure her. "Truly, I do not believe Lord Chatham would exaggerate our reasons to hope. Quite the opposite, in fact, I feel he strove to keep my hopes within the realm of the possible."

Ariane gave her friend a grim little smile. "No," she agreed ironically. "Lord Chatham is not so evil as to lie for no good reason. When Lord Chatham deceives, it is to some laudable purpose, to be sure."

Mary winced at Ariane's bitter tone. She was the only one to whom Ariane had confided how the Marquess of Chatham had used her to entrap the Comte de Triens. Having a more-than-passing understanding of Ariane's capacity for loyalty, she understood very well how such a ruse would affect her friend.

To have been used unwittingly to make a friend of a man so that he could then, solely as a result of his friendship with her, be taken captive must inevitably distress her deeply. And not to have been trusted with the truth of the matter from the first must, also inevitably, cut her to the quick.

They were coming to the bookseller's, the one shop both girls wished to visit, when Mary felt Ariane stiffen. The sound of an approaching curricle made her look to the street, and though she did not much care for horses, she paused to admire the pair of blacks pulling it. It was then she had her answer as to what had affected Ariane.

The Marquess of Chatham handled his restive pair with an ease Mary could not help but appreciate. The merest flick of his wrist brought them away from a dray that had drawn up unexpectedly. The movement also brought his curricle closer to them, allowing Mary to note what she had not before: A very pretty, blond girl was perched beside him, holding tightly to the seat with both her hands. Mary sympathized with the girl's obvious uneasiness. She'd have thought the light curricle and restive animals an unstable combination herself.

Something brought them, or rather—Mary corrected herself, for the marquess did not seem to see her—something brought Ariane to Lord Chatham's attention. His gaze narrowed sharply upon her friend, while Ariane, seemingly oblivious to his regard, stared fixedly before her.

As Mary watched, the marquess cracked his whip, bringing the left of his pair back into line and simultaneously bringing Ariane's head around with a jerk.

When their eyes met, the marquess's mouth curved slightly as he inclined his head in a brief, faintly mocking salute.

"Who is the girl with Lord Chatham?" she asked curiously when the curricle had passed on.

Ariane's walking pace increased perceptibly. "She is Miss Cecily Ashton, the marquess's intended."

"Intended?" Mary repeated, astonished. There had never been any mention of a betrothal in regard to Lord Chatham.

Ariane glanced at her friend briefly and then gave a small, mirthless laugh. "I have surprised you, I see. Actually I overstated the matter. It is only an understanding they have between them."

"Did Lord Chatham tell you of it?" Mary asked, still quite obviously taken aback by the news.

"He did not deny it," Ariane said soberly, recalling with painful clarity the moment when she had first learned Damien had plans to marry. "Aunt Chloe and Corinne spoke of it as well, though my elder cousin seems to have forgotten since then. Their lands march or their fathers were the best of friends, something anyway, I can't quite . . ." Ariane came to a stumbling halt, leaving her sentence unfinished. "Mary, would you mind awfully if we missed the bookseller's?" she asked in a strained voice, her eyes on the doorway of the shop.

Mary scarcely needed to look to know it was the marquess who had again thrown Ariane off her stride. With the perfect, diminutive Miss Ashton on his arm, he was making his way into the bookseller's himself. Just before they disappeared from sight, he bent solicitously to hear something his partner was saying. Whatever it was made him laugh, and the low but rich sound carried clearly down the street.

Without waiting for Mary's agreement, Ariane turned on her heel. Mary followed her quietly. She had no need to ask what was amiss. Now that she knew Lord Chatham was betrothed to another, she understood rather better than she had before why the least mention of the marquess could make sparks fly from Ariane's eyes.

24

At Lady Grantham's dinner the following night, Miss Ashton looked as pretty as an angel, or so Dora thought, and when she whispered her admiration to her cousin, Ariane had to agree that everything about Cecily Ashton seemed angelic, from her finely spun golden hair to her gentle, demure expression.

Even her singing voice was sweet enough to earn her a place in a heavenly choir. A generous person, Ariane did not begrudge Miss Ashton her talent. Her failure to enjoy it as she should, she laid directly at Damien's door.

To watch Cecily meant she must, perforce, look upon Damien as well, for he was doing his betrothed the honor of turning the pages for her.

Ariane tried mightily to keep her gaze trained on an

indeterminate spot on the wall, one well above the pair. She could then listen to Cecily while avoiding Damien.

But her eyes refused to remain lifted, no matter how sternly she commanded them. Before she knew it, those treacherous orbs would lower their sights, and she would find herself gazing raptly at Damien.

Her regard fastened hungrily upon him, she would note how charmingly his black hair curled over his neckcloth in the back, or how gracefully he held his body, or at last, how disturbingly sensual his mouth was.

Vowing it was the last time, Ariane wrenched her gaze away, angry with Damien for affecting her so, and angrier at herself for being so affected, after everything that had passed between them.

Biting her lip, she recalled how she'd reacted when he first entered her aunt's drawing room. The look they'd exchanged then had been the only communication between them all evening, for Ariane had taken care otherwise to remain aloof from him, moving from one cluster of guests to another whenever she even suspected Damien might be approaching.

Still, that one look had been enough. And most frustrating of all, she knew she'd angled for it!

Why otherwise would she have taken such pains with her appearance? Ignoring the unpleasant little voice that derided her for doing so, she had chosen a silk gown of dusty rose that was cut low and square at the neck. With its high waist it emphasized her swelling breasts more than any other gown she had. And she knew it.

The maid, after dressing her hair in artful disarray atop her head, had sighed at the picture she made in that dress with a thin circlet of diamonds gleaming around her neck. She'd called her the "loveliest vision ever," and if Ariane thought that a bit strong, she did think she would do.

She'd been standing by the window in the drawing room when he came. Only a few feet from the door, she'd watched as, Miss Ashton dangling from his arm, he had greeted her aunt and uncle.

She ought to have looked away then, but she had not. He had looked so very handsome, her treacherous eyes would linger on his face. And so, when his host and hostess turned from him to greet Miss Ashton and her mother, his bold, dark eyes had found her.

From where she stood she'd not been able to miss the momentary, involuntary widening of those eyes as he took in her appearance. His gaze had lingered, obviously, upon her décollatage, and then, flicking his gaze upward, he'd looked directly into her waiting eyes.

To her very toes she had felt the force of that brief, penetrating, and—or so it had seemed at the time—possessive look.

Though she'd not have admitted it, there was, when she turned back to attend to Dora's chatter, a decided sparkle in her eyes. The knowledge that she had affected Damien—and she had, she knew—was heady stuff.

The effect had not lingered overlong. However appealing he found her appearance, it was Cecily who remained by his side all evening. And it had been exceedingly difficult to be obliged to see them together. The same intensely painful sensation she'd experienced when she'd seen them laughing together at the bookseller's overcame her whenever she looked up to see his dark head bent close to his betrothed's golden one.

Ariane's discomfort had only increased after dinner during the musical interlude. There was no way to avoid the sight of them together, when she must sit staring at them. Feeling drained and weary, she found it increasingly difficult to resist her attraction.

Luckily for her nerves, Miss Ashton could not sing overlong—her voice was not so strong—and the tea tray was soon brought in, Dora and Corinne having preceded Miss Ashton at the piano.

Ariane helped hand around the teacups, and sending up a prayer of thanks that the evening was almost at an end, she settled herself beside an old friend of her uncle's, a former admiral in the navy whom Ariane had always liked greatly.

"Well, my dear child, this is heaven itself," the admiral boomed at her fondly in a voice made more for a quarter-deck than a drawing room. "A cup of your aunt's fine tea handed me by a lovely chit like you. But tell me, sweeting, why did you not join the other young ladies in entertaining us? I'd not have thought you shy."

Ariane laughed at the thought, but before she could answer him, a soft, hesitant, little voice was saying, "Yes, Miss Bennington. I, too, am concerned that you did not sing for us." Amazed that Miss Ashton, who had never spoken to her before, was voicing such a sentiment, Ariane was momentarily struck dumb. "I hope I did not take overlong at my turn," the girl added, her brow knit with concern.

She seemed such a small, sincere creature that Ariane could not hold her in dislike. It was not her fault, after all, if she had property that marched with Damien's. "Do not distress yourself on my account, Miss Ashton." Ariane smiled easily. "Truly, I've not the least proficiency. That is why I did not sing or play." Making a comical face, she admitted, "I am afraid, you see, that I spent most of my childhood music lessons on horseback, assiduously avoiding my tutor."

The admiral whooped lustily, saying that he'd seized on the least excuse to avoid doing his scales as well, while Cecily seemed at first startled by the thought of such headstrong behavior, and then, beguiled by the others' laughter, she laughed, too, though it was a gentle, tinkling sound.

Unaccountably pleased to have elicited such a spontaneous response from the demure girl, Ariane's eyes sparkled merrily, until she chanced to glance up and see Damien was watching them, a ghost of a smile tugging at his mouth. On the instant her pleasure cooled.

It was simply too much to see Damien smiling with such tenderness on his future wife. Veiling her eyes with her lashes, she consigned him to a long, uncomfortable stay with the devil. How dare he come here, she fumed to herself, parading the lady he would wed before her. If he had come to Bath, as she suspected, to apprehend Deparens, why was he not off doing that? Why was he cozying up to her family, insinuating himself into her circle? And in the process reminding her how vastly compelling he was.

After what seemed to Ariane to be an interminable amount of time, the guests finally rose and began to mill about saying all the last-minute politenesses that guests generally do before taking their leave.

Miss Ashton had gone to her mother and the admiral to his wife, so that Ariane was left alone for a moment before she went to make her own adieus. She'd have done better to go to the others at once. Like the unholy spirit to whose company Ariane had condemned him, Damien suddenly materialized by her side, though she had not thought he was even in her part of the room.

"Though you denied it to Cecily, I think you must be growing shy, Rie. I know your voice is not so bad. I've heard you sing, if you recall."

His reference to a particularly enjoyable evening in Brighton when Ariane had joined Solange in song caused her to flush. Briefly she was reminded of a boy in Appledyne who had enjoyed taking the wings off flies while they still lived. Like him, Damien seemed to enjoy causing pain.

In the circumstances it seemed a particularly cruel thing to do, to remind her of the sort of evening she could never have again with him.

"I had Solange to accompany me then," she replied, her cool tone worth every bit of the effort. "By myself, I'm afraid I'm hard put to carry the simplest tune."

Occasionally, the mind will play tricks when it is least expected to do so, which is what Ariane's mind did at that precise moment. Unbidden, a memory of Toby came to her mind, surprising her into a chuckle.

Feeling more than seeing Damien's brow lift faintly, Ariane risked glancing at him. She nearly lost the train of her thought. His eyes, as he looked down at her, were meltingly warm.

"I, ah, I was only remembering a remark of Toby's on the subject of my voice," she explained vaguely, her gaze skittering away to rest on the others, some of whom were now advancing toward the doors.

"And he said?" Damien prompted when it seemed Ariane would not continue.

She shrugged, unable to return her gaze to him no

175

matter how firmly she told herself that not to do so was a sign of cowardice. "He said I sounded like his frog."

She'd not delivered the line well. Distracted by the effect he had on her, she'd said it flatly, leaving it to fall between them like a stone.

Damien made no attempt to laugh, lighten the atmosphere, and depart as she wished mightly that he would. "Rie."

Ariane heard his quiet pronouncement of her name, but she absorbed herself with an imaginary piece of lint on her gown.

"Rie." There was nothing for it. When she looked up, she found his black eyes gleaming more than merely warmly. "I have more that I would say to you." His voice was so low and lazy, the sound of it sent Ariane's blood licking warmly through her veins, making it impossible for her to think to register a protest of his intent. "It is only fair to warn you that I shall come to claim you and that I shall do so when you have not surrounded yourself with an army of friends and family. Be prepared for me, infant."

Having flung down his soft challenge, Damien lifted her hand, and kissed it before she could jerk it from his grasp, his eyes gleaming wickedly into hers all the while.

25

Not knowing why Damien should desire to speak further with her—and in private—did not make the following days easier. Considering one possibility after another, Ariane tossed them all aside, wanting to scream from frustration. He had no right to set her on pins like this, she swore unhappily. They had nothing to say.

Still, when he did not make an appearance at Grantham House that day or the next, nor come to the Pump Room when she accompanied Mary, nor even pass by her in Mr. Huntsleigh's carriage when he took her and Dora driving, Ariane became annoyed.

She was not angry, she told herself, merely annoyed, and that only because she felt bound to be on the lookout for him. That he seemed in no great haste to seek her out did not affect her in the least.

When a fourth day passed and she was telling herself yet again how little his absence affected her, Ariane pulled herself up short. It was time she find something or someone else to occupy her.

A nicely timed summons from her aunt provided her some hope of distraction. Lady Grantham, the maid said, wished her advice on what dress she should wear that evening. With an amused smile curving her lips, she went along to Lady Grantham's rooms, thinking as she went that it had not been so very long since her aunt had reprimanded her for going out in a dress with a disgracefully frayed hem.

With a mental salute to Solange, Ariane helped her aunt decide upon a very handsome gold brocade evening gown that they both agreed would flatter Lady Grantham's dark coloring nicely.

Her aunt was judging the effect of her pearls with the brocade dress when Ariane remarked casually, "Do you not find Mr. Huntsleigh an amiable young man, Aunt Chloe?"

"Why, I find him most amiable, indeed," Lady Grantham replied, looking quickly at Ariane, her pearls momentarily forgotten. "He has adequate address, particularly for a man of his age, and most pleasing manners." She smiled at her niece, of whom, despite their differences, she was fond. "He seems taken with you, my dear, thus demonstrating he possesses discernment."

Ariane laughed. "He does not seem indifferent," she allowed. "Of late, however," she continued—and something in her tone made her aunt lay down her pearls altogether—"I believe there has been a change in Mr. Huntsleigh's interests. He seems to be awakening to the fact that Dora would make him a far better wife than I."

"Dora! But Dora is so young," Lady Grantham protested, addressing a point that was somewhat beside the issue.

"I do not mean to imply that Mr. Huntsleigh plans to speak to Uncle Randall tomorrow," Ariane assured her. "I only want to warn you that when we three are together, it is to Dora Mr. Huntsleigh turns."

Lady Grantham sank down upon a soft chair the better to assess Ariane's news. "He is wealthy," she allowed tentatively, "and at his majority will be wealthier still. I suppose if Dora cares for him, it would not be such a bad thing . . . Well, we shall have to see," she said, shaking her head as if she could not quite believe they were speaking of such a serious matter in connection with her little Dora.

When she looked back again at her niece, she was frowning. "You do not seem to mind overmuch, Rie," she observed, clearly puzzled.

It was not the time to inform her aunt she intended to marry no one, but Ariane did confess she was not vastly overset by Mr. Huntsleigh's desertion. "I am persuaded we would not suit."

Lady Grantham did not look much pleased with Ariane's explanation, but she did reluctantly have to agree. "I doubt you will make anyone a comfortable wife, my dear," she sighed. "You are too much like your father."

Whether she was too much like her father Ariane could not know, but she did not imagine that he would have been such a goose that, immediately upon entering Lady Dorster's crowded ballroom that evening, he'd have searched the room for Damien.

Damien was not present, though Miss Ashton, sitting close beside her mother, was. Ariane was uncertain whether she was relieved or not, and she decided he would be as absent this entire evening as he had been the previous few, so that when Damien did arrive much later, she was not at all prepared for him. And unprepared, she was powerless to resist the rush of pleasure she experienced seeing him there at the door executing a graceful bow over his hostess's eagerly extended hand.

He made no effort to approach her, but Ariane kept a wary eye upon him nonetheless. He danced first with a curvaceous woman of his own age whom she did not know, then with Miss Ashton, Dora, Corinne, and again the older woman.

When she saw him lead Miss Ashton out for their second dance, Ariane had had enough. Turning abruptly, she asked Dora to make her apologies to Mr. Huntsleigh, who was to partner her next, and slipped out the doors to the terrace.

Breathing deeply of cool night air that did not smell particularly sweet, Ariane experienced a wave of longing for the Willows. The gardens there would smell of apple blossoms now.

Sighing at the thought of how very little say she seemed to have in her life, she descended to the graveled walk. When she came to a bench, she sat, deciding she preferred the town-scented air to the close atmosphere of the ballroom for the time being.

"You'll lose young Huntsleigh if you leave him to your pretty cousin."

Ariane started, then ground out an oath she'd learned from Jed Tregan. How dare Damien ignore her the night long, then seek her out when she sought privacy.

"Mr. Huntsleigh is not the prize in some contest between Dora and me," she retorted hotly, rising on the instant to go. If Damien wished to speak to her, then he could do so in the usual way and before his betrothed.

But Damien had warned her he would speak privately to her, and she ought to have known he did not make idle threats. "Don't be so hasty, Rie," he chided, amusement lacing his voice as he clasped her arm lightly and returned her to her seat. "Most young ladies would be excessively flattered if I sought them out."

Ariane did not care that it was a deliberate provocation. She welcomed the flare of anger his conceit incited as a protection against the treacherously happy warmth his presence so close beside her in the cool night aroused in her weak breast.

"Waiting two hours to track me down when it is obvious

I have come outside to be alone is not the least flattering," she informed him, knowing the moment the words were spoken that she'd been overhasty. Even to her ears, her words sounded more complaint than set-down.

Apparently Damien thought so as well. "Tsk, tsk, Rie." His soft chuckle intensified her chagrin. "I had not realized you kept such a close account of my comings and goings."

"Oh!" Ariane once more sought to depart.

Before she could do more than lift herself slightly, Damien had linked his arm through hers. "You may not go just yet, my dear," he informed her, all amiability. "I've been away a few days on business that concerns you."

Even as she registered the explanation of his absence, she bristled. She must, or risk acknowledging how right his arm felt beneath hers. "Do not confuse my business with yours, my lord," she directed him tartly. "I do not work for you any longer. If your business has to do with Deparens, then it concerns you, not me, for it is you who want him."

"Sit down, Rie."

Ariane did not mistake the steel in that soft command. She did not try to leave again, but she did wrench her arm from his grasp. "You do not have my permission to call me that," she snapped irritably.

Ariane rubbed her arm, more to imply that it hurt than anything, and waited for Damien's response, ready to find fault with whatever he said. When he did not oblige her, the silence lengthened, setting Ariane's nerves on edge.

To calm herself, she drew a deep breath, the ragged sound of it loud in the quiet.

Softly, on the heels of her sigh, Damien spoke. "Did you care for Triens so much, Rie?"

She had not expected it, not the question or the grave tone. She did not pretend to misunderstand, though to answer she had to shut out her response to the deep note in his voice. "What is 'so much'?" she asked, facing him directly despite the fact that in the faint light of the garden it was impossible to read his expression clearly. "The count became a friend, a good friend." Suddenly bitterness overcame her and she hurled her next words at him angrily. "But of course you know we were friends, did you not? You put us together: the green girl and the spy! And you even worried over how deeply he might engage my feelings, as I recall. Such a thoughtful man! I wonder, if *monsieur le comte* had asked for my hand, would you have told me then what he was?

"No, likely not," she answered herself, sarcasm dripping from her voice as she rushed on. "It might have been useful to mark down the names of those attending the wedding. Ah, my lord, what a comfort it must be to the War Office to have you, a master at manipulations . . ."

Damien caught her by the shoulders, jerking her up close to him. "I resent all that!" he growled harshly. "Nothing I did was done to hurt you, and well you know it. I did only what had to be done."

"You might have trusted me," Ariane cried, revealing there in the darkness what had hurt her the very most in the matter of the Comte de Triens.

How Damien might have replied, she was not to learn, for suddenly the terrace doors opened, spilling a flood of light into the gardens.

Taken by surprise, Damien momentarily loosened his hold on her. It was enough. Whirling around, Ariane made good her escape, wiping the painful tears from her eyes as she fled into the crowded ballroom.

Dazed as much by the turbulence of her emotions as by the sudden onslaught of the lights, she accepted the first young man who asked her to dance. He had not signed her card, but the only issue of importance to Ariane was that she reached the safety of the dance floor before Damien returned.

Only a heartbeat later he came. Over the young man's shoulder she watched as he rapidly scanned the room. Unerringly he found her. His dark gaze clashed with hers, promising a future, stormy meeting, but he made no move toward her.

Turning abruptly, he sought out her uncle instead. After

181

he'd spoken quietly to Sir Randall for some little while, he departed the ball altogether.

Ariane watched him pass through Lady Dorster's doors with a sigh of relief. It did not seem likely that he could have gotten her off alone again—she'd have been prepared —but she did not care to chance it. She had come too close as it was to revealing how very deeply he had hurt her.

26

Ariane tossed off her thick bedcovers with a frustrated moan. Though she'd returned from Lady Dorster's only a few hours earlier, she was irrevocably awake.

Not bothering to ring for her maid, she dragged out her habit. A ride would be just the thing to settle her over-wrought nerves.

They needed settling. As clearly as if he still touched her, she could feel the warmth of Damien's hands on her shoulders . . . She shivered at the memory. Damien's touch was something she must not allow herself to dwell upon.

It was better to recall how angrily he'd told her he had not meant to hurt her. Ariane shoved her slender foot into a boot with unnecessary force. Did he think lack of fore-thought an adequate excuse?

Even children were told where good intentions led. Let him answer why he had not trusted her—or a more difficult question, surely, why he had gone out of his way to make her feel trusted.

And if that were not enough, she addressed a mental image of Damien, suitably chastened with his head hanging down, he might clarify why, though he was betrothed, or nearly so, to another, he'd played fast and loose with her feelings.

How was she to have known his teasing, his indulgences, his kisses, meant nothing, that he felt no more for her than any rake might feel toward any passable-looking female?

Of the two of them he was the experienced one, possessing a fine understanding of his effect upon women. What had he expected her to think when he'd kissed her so that her head spun? That she'd have bethought herself of Crissie's warning?

Knowing that was exactly what she ought to have done, and recalling her own boast that she was safe from a man who had admitted he was a rake, did not sweeten Ariane's mood. Scowling, she stamped off down the hallway and did not hear her uncle until he had called her twice.

"You are up early," she said, smiling curiously after she'd bid him good day.

"Unusually so," Sir Randall acknowledged, returning her smile. "It occurred to me that you might take it into your head to go riding, and I must speak to you before you do, Rie. I should have done so last evening, but you rushed off to your room so quickly, I could not catch you."

Beneath her uncle's sapient as well as kindly gaze, Ariane flushed slightly.

"Well, that's unimportant now." Sir Randall dismissed the matter of her oddly subdued mood with a wave of his hand. "Come along to my study, there should be a good fire there."

Without preamble when they were both comfortably seated, he began, "Rie, Lord Chatham has explained to me the truth of your relationship. Don't be alarmed." He smiled gently when Ariane gasped in dismay. "While I wish you had trusted me enough to tell me yourself, I do understand the circumstances. You have always been a spirited child, and I found, after my initial shock, that the marquess's story did not surprise me terribly."

"I, that is, Colin—"

Her uncle halted her fumbling attempt at an explanation by holding up his hand. "Lord Chatham explained about Colin, Rie. As I said, I understand." He paused, frowning slightly. "I shall not tell your aunt, by the by. Chloe would not view the matter as I do, and I do not care to have her

183

upset." Thinking her uncle's assessment was as great an understatement as she had ever heard, Ariane hastily nodded her agreement. "The marquess's primary intent in speaking with me was to inform me of this Frenchman whose been seen in Bath. He believes, as I think he told you, that he may intend you some harm."

"Did he say why?" Ariane asked, for she had not been able to think why Deparens would be interested in her.

Sir Randall nodded. "I gather the marquess believes the villain hopes to hold you hostage in return for the freedom of his master. He's not certain, you understand, but he thinks the possibility is strong enough that he has asked me to curtail one of your favorite activities. I am sorry, my dear, but I must ask you not to ride out for the time being. Lord Chatham believes old Higgs would not be adequate protection."

Ariane, to her credit, stifled her instinctive protest. Mustering the smile Sir Randall's forgiving nature deserved, she advised him she would do as he asked.

It was not easy to give up her ride, however, and when she was out of her uncle's sight, her shoulders drooped rather markedly. Crissie, who met her on the stairs, inquired at once what was amiss, and when Ariane had made her an explanation, she offered to accompany her on a walk.

"It won't be quite the same as a ride, I grant, but at least we shall be out of doors."

Ariane's response was to hug her old governess tightly. "You are the greatest dear, Crissie."

"Don't thank me yet." Crissie returned the affectionate embrace with a sweet smile of her own. "It looks like rain. If we are to return as dry as we leave, we shall have to go at once."

"Corinne seems to have had a grand time last evening," Crissie remarked a trifle hesitantly when they had been walking briskly some little while. "She was quite in alt that Lord Chatham danced with her." To Crissie's surprise, for she knew from Dora that the marquess had not danced at all with Ariane, her companion only shrugged.

184

"My elder cousin is a fool," Ariane replied tersely. "His lordship may have danced once with her, but he danced twice with Miss Ashton. In her excitement, Corinne seems to have forgotten the marquess has an understanding with someone else."

Indeed, thought Crissie, she, too, had somehow forgotten Miss Ashton. "She seems such a timid little thing," she murmured half to herself.

"You've seen her?" Ariane asked, surprised.

"Yes." Crissie reddened slightly. "Toby would speak to Lord Chatham when he came to dinner, and I saw no harm in allowing it."

"And, by chance, you were able to meet the future marchioness."

"I could not allow Toby to go alone," Crissie responded reasonably, quite ignoring Ariane's knowing look. "Lord Chatham was as handsome as ever, I must say," she added, watching Ariane from the corner of her eye. When Ariane made no reply, Crissie returned to the marquess's future bride. "I thought Miss Ashton quite pretty with her porcelain complexion and blue eyes, but I find it difficult to imagine her married to Lord Chatham. She seems so small in comparison to him."

"You yourself said he would marry where he must," Ariane replied shortly, reminding Crissie of a statement she had all but forgotten. While Crissie considered how best to explain her change of feeling on the matter, Ariane muttered half to herself, "Certainly he would do a great deal better to marry her than Corinne. Miss Ashton, at least, possesses a pleasant disposition."

"Ah!" Crissie's wail was not in response to Ariane's less-than-charitable observation upon her cousin. A gust of wind had nearly taken her hat. "Oh, dear! The rain is here sooner than I'd expected."

She cast an anxious look at the sky as a drop of rain splattered on her extended hand. The single drop was followed by another, and before she and Ariane had made much progress toward home, they found themselves assailed by a downpour against which their fashionable parasols were little protection. Ariane took the brunt, putting Crissie behind her, but she was too slender to be more than inadequate as a refuge.

It was with extremely mixed feelings, therefore, that she recognized the crest emblazoned upon the carriage that pulled up beside them only a few moments later.

With easy grace Damien leapt down to hold out his hand to Crissie. "Allow me, my dear Miss Crisswell," he said with a smile whose power was not diminished by the storm.

Ariane made no move to follow Crissie's scramble to safety. With a beaver hat set at a rakish angle on his head and a many-caped driving coat thrown about his shoulders, Damien was more imposing than ever.

The scene in Lady Dorster's garden as strong in her mind now as it had been earlier, she was hard put to view the Marquess of Chatham's sudden appearance with the same welcome Crissie did.

Her hesitation did not go unremarked. "Coming, Rie? Or shall we follow along beside you as you maintain your distance?" he asked, an infuriatingly wicked light dancing in his eye.

With the rain dripping from the brim of her sodden bonnet onto the tip of her slim nose, her damp hair a riot of unruly curls, and her feet wet through, there was little Ariane could do but allow her eloquent green eyes to cast him a speaking look. Pointedly ignoring the hand he placed beneath her elbow anyway, she then joined Crissie in the lion's den.

"You were the very sight I wished to see, my lord," Crissie informed Damien with a grateful smile when the carriage was once more on its way. "We are both soaked to the bone, though Rie took the worst of it. Oh, my, just look at my boots!"

Damien murmured some sympathetic remark as he followed Crissie's mournful gaze. Her boots, which must have once been blue, he thought, were now an earthen brown.

When he glanced up, he caught Ariane's gaze upon him, her expression unreservedly baleful. "I wonder you are looking so put out with me, Rie?" he asked pleasantly. "I did not cause the rain, though I cannot deny I am pleased to see it kept you from riding."

"You must know very well it was you, not the weather that kept me in town," she retorted, nettled by what she thought was a smug note in his voice.

"Then you have spoken to your uncle." It was as much question as statement, and Ariane nodded curtly. "I am relieved you heeded my warning," he said, his voice so suddenly grave that Ariane felt for the briefest instant that he did, in a vital way, care about her.

Afraid he would see some sign of the confusion into which he'd thrown her, she gave a shrug as if to say it was nothing, and took refuge in looking out the window. Damien did not press her, turning instead to engage Crissie in amicable conversation, his deep voice stirring Ariane's senses more than she wished to acknowledge.

Eager to escape being in such close confines with him, she only just kept herself from springing out before Crissie when the lackey opened the carriage door at Grantham House. Politeness demanded that she allow the older woman to descend first, and though poised to follow, she curbed her impatience.

At last it was her turn to thank Damien and descend. "I am grateful . . ." she began as she slid toward the door.

The edge of her seat was as far as she got. Quicker than she, Damien leaned forward, barring her way with his body. "You go along, Miss Crisswell," he called to Crissie's quickly retreating back. "Ariane will follow in a moment. Just now, I must speak to her."

"No! You cannot keep me here," Ariane cried with real dismay, though Damien was already directing the coachman to drive around the square slowly.

"You cannot—"

But Damien interrupted her. "I have things I wish to say to you, as I told you. Coming upon you in a downpour has saved me the trouble of dragging you into your uncle's study."

"This insistence on conversation seems sudden, indeed, my lord!" Ariane's eyes flashed with her frustration.

"Pray forgive me if I fail to understand it. But, then, for all these months, you have seemed well content with silence."

Damien flicked Ariane an ironic glance before pausing to toss his hat onto the seat beside him and stretch out his long legs. Settled to his apparent satisfaction, he looked with disconcerting detachment into Ariane's glaring eyes. "I am surprised you would call me to task for not presenting myself at your doorstep, Ariane. Neither your hasty departure from Brighton nor your reception of me here in Bath has given me the impression that you'd have welcomed me. However, even had you importuned me for a visit, I admit I could not have accommodated you. You see, I have been a trifle busy."

Of a sudden Ariane had the unhappy notion that she was about to feel the veriest fool. "First"—Damien ticked off his point on one long finger—"there was the matter of your brother's whereabouts to occupy me. It took time, most of it spent in evil-smelling, raucous seamen's haunts, to learn that foul captain's name and destination.

"Then, a man had to be recruited to go after Colin. I could not go myself as I had, I am certain you will appreciate, other business.

"There was, as yet, one member of the Comte de Triens' spy ring to apprehend. To that end I spent more nights than I care to remember in cold, damp, rough inns, following the trail of the man you know as Deparens. You do recall Deparens?" Damien inquired, but Ariane, recognizing a rhetorical question when she heard it, made no answer. "I mean," he continued helpfully, "the count's butler, the man who was able to escape our net in Brighton only because you, Miss Bennington, did not keep your word to me."

Feeling as foolish as she'd feared she might, Ariane could not hold his gaze.

"And now," Damien continued coolly, his mood not the least softened by her downcast eyes, "I hope you are able to understand why I did not have the leisure to hurry to the Willows to insist upon a talk."

Ariane forced herself to look at him. Having to address

his closed, forbidding expression was her penance for her actions at the count's ball, she decided. "I am sorry about Deparens. I know I promised to keep out of it, but when I didn't see you and Sir Henry left the ballroom, I thought . . ." Her voice trailed off. It didn't matter what she'd thought, she'd been wrong and she knew it.

"You thought foolishly," Damien finished, more dampeningly than Ariane thought was strictly fair. She had acted hastily, it was true, perhaps even foolishly, but had Damien trusted her with his plans, she'd have had the confidence to keep away.

"You may look affronted all you like," he continued, easily reading her expression. "The fact remains that a dangerous spy escaped because of your ill-considered actions. Which brings me to the present. I am pleasantly surprised to find you are behaving wisely today, but I wish some assurance that you will show the same good judgment tomorrow. I am not at all sanguine you will be so reasonable two days in a row."

In fact, Ariane did think he was being unduly cautious. "Well—" she began.

Damien interrupted her. "No hesitations. Deparens is a very shrewd, ruthless man."

"But I cannot believe I could not outdistance him on horseback."

Damien did not disagree. "No doubt you could, if the race were equal. But I assure you Deparens will take care that it is anything but equal."

"Truly I do not think he could ever catch me on my uncle's stallion."

"Damnation, Ariane!" Uncoiling with a violent start, Damien caught her by the wrists and shook her. "I vow you can provoke me more than is wise." His black eyes glittering with his irritation, he shook her again. "Can you really not imagine the agony I suffered when I saw that cutthroat with his knife at your throat?"

Ariane's eyes widened. She had not thought he had suffered at all, much less agony. Appallingly, it was elation that swept her.

They were sitting very close together, Damien's thighs

189

holding her in place. At such close quarters the achingly masculine lines of his face seemed more compelling than ever, and it was only by the greatest effort that Ariane could keep from lifting her hand to trace the strong line of his jaw.

"Did you ever intend to tell me what you were really about?" she asked quietly.

Though Damien displayed no surprise at the change of subject, she did see the jaw she had wanted to touch clench. "I was about the business of stopping a devilishly successful spy ring."

She did not make an answer, did not even blink, only continued to search him with her wide emerald gaze.

"No," Damien answered that look his grip on her wrists relaxing slightly, "I had not thought I would find it necessary to tell you about Triens."

"Why," she asked, "did you not trust me?"

"By entrusting you with my identity, I trusted you with my life," he contradicted her forcefully, his black eyes fixed upon her, compelling her to understand. "I did not, it is true, trust you with my suspicions of Triens. I did not then, and still do not now, for that matter, believe you are capable of carrying on a flirtation with a man you must distrust. I would that I might have used Solange. But Solange would not do. Triens does not have a penchant for mature beauties, only young, innocent ones."

Startled, Ariane gave him a quick, piercing look, then veiled her eyes with her long lashes. Damien's frank remark brought to her mind the evening Triens had shown her his collection of objets d'art. The Chinese girl, preening before her mirror, had been young and innocent, too.

Impatient with her withdrawal, Damien cupped her chin, tilting her head back. "Do you understand now?" he asked softly. "I very badly needed to find an approach to the count, and you were the best one I found after months of thinking on the matter. I regret that I could not tell you," he said, his low voice working its magic on Ariane's senses. "But you are not made for subterfuge, love. Every feeling you have is reflected too clearly in those great green eyes of yours."

Later Ariane was to compare herself scornfully to the victim of the cobra, an Indian snake she had lately read of. The cobra did not attack its prey directly, the book said, but instead performed a swaying dance so mesmerizing the victim that it did not attempt an escape, but stood meekly, instead, waiting to be taken up for dinner.

Like that prey, Ariane, her senses assaulted by the velvety warmth of Damien's eyes, gave no thought to flight as he brought her slowly toward him.

His lips, when they captured hers, seared her, his forceful touch lighting an irresistible fire inside her. Without thought she put her arms around his neck and entwined her fingers in his thick, dark hair.

When the coach rocked to a stop, Damien pulled back. Her mind still not functioning properly, Ariane encountered the hot, demanding gleam in his eyes with a responding surge of longing.

Unfortunately her eyes fell next to his mouth. Though she was yet dazed, she could discern still the triumphant tilt to his charming half-smile.

That the lackey appeared to open the door at that precise moment was the merest luck. If he'd not come she'd have had to jumped down completely unaided. As it was, her foot touched the steps before they were entirely unfolded, and feeling them give way, Ariane was forced to grab inelegantly onto the boy's arm or else tumble into the mud.

It was some distance from the carriage to the steps of Grantham House, but nonetheless, as Ariane fled up them, her body stiff with self-reproach at the scene she'd allowed to occur, she could hear with humiliating distinctness a deep, amused chuckle floating in the air behind her.

27

Crissie said Lord Chatham brought you home.''
Corinne stood just above her cousin on the stairs, interrupting Ariane's flight to her room as she craned to look at
the doorway. Seeing no one but the butler, she looked
again at Ariane and was for a moment diverted. "Why,
you look a fright," she exclaimed, wrinkling her thin nose
at Ariane's sodden bonnet and muddy boots. "Well! Now
I understand why Chatham did not escort you inside. The
way you conduct yourself, he must think we are all
barbarians."

Ariane had quite forgotten how bedraggled she must
look, and a touch of red suffused her cheeks. It was two
farthings to a brass monkey that Miss Ashton had never
looked a wet, muddy mess.

"Don't be more fool than you can help, Corinne," she
sighed, dispatching thoughts of Cecily Ashton and moving
by her cousin. "If Chatham had wanted to visit, you may
be certain he'd not have allowed my appearance to keep
him."

Gaining the privacy of her room at last, Ariane locked
her door and leaned against it for support as the scene with
Damien threatened to overwhelm her.

How could she have responded so? How could she?
After everything, even knowing he was intended for
another!

She pressed a trembling hand to her lips. They were
sensitive to her touch, each nerve ending tingling still. Even
now a part of her longed to receive his kiss again.

And he had known how lost to all reason she had been.

Oh! She kicked the leg of the chintz-covered chair
nearest her, wishing it were Damien's leg instead.
Succeeding only in bruising her toe, Ariane collapsed into
the depths of the ill-used piece of furniture.

Why? Why should he wish to press his attentions upon her when they both knew he was engaged? Did he intend to make love to her, to make her his mistress? Mistress indeed, she addressed herself tiredly. No man would want an inexperienced girl of eighteen as his mistress. Particularly not a man who attracted the sort of ardent lures Ariane had seen more than one, enticing, experienced woman cast out to him.

No, the only explanation was much simpler, and yet, it was one she felt loathe to face. Rake that he was, he merely wished to mark another conquest.

Tears in her eyes, for she had never felt so confused, she tried to give thought to what she must do. The brave answer was to say, Forget the matter, go on, and if she should find herself alone again with the Marquess of Chatham, be prepared to fend him off.

But would she? She could not know with any surety that she would repulse him, and not knowing made her want to die of shame. It seemed she had no control over her response to Damien.

Sighing morosely, she thought how very much she'd have liked to ride. Before, the magic of being outside, concentrating on the animal beneath her, had always helped her to see matters more clearly. And she certainly needed clarity now.

The remainder of the morning brought no solution to the dilemma posed by Damien, but it did, in the unlikeliest of places, present her with an answer to how she might get her ride.

When she entered the Pump Room with Mary and Lady B, however, there was no indication of her coming fortune. Quite the opposite, her cheeks paling suddenly, Ariane recognized Mrs. Ashton in Lady B's little group.

When a quick survey of the room assured her that Damien was not present, she relaxed fractionally, enough to respond politely to the lady's greeting. Looking to Mary, she thought to leave then, but espied Mr. Huntsleigh and his mother coming to speak to her.

Suppressing a vexed groan, she smiled as sweetly as she could and was just going to say that she and Mary must be excused to do their errands when Mr. Huntsleigh inquired, as a mere politeness, if she'd been riding that morning.

His question sparked a more than merely polite response in Ariane's green eyes. Her uncle might object to her going for a ride with only Evan Huntsleigh as escort—likely he would, for Evan was not strong or burly or given to carrying cudgels—but Ariane thought he would do well enough. From a distance, she did not think Deparens would recognize how little threat Mr. Huntsleigh posed.

Giving Mary a glance that pleaded with her to be patient, she drew Mr. Huntsleigh off to the side and forthrightly asked if he would provide her escort on her ride the next morning. "I hope you will not think me excessively forward," she said quickly. "It is only that my uncle's groom is, ah, unable to accompany me just now, and I hoped that as you are my friend, you would not mind my asking for the favor of your company."

Mr. Huntsleigh looked into her entreating green eyes with a gallant smile. "By jove, I know you too well to think you forward, Miss Bennington. And I am honored that you should think of me."

In happy agreement, they made their plans, Mr. Huntsleigh assuring her in passing that he would bring his groom, a point of propriety that had not occurred to Ariane. After some discussion he also allowed himself to be persuaded to meet her in the mews behind Grantham House.

Though Mr. Huntsleigh had frowned at her request that he not call for her at the door, Ariane persuaded him at last to do as she wished. "Let us, do please, have an adventure from start to finish," she had pleaded, and he'd been no proof at all against her entreating smile.

When she bid Mr. Huntsleigh farewell, Ariane knew a twinge of guilt. She had not been so easy with him in some time, and was only being so now because she wished something of him. With a thought for Dora as well, she determined she would make her feelings on the subject of marriage clear to him—tomorrow, when they were safely on their ride.

Ariane waved to Mary, feeling well-pleased with herself.

At least a part of her life seemed once again in her control.

"Oh, look!" Mary waved happily. "It is Lord Chatham."

Ariane's heart seemed to stop beating altogether as her gaze found Damien. Leaning comfortably against a column, his arms folded over his chest, he was, she saw with a rush of alarm, regarding her with a particularly keen, speculative gaze. How long he had been watching she couldn't know, but he looked to have been there for some time.

To her fury, she felt her cheeks heat painfully. It had been too few hours since she'd felt his mockingly curved mouth on hers. Abruptly she jerked her head about and lifted her chin to a dangerous angle. Sweeping regally out the door, she ignored Mary's friendly interchange with the devilish man completely. And she told herself that even had Damien seen her with Mr. Huntsleigh, he could not know what she had been about. She would get her ride despite him!

Good to his word, Mr. Huntsleigh presented himself precisely at eight o'clock the following morning, his short, wiry groom in tow. Following Ariane's suggestion, for she particularly liked a forested section that lay along it, they took the Radstock Road. It was a beautiful day, the rains of the day before having cleared the air so that the sunlight shone like crystal.

"Shall we move along?" Ariane called, her spirits infected by the day. They had reached the part of the road where traffic had thinned considerably and the woods were in sight, beckoning. Without waiting for Mr. Huntsleigh's reply, she urged her stallion to a canter.

Startled, Mr. Huntsleigh cried out for her to wait, but Ariane was lost to everything except the feel of the fresh breeze on her face. Not aware she would be testing her escorts beyond their powers, she gave her mount, a fine stallion her uncle had owned only a year, his head, and streaked away down the road.

Mr. Huntsleigh stared after her aghast. Unlike most other young men his age, Evan Huntsleigh had attended more assiduously to his studies than to athletic pursuits, and was, he would have admitted himself, a most indifferent horseman. Ordinarily, he could acquit himself well enough, but riding with Ariane, he realized too late, was altogether out of the ordinary.

Groaning aloud, Mr. Huntsleigh had a sudden, daunting recollection of the fierce light in the Marquess of Chatham's eyes as he had commanded him to stay with Miss Bennington at all costs.

The order had come after the marquess had intercepted him and as cool as you please had demanded to know what Ariane had wanted of him. By no means a timid man, Mr. Huntsleigh would have informed anyone else the question was presumptuous in the extreme. There had been, however, a certain flat steeliness in the marquess's eye that had decided Mr. Huntsleigh to tell him exactly what he wanted to know and to agree obediently to all the instructions he was given afterward.

Seeing that Ariane would soon disappear around a bend that led into the forest, Mr. Huntsleigh spurred his horse, making a valiant effort to close the lead she'd opened. Unused to a pace much beyond a walk, the gentle creature responded reluctantly and Ariane was lost to his sight in the next moment.

His attention taken up entirely with the effort of catching up to Ariane, Mr. Huntsleigh did not hear the approach of the man who had been following their group some little while. It was only when the man drew up with him that Mr. Huntsleigh turned, and even then he expected to see his groom. Most assuredly he did not expect the large hamlike fist that shot out to cuff him squarely on the chin, catching him completely unawares and sending him in a high arch to the ground.

With the wind knocked out of him, Evan Huntsleigh lay gasping and made no effort to pick himself up until he heard at least one and possibly two riders approaching from the direction Ariane had taken. Thinking he must prepare to do battle with a madman, he stumbled, breathing hard, to his feet.

He was not at all certain, when he recognized the first of

196

the two riders, whether he would not rather face his anonymous assaulter.

"Where is she, man?" Chatham shouted, dragging his plunging mount to a halt.

A wary eye on the dangerous animal, Evan Huntsleigh faltered a step. "She, she rode on," he stammered, only gathering his wits when the marquess's dark brow drew down thunderously. "She raced around that bend, sir, and then I was attacked."

"He must have gone through the woods here to cut her off," cried the second man, a stranger, as he pointed to a small path that seemed to lead through the trees.

Mr. Huntsleigh watched in awe as the two riders wheeled their mounts about and crashed away down the narrow opening, the marquess taking the lead. Knowing he could do nothing to assist them, he found his horse, fortunately standing only a little distance away, and went to see to his groom, whose prone form seemed to indicate he, too, had had an encounter with the stranger's fist.

Having taken a shortcut through the woods, Deparens was able to burst out of the trees just ahead of Ariane. There was nothing she could do to avoid him with her mount rearing in fright and all her concentration by necessity on keeping her seat. Before the animal had quieted fully, Deparens lifted her from her horse and flung her facedown before him like a sack of grain.

Clamping her in place with his hand, the Frenchman charged back into the forest, not caring in the least that low-hanging branches on the narrow path tore viciously at Ariane's hair.

It was that pain to her head that roused her. She'd been stunned by the force of being thrown over his horse, but made aware of her awful predicament, she instinctively lashed out, beating on the horse beneath her with her fists and feet until it began to shy.

Deparens retaliated by grabbing a handful of her hair and shaking her. The pain was considerable, but Ariane was too frightened to be deterred long. Straining frantically, she caught the rein nearest her and pulled hard, creating such confusion that the horse reared.

To regain control, Deparens was obliged to loosen his hold on her, leaving her free to push herself away.

Unfortunately she had not realized how little control she would have. Tumbling wildly, she never saw the rock upon which she hit her head. One moment she was aware and struggling, and the next she was insensible.

Unconscious, she could not appreciate the efficiency with which Deparens quieted his frightened mount, slid to the ground, and began to tie her hands with a rope he had brought for that purpose.

Nor could she appreciate the irony that he was thus occupied with her prostrate form, when a bay stallion charged like a cannonball into the clearing. Too late Deparens dropped the rope and reached for the pistol in his waistband. The tall, dark rider had his pistol at the ready. Easily getting off the first shot, he hit Deparens in the shoulder at close range and sent him sprawling backward in the dirt.

"Rie!" Damien leapt to the ground, though his horse still moved, and coming to a skidding halt beside Ariane, he gently cupped her still, white face in his hands. At his touch, she stirred, but did not open her eyes.

Reassured by her movement, he carefully laid her head down and whirled upon Deparens, who had begun to stir in earnest. His eyes blazing with a murderous rage, Damien dragged the large man half upright.

"If you've hurt her badly, *mon ami*, you'll wish to God I'd killed you with that bullet," he swore savagely. Prematurely making good his threat, he crashed his fist into the Frenchman's jaw. It connected with a satisfying crack and laid Deparens out cold.

Damien, with Ariane's head cradled in his lap, was removing the rope from her hands when the second horseman came pounding into sight.

"Is she hurt badly?" he cried anxiously.

"Nothing seems to be broken, but she must have hit her head on that rock there. I cannot tell how bad it is." As they both watched, Ariane stirred again.

As did Deparens.

"I'll have his murder on my hands if I go near him again," Damien growled, jerking his chin toward the wounded man. Probing Ariane's head, he found a lump the size of a goose's egg. His mouth tightened grimly at his finding. "Take that rope he brought for her and tie him tightly," he ordered peremptorily.

His companion made no argument. When he'd bound their captive's hands, he also stopped to tie a makeshift bandage around his bullet wound, for it was bleeding badly.

The second time Damien probed her lump, Ariane groaned and, opening her eyes, blinked against the painful brightness of the light. "Damien?" she whispered with a puzzled frown as the dark shape above her swam into focus. Seeing his jaw tighten, she reached up to touch it. It seemed she had been wanting to that for some time, she thought confusedly.

Damien covered the slender hand offering him comfort with his own and, taking it to his mouth, kissed it softly. "Yes, sweeting, it is I."

Ariane smiled faintly and wondered at Damien's grim look, but the effort of keeping her eyes open was too much. A little sigh escaping her, she retreated into darkness.

"Can we move her, do you think?"

The voice was familiar to her. She knew it . . . though she could not think whose it was. Cradled in arms she knew instinctively to be Damien's, she found it annoying to try to think. It felt best to lie quietly . . .

Her eyes flew open. "Colin!" Ariane cried, starting up. At her sudden movement the most shattering pain pierced her head. Wincing, she fell back, closing her eyes until she thought it safe to try again.

Her handsome brother was there kneeling beside her, looking most anxious, though he was making every effort to smile a greeting. Wordlessly she held out her arms, and Damien passed her into Colin's embrace. "Is it really you, Colin?" she cried, her voice muffled by his chest.

"The one and only, back from points west, my love," he

confirmed with credible cheerfulness despite the way he frowned at her as he stroked her tangled curls. "And imagine," he continued with a wavering chuckle, "I arrived at Lord Chatham's just in time to find you up to one of your escapades."

"I was only riding," Ariane managed to retort, though her protest was a mere whisper.

And with that, to her horror, she began to cry. Why exactly she became such a watering pot, she'd have found it difficult to say. There was the unmitigated joy of having Colin solid as a rock beside her, and the reaction of the fear she'd suffered when Deparens had captured her, and not least of all, the throbbing pain in her head.

Likely they all combined to make her soak her brother's coat through, though, if truth be told, the only thought clear in her mind was the sudden realization that with Deparens captured and Colin returned, Damien had no reason at all to see her ever again.

28

Ariane rode home mounted before Colin, feeling so spent and achy that she was scarcely aware of Damien and Deparens behind them. Nor was she able to give Mr. Huntsleigh the greeting he deserved when Colin's shout signaled they had overtaken him.

For his part, Evan Huntsleigh may well have felt some embarrassment. He'd been left behind by Ariane, her attacker, and her rescuers, and now was to be found riding double with his groom, whose horse had run off. Yet his expression conveyed nothing but concern for Ariane.

"I would never have forgiven myself if anything had happened to you," he told her, his young face very grave.

"Please, Mr. Huntsleigh." Ariane shook her head, an ill-advised movement that brought her fresh pain. "It is I who should apologize for causing you concern. I am well enough, I assure you, but for this plaguey bump on my head. You will come to Grantham House tomorrow, I hope, that I may apologize as you deserve?''

Though Mr. Huntsleigh assured her no apologies were needed, Ariane insisted, and seeing how pale she was, Mr. Huntsleigh capitulated, saying that he would come, at least, to inquire after her recovery.

Reading the question in his eyes as he glanced at the stranger holding her closely, Ariane begged pardon for her lapse in manners. "This is my brother, Colin Bennington," she explained.

It was all she could do. With her eyes closed, Ariane listened only distantly to the two young men exchange greetings. Mr. Huntsleigh asked just who "the man" was, and Ariane thought Colin said that he was a Frenchman the War Office had been seeking for some time.

At the edge of town, Damien took his prisoner off, saying nothing beyond "Until later, Miss Bennington," to her. It was a measure of the uncommonly unsettled state of her nerves that his brief, formal remark brought tears to her eyes. To conceal them she nodded a farewell with her eyes closed, as if she were in great pain, and then when he had left, she buried her face in Colin's still-damp coat.

At length, Mr. Huntsleigh and his groom had bid them adieu, and when she and Colin arrived at Grantham House, it was a vast relief to find only her uncle about. She'd never have thought of a satisfactory way to explain her wild appearance to her aunt.

Sir Randall was trying enough. Frowning anxiously, he preceded Colin up the stairs to her bedroom, and though he did not say a severe word to her, his obvious chagrin that she would ride out without informing him made her feel quite as wretched as she knew she deserved to feel.

When she was tucked in her bed, the pillows piled high behind her, she sought to make amends. "I know it is little excuse, Uncle Randall," she told him, silly tears forming in her eyes, "but I did think that with both Mr. Huntsleigh and his groom for escort, I should be safe enough."

"I am only glad that you came to no lasting harm,

Ariane." Sir Randall shook his head, his restraint making Ariane feel worse, if possible. "Is Mr. Huntsleigh unscathed?"

Ariane flushed. "Not entirely," she admitted in a small voice. "Deparens knocked him from his horse. I hope he will not be completely out of charity with me when he awakens tomorrow, for he will be very sore."

"He'd not be the only one—out of charity with you, I mean," Colin spoke up, a half-smile tugging at his mouth as he regarded his sister's wan but still-lovely face. "When he discovered you had ridden off from Huntsleigh, Chatham was so angry I thought he intended to beat you, not Deparens, to a pulp."

Ariane sniffed but otherwise ignored her brother's confidence, stated in a remarkably cheerful tone, considering. Whether Damien was or was not put out with her was of little importance, after all, for she was not likely to ever see him again. "How did you and Lord Chatham come to be there, Colin? It could not have been lucky chance, surely."

Her effort to change the subject earned her a knowing smile, but Colin was not reluctant to answer. "No, luck was not involved," he acknowledged wryly. "It seems Chatham became suspicious when he saw you in conversation with Huntsleigh yesterday. He thought you were smiling the way you do, when you are wheedling something."

When Ariane made to protest with visible indignation his choice of words, he only laughed at her. "You needn't waste your reproaches on me, Rie. It's Chatham I am quoting. At any rate, when he learned your plans, he decided not to prevent your going, but to try to use you to lure the Frenchman into the open."

"And he didn't deign to tell me," Ariane cried, the use of the word "wheedle" still rankling.

Ignoring her unhappy tone, Colin looked at her curiously. "Chatham said he couldn't be certain you'd be inclined to cooperate with him if he did tell you."

Ariane's eyes fell briefly. Recalling the way she had felt toward Damien the day before, it was entirely possible she

202

would have refused to assist him. Not feeling at all like explaining the whole to Colin, she asked how they'd known which road she would take.

Seeing he would not get an answer to his unstated question, Colin shrugged. "It is the one you always take, so Chatham said. He guessed that Deparens would know as much as well. The only cover on the road is those woods, and to spring his trap, Chatham instructed Mr. Huntsleigh to stay with you until the second bend in the woods. There he was to seem to have some trouble and leave you to ride on alone. Of course, you'd not actually have been alone at all; we were there secreted in the trees, ready to accost Deparens when he moved after you.

"Unfortunately the lad couldn't keep pace from the beginning, and Deparens had his opportunity before you were in our sight. You should give thanks, my impetuous sister, that Chatham did not hesitate when we heard horses galloping, but then saw no riders."

"I am indeed grateful," Ariane sighed, gingerly rubbing the bump on her head. Unconscious, she'd have been little burden to Deparens. "Oh! Colin!" Suddenly she clapped a hand to her mouth. "Mary! I have forgotten Mary! Did Da, er, Lord Chatham tell you that Mary Mowbry is in Bath?"

For the first time, as he grinned happily, Colin's deep brown eyes lit with a bright sparkle. "He did, and as soon as I've cleaned up a bit and greeted my aunt, I shall be going to see Miss Mary Mowbry. It was only the thought of how sad she'd be, if I did not return, that kept me alive."

"You are an insufferably conceited beast," Ariane castigated him with a fond, if tired smile.

"And thinking of you and Toby," Colin added, returning that smile.

"I am glad to see you, Colin," Ariane told him softly, her eyes becoming misty.

Unable to trust his voice, Colin simply kissed her on the forehead.

"And," Ariane continued, trying for a lighter tone, "I am glad to see that you were not playing Mary for a fool, for I have come to love her dearly."

"Of course I would not play that dear, sweet girl for a fool!"

When Ariane forgot herself and laughed at her brother's bristling and welcome reply, she experienced another sharp pain. Seeing her wince, Sir Randall intervened to say it was time she rested. Clapping Colin affectionately on the back, he told her she'd have time to catch up with her scamp of a brother later.

As she drifted off to sleep, Ariane cheered herself with thoughts of Colin and Mary married. They would live at the Willows, as, of course, would she and Toby. All of them together would be a merry, cozy group.

Somehow, when she awakened, Ariane did not feel as comforted by the picture she had conjured, but Toby ran in just then and she gladly put consideration of her change of heart aside. With Toby jumping around exclaiming over Colin's return, there was little else she could do.

The next afternoon when Mr. Huntsleigh came, Ariane was greatly recovered. Her head, as she told him when he asked, was only sore to the touch.

There was no one else present but Crissie, who sat at some distance with her needlework, for Ariane had asked Dora if she might speak to Mr. Huntsleigh privately. "I have used him in a scheme of mine, and I must apologize," she'd explained.

It was an indication how well Dora knew her cousin and how much she trusted her that she had asked no questions nor made any argument, but simply said, "You will invite him to stay for tea, I hope?"

Grateful, Ariane hugged Dora tightly. "You are a dear not to ask just how I've misused the poor man, and just for that I promise that, if I have to tie him hand and foot, I shall present him to you at tea."

Though Mr. Huntsleigh once again protested that Ariane owed him no apologies, she firmly insisted that she did. "I knew that there was a danger of our being accosted, you see, but I did not tell you for fear that you would refuse to go. It was inexcusable, and to top it all, though I knew not to, I allowed the joy of riding to get the better of me and raced away, giving Deparens the chance to deal you a brutal blow.''

"You did not behave with the greatest wisdom then, it is true," Mr. Huntsleigh allowed, rubbing his chin with a rueful grimace. "But that is your only responsibility. I knew from Lord Chatham that there was danger. It all had something to do with Brighton, I gather.''

Though Mr. Huntsleigh eyed her hopefully, Ariane resisted the impulse to enlighten him. "You must ask Lord Chatham to tell you the whole," she said. Immediately a roguish twinkle lit her eyes. "No, perhaps you should not apply to him," she corrected herself with a laugh. "I'm afraid to say I acted rather rashly there, as well.''

Noting the uncertain look her companion's open countenance could not hide, Ariane laughed unself-consciously. "My brother calls me a minx, and I fear he's not much mistaken," she admitted, "but I would not have you think I take your bruises lightly. I am sorry to have involved you, a friend, in one of my escapades. I hope you will continue to feel forgiving as your bruises darken.''

When Mr. Huntsleigh with a truly endearing smile replied that her only hope of offending him permanently was to continue to doubt him, Ariane smiled happily. "Then, I hope you will give proof of your forgiveness by staying for tea. Dora particularly hoped you would," she added, watching him closely.

To her great relief, he reddened.

"Dora is a charming girl who is not given to wild starts," Ariane remarked, looking directly into Mr. Huntsleigh's nice, blue eyes.

Proving there was more to him than first met the eye, Evan Huntsleigh did not shrink from the significance of her level look. "If you are trying to warn me off, you needn't," he said with a faint smile that, surprisingly, put Ariane to the blush.

Seeing the pink rise in her cheeks, he grinned. "By Jove, I never thought to see you look at a loss, Ariane!" He teased with such relish that she was immediately put at her ease and laughed. "I may call you Ariane now, I hope?" When she nodded, he continued to address her, his tone unexpectedly wise. "I am glad to know you, Ariane—you are alive in a way few people are—but I have been aware for some time of the limit of your feelings for me. I suppose I can hardly blame you with . . ." Suddenly, he pulled himself up short and changed his tack, or so it seemed to Ariane. "At any rate," Evan Huntsleigh said with such warmth she forgot to be puzzled, "I am glad we shall be friends."

Watching Evan and Dora at tea, Ariane was enormously pleased. They were a charming couple, each one as kind and open as the other, and they would make a good marriage when they got around to tying the knot, an event she thought would happen sooner than later, no matter Dora's youth.

"It would seem Mr. Huntsleigh's sentiments have undergone a change," Corinne remarked to Ariane as they went up to their rooms after tea. Her statement reminded Ariane that Corinne had not been in company with Mr. Huntsleigh and Dora in some time, and she could not keep from having some fun at the girl's expense.

To that end, she frowned elaborately. "You think he no longer cares for Dora?" she asked with great concern.

"No! I mean, yes! Yes, yes, I do think he cares for Dora," Corinne stuttered, discomposed by Ariane's question. "He seems to like her very well indeed."

A spasm of irritation crossed Corinne's face. "You seemed to think before that he was interested in you, Rie."

Before Ariane could say, "Why, no, indeed" in the airy way she knew would infuriate Corinne further, Toby, who had been waiting in his sister's room for her, literally leapt into the fray. Bounding into the hallway, he defended his sister stoutly. "Rie doesn't like that boy at all! He can't even ride! She—"

"Toby, that is enough," his sister rounded on him firmly. "Mr. Huntsleigh may not be a bruising rider, but he is a very kind, delightful person whom I like exceedingly. In my opinion, he is the perfect match for Dora and will make her a fine husband. And, now that's all settled, Corinne, we shall bid you adieu until dinner."

With a brief nod in Corinne's direction Ariane scooted

Toby before her and quickly closed the door to her room, thinking she'd almost been served what she deserved for goading her cousin.

She had a strong suspicion about what her little brother had been going to say, and she knew she was not up to keeping all emotion from her face, if Damien de Villars' name were mentioned.

She had not long to wait to have her suspicion proven right, for no sooner had she closed the door than her little brother turned to her with a worried expression. "Rie, I had thought that, perhaps, you and Lord Chatham . . ." His high voice trailed off when Ariane shook her head.

"There was nothing between us but this business with the spy, Toby."

"Will we ever see him again?"

"I cannot say," she replied truthfully. "With Colin returned to us, there is no longer any need for Lord Chatham to act as our, ah, as our older brother."

Toby's shoulders slumped. "I suppose you're right," he allowed, scuffing at the floor with the toe of his shoe. "He hasn't even come around to see how your head is getting on." Suddenly he looked up, his lower lip thrust out mutinously. "I don't think it's fair people coming and going without a word. I liked him!"

"I know," Ariane answered him softly. "I liked him, too."

And with that Toby did something he'd not done in some little time. To hide his tears, he ran headlong to bury his head in her chest and hold her tightly around her waist.

29

"Why must I go, Colin?"

Colin eyed the stubborn thrust of his sister's delicate jaw with genuine surprise. They were only discussing an invitation to a garden party, after all. "I have it," he announced suddenly, his brow clearing. "You're piqued because Chatham's not been 'round to inquire after your health, aren't you?" Before Ariane could inform him she'd not given Lord Chatham's absence a moment's thought, Colin was explaining that Damien had not come because he had personally escorted Deparens to London. "He'll be returned in time for his godmother's party, though," he added, unwittingly assuring further contention.

"Lord Chatham's absence has nothing to do with anything," Ariane told him sharply when she was given the opportunity to do so. "I simply do not feel up to such entertainment."

"Leave off, Rie," Colin commanded, quite out of patience with her nonsensical stubbornness. "If you are up to riding, you are up to a garden party. You will go. No." He stilled her protest with a sharp movement of his hand. "You do not understand. I owe Lord Chatham a very great deal."

Raking his hand through his hair, Colin paced to the window and back before reluctantly addressing Ariane again. "Rie, Chatham's the only one at the War Office who didn't give me up for dead. Maccauley absolutely refused to waste a man on tracking me down, said I was past hope. But Chatham, who does just as he pleases, would not give up, and when he suspected I'd been sent to the Indies, he sent his own man, a secretary of some sort, after me.

"You understand, of course, that the marquess said

nothing of this to me. My authority is Maccauley himself. When I tried to thank Chatham, he would have none of it, asking only that I make no mention of it to anyone. I've broken my word to him, but only because I wish you to understand why we owe him and his family every courtesy. I can only guess at the reason for his persistence, but I do know beyond a doubt that the man saved my life.''

As Colin made his explanation, Ariane stared at him in growing horror. All too clearly she remembered calling Damien a callous, unfeeling monster, and that on her most forgiving days. Yet, while she'd been railing at him for not caring whether Colin lived or died so long as his own schemes came out successfully, Damien had, in fact, been doing everything he could to return Colin to her. Just as he had told her he would do.

"Too, Rie," Colin continued, frowning slightly because Ariane had not reacted visibly to his revelation, "Crissie will need help with Toby. I've not had the chance to tell you that I shan't be able to keep much of an eye on him. I've at last persuaded Mary to go, and I shall need to be with her, of course."

"Oh, Colin, I am glad! It is time she quit hiding away. So few know Sir Henry's crime it isn't likely she'll have the least problem. And you needn't say any more about my attending. After what you've told me, I understand your insistence that I be present."

Relieved to have the matter settled to his liking, Colin dropped a fond kiss on his sister's cheek, vowing that she would not regret her decision, and left to keep an appointment with Mary.

Ariane's brave smile faded as soon as the door closed. She'd actually forgotten that Toby had been included specifically in Lady Bandbrooke's invitation. He had been in alt, but she'd been so determined to avoid the sight of Damien with pretty, petite Miss Ashton on his arm, she had forgotten.

Clenching her hand in a tight fist, Ariane dealt the arm of her chair a hard, painful rap. The thought of facing Damien after the shameful way she'd responded to his kiss was not at all easy to contemplate.

And there had been her response to him in the woods, though at least in that instance it was only she who was aware how she'd responded. When she had first opened her eyes, before she'd had time to remember all that was between them, it had seemed to her that she would burst with love for the tender look he gave her.

Of course she realized now, in full possession of her faculties once more, that she had mistaken his ordinary concern for something more. Still, the episode had been proof of something she'd wanted to deny. She had been telling herself that her interest in Damien was merely an attraction she would overcome in time.

But it seemed her feelings could not be so lightly dismissed. Out of all reason, she loved him. He was the man whose spirit matched hers, just as she had thought that oh-so-long-ago morning after they had gone sailing.

The garden party would be torturous. Seeing the man she loved with the woman he was to marry . . . A pained smile curved her lips briefly. The situation sounded as melodramatic as something to be found in a penny novel.

Abruptly she rose and paced restlessly to the window. These morbid musings could do her little good. Damien was not for her, and never had been. There was nothing to be gained from fretting over him in this absurd way. She must put her feelings for him behind her, for only then could she get on with her life.

But first, as her sense of honor obliged her to do, she would go to his godmother's garden party and give him the thanks he was due for returning her brother to her.

Lady Helena Bandbrooke, standing quite alone, Ariane was relieved to see when the Bennington party was shown out to the terrace, was a formidable figure with a fortune in diamonds sparkling at her throat and ears, her white hair arranged in an elaborate coiffure, and her clear, penetrating gaze frankly evaluating her newest guests. She carried a cane, having not entirely recovered from the ankle injury that had kept her from the social rounds, but she said she was coming along nicely, thank you, when Colin inquired. Indeed, it amused Ariane to note that their hostess used her cane more to punctuate her conversation than as a walking aid.

"I knew that dashing father of yours, you know," she announced with a smile whose warmth surprised Ariane. "And despite my failing eyesight I can see that you've all been blessed with his good looks. What a dash he cut, my dears!" She chuckled richly as if relishing some particular memory before waving her walking stick toward David Bennington's three children. "But as I hear it, David's not entirely lost to us. He was fortunate enough to pass on his admirable spirit to you young 'uns, it would seem."

It was Colin who answered, giving Lady Bandbrooke a charming grin that put her very much in mind of his sire. "Knowing your source of information can only be Lord Chatham, I am relieved to hear that he describes our spirit as admirable and not trying, my lady. Lord knows, we could scarce blame him if he did."

Lady Bandbrooke smiled dryly. "I think it safe to say my godson's a rare one, Mr. Bennington. From the cradle he's sought out challenge, particularly"—here her shrewd, twinkling eyes came to rest lightly upon Ariane—"when it is as charmingly presented as in this instance."

"Why, thank you, Lady Bandbrooke, you are too kind." Ariane was startled into blushing fiercely as she dropped into a graceful curtsy. Then, summoning the spirit Lady Bandbrooke had extolled earlier, she added with a smile whose charm rivaled that of her brother's, "I do believe your godson could learn something about diplomacy from you."

Lady Bandbrooke chuckled heartily and remarked that it was refreshing to meet a chit with the spirit to see Damien had a fault. With new arrivals approaching, she then gestured with her walking stick to the guests disporting themselves on the lawn.

"Go on and enjoy yourselves, my dears," she urged. "We've a grand announcement to make later, and I demand that everyone be in the best of spirits to receive it."

Had she been alone, Ariane knew she'd have turned on her heel then and there, no matter what she owed Damien in the way of thanks. Lady Bandbrooke could only mean that Damien's engagement to Miss Ashton was to be formally announced at long last.

"Look, Rie," Toby cried, jerking her from her thoughts as he descended the steps to the lawn between her and Crissie. "It's Lord Chatham!"

Ariane forcibly restrained her younger brother's impulse to dash away in Damien's direction by holding tightly to his hand. It was difficult to see—the sun was in their eyes—but there seemed little doubt that the tall man with dark hair at whom Toby was gesturing was Damien, particularly as there was a small girl with golden hair clinging to his arm.

"There's such a crowd about him just now, perhaps we should go to the refreshment table first."

Ariane's simple ploy worked. "That's a capital idea," Toby approved, freeing himself to bound off for a Bath cake, a favorite treat his alert eye had spotted even from a distance.

"Now, Toby, you mustn't mound your plate!" Crissie's reminder was given to her charge's back. "That scamp will have two of everything . . ." Shaking her head, she hurried after him.

Ariane felt some guilt when she did not follow. She was responsible for Toby's running off like that, after all, but the thought of food was so unappetizing, she did not much even want to look at it. She would relieve Crissie later, she promised herself.

It was just as well she did not go, for just then, Colin turned to address her. He and Mary had been whispering to each other, Colin no doubt encouraging his shy love, and they had not heard the exchange with Toby. "Look, Rie!" Ariane's heart stopped. It would not be so easy to divert Colin. "It's Jeremy Heathcote!"

She let out a sigh of relief. Jeremy was a friend of Colin's from his school days. "So it is." She followed his gaze before linking her arm with Mary's. "You'll like him, Mary," she said, aware that her friend was facing her first introduction with some hesitation. "He's not half the rascal my brother is."

"You only liked him, Rie," Colin said, grinning down at her, "because Jeremy took your part against me, though you were an unruly child forever trailing after us when you should have been at home doing your lessons."

"Yes, I always thought Jeremy displayed the greatest good sense." Ariane nodded sagely as Mary smiled at the two of them, losing her self-consciousness as she followed their banter. "From the beginning he knew which one of us merited listening to."

They were still squabbling when they came to Jeremy Heathcote. With Colin and Ariane by her side, Mary found the introductions remarkably easy and could even stand back to observe Mr. Heathcote's reaction when he realized the beauty beside her was, lo and behold, Colin's little sister.

"Good Lord, Ariane! You've certainly changed." The appreciative look in his eye indicated that he found her transformation charming indeed.

Mary was not the least surprised that Ariane should only laugh, saying, "I hope I am not still the unruly child Colin just called me."

As if he could scarcely believe she was actually the same person, Jeremy recounted the first time he'd encountered Ariane, then a child of twelve. "What a scamp you were, dressed in breeches like a boy! And insisting on taking that mare you couldn't mount without assistance over a wall almost as high as you were tall. My heart was in my throat until Colin told me you'd been taking it since you were ten."

They all laughed, and then Colin had some story to tell of their school days together. It was amusing, but Ariane found it impossible to keep her mind on the conversation. From where she stood, she had a clear view of the area around the refreshment table and, therefore, of Toby and Crissie. They were, she saw, greeting someone, and even if she had not been able to see full well who it was, she'd have known it was Damien, because they were both smiling so broadly.

While Crissie beamed, Toby clambered upon a bench simply to show his idol how neatly he could jump down, and chattered all the while he did so.

With a sinking feeling, Ariane thought she could almost hear her little brother. "Rie wouldn't let me come to greet you while you were standing with Miss Ashton . . ." he would as likely as not say. Or, lowering thought, he might inform his hero how bereft they'd *both* been at the thought of never seeing him again.

As if on cue, Damien turned, catching her eye. His smile, as he bowed in her direction, seemed odiously knowing, and Ariane, to her fury, felt her cheeks heat.

"Rie, we've been looking all over for you!"

Her heart thudding painfully, Ariane made some greeting to Dora, Evan, and Corinne as they arrived. Introductions had to be made, but Ariane let Colin do the honors. Careful not to look again at Damien, she tortured herself with wondering if Miss Ashton had gone to join him—and if she had, imagining what Toby might say to her.

The thought was dreadful enough to send her gaze straying cautiously back to the refreshment area. Toby and Crissie were nowhere in sight. She gave their absence only a moment's thought and looked away.

She found Damien alone only a little distance further on. Though surrounded by a knot of people, it was clear he was the center of attention. It was little wonder. He was smiling as he entertained them with some story, and even from a distance Ariane could feel the effects of that flashing smile down to her toes.

He was a compelling figure. There was no denying that. Like most of the gentlemen present, he was dressed in a coat of superfine, a pair of buckskin breeches, and gleaming Hessians. But what Damien did for that coat and those skin-tight breeches, no one else could.

It was almost too much, she thought, the way a lock of his black hair had fallen forward to curl onto his brow. It made him seem approachable.

"We've just been speaking with Cecily Ashton." Ariane's attention was returned abruptly to Dora. The Granthams having come earlier by separate carriage, there had been some discussion of whom they'd seen that afternoon. "She's quite as pretty as always, and you won't credit it, but—"

"Why, look! Someone is taking out a rowboat," Ariane ruthlessly interrupted her younger cousin's bubbly remarks. Though she knew she must eventually, she could not just now bear to hear the news of Damien's betrothal confirmed.

To her relief, Jeremy Heathcote at once voiced the opinion that they should go down to the little lake that lay at the foot of the garden, and hold races. Dora's unfinished remark was forgotten as everyone rushed to agree. "Come, Rie." Jeremy extended his hand. "We shall be a winning combination, I'm sure."

"I shall join you a little later," Ariane improvised quickly. "I promised Crissie I would relieve her with Toby about this time. Take Corinne in my place, however, I vow she's lightning in a rowboat."

Jeremy took her suggestion with good grace, as, surprisingly, did Corinne. Why Ariane had recommended her cousin, she wasn't certain, though the sight of Corinne standing a little apart from the others had somehow pulled at her sympathies.

But Ariane did not spend much time thinking of Corinne. The thought uppermost in her mind just then was that she must escape the gay and amiable gathering.

Unlike the other guests, her spirits were so grim she was afraid she'd soon betray herself to those who knew her well.

She'd accepted when she came that she would have to endure the sight of Damien and Cecily together, but she'd not counted upon having to extend them felicitations.

Felicitations meant a date had been set, and a specific day made their wedding seem of a sudden very real. Made almost ill by the thought, she'd not been able even to bear hearing it mentioned in casual conversation.

At least for a time she must retreat. Perhaps alone, she could recover some degree of equanimity and then make her return with, if not a smile, at least her head held high.

30

It was not so easy to get away as she'd hoped it would be. First, she had to respond brightly to her Uncle Randall, who came to greet her with an old friend who had known her parents. Then, she had to appease her Aunt Chloe, who hurried over to demand anxiously why she was not with the other young people down by the lake. Told that her niece's head injury was the result of a fall from her horse, Lady Grantham had worried that Ariane had sustained some permanent, if undetected injury.

From her aunt Ariane learned that Damien had saddled a pony for Toby's use and that her brother and Crissie were at the stables.

Keeping a wary eye out for Damien and Miss Ashton, Ariane hurriedly made the excuse that she wished to see to Toby, something she did intend to do later, and escaped her aunt and the party at last.

The air that day was soft, its faintly sweet scent reminding her of Appledyne and awakening a longing to be there, where there was nothing very difficult to face.

Choosing the path that seemed least used, Ariane followed it until after a time she came to a summerhouse whose very isolation appealed to her. After dusting off a step, she took a seat, a wild rose she'd picked along the way in her hand. Relieved that she could do as she liked, she tossed her straw bonnet down beside her.

Absently, as she lifted her face to the sun, she worried at the flower's petals. If only she had summoned the courage to approach Damien when he was with Toby and Crissie, she might have stayed where she was for the rest of the afternoon. It was not so difficult here alone, in the sun.

She could almost forget Damien and his bride-to-be. Ariane closed her eyes tightly, the tears lurking just below the surface, pricking at her lids. She would eventually have to search him out. She would thank him, then bid him farewell, long life, good health, a lovely wedding, and the goal of it all, a sound heir. At the thought, the last waxy petal from her rose floated to the ground, leaving a thorny stem in her hand.

"Does he love you?"

Ariane whirled furiously about, her heartbeat suddenly trebling its pace.

Staring dumbstruck, she saw it was, indeed, Damien, propped comfortably against a tree only a few feet away from her, who had spoken. She might have cried her frustration aloud, she was not certain, but she did rail silently at fate for allowing Damien to happen upon the path she'd taken. She was not yet ready for him, she upbraided chance.

Damien uncoiled himself and nodded toward the naked stem. "Does he love you?" he repeated, unsmiling.

Ariane looked down at the stem as if she had never seen it before. "No," she said abruptly, her voice cool. "It would seem not." She reached for her hat, intending to go.

Swift as a cat, Damien scooped it up, then dropped down beside her. "He would be a fool not to love you," he said, his voice soft as the air.

It seemed to Ariane a cruel game to tell her she was desirable on the day when he would announce his intent to wed another. "Pulling petals is nonsense," she informed him shortly, rising. "As childish as were my feelings." She extended her hand for her hat.

It was child's play for Damien to catch her hand and gently but firmly pull her down beside him. "I like children's games. Don't go, we've yet to talk."

After a moment's unequal struggle, Ariane conceded him the victory and let her hand lie limply in his. Damien squeezed it gently. "If you fear I shall scold you over Deparens, I promise to reserve my remarks for another day. This afternoon is far too lovely to cloud with bygones."

Ariane could sense his smile and cast him a tart look. "You've not such a sharp tongue that I'm afraid of it, sir."

217

"We are making progress, I've won an entire sentence."

Unable to resist, Ariane glanced at him again, her eyes resting for a heartbeat on his curving mouth. When his smile deepened under her scrutiny, her gaze flicked upward.

"What is it, Rie? You've never been reticent before." His eyes were as soft as velvet.

She tore her gaze away and with the tip of her tongue moistened her dry, stiff lips. Damien watched, a new gleam in his eye, but Ariane was so intent on gathering her courage, she did not notice. "I feel the most frightful fool," she admitted at last in a rush.

Damien's mouth twitched. "No wonder you're blue-deviled."

At once she rounded on him irritably. "I do not find it the least amusing to be in your debt."

When Damien's brow lifted in surprise, she took a deep breath to settle her nerves. "It's about Colin. He has told me what you did for him, Damien. I-I can never thank you adequately."

Damien was no longer smiling, though he was doing something almost as disconcerting. With his thumb he was gently tracing circles on the palm of her hand, the seemingly simple gesture sending shivers up and down her spine.

"You owe me no thanks, Rie. I gave you my word that I would find Colin in return for your efforts in Brighton."

"But I didn't trust you," she blurted out, shamed. "And you know as well as I, I thought the most dreadful things."

"As I recall, when Mowbry announced Colin's fate, I gave you little reason not to believe him. With Deparens holding you hostage, it did not seem the time to give you a reasoned explanation of the vague theory I had."

Damien's tone was so reasonable, Ariane couldn't withhold a rueful smile. "And I ran off before you could come to give it later. I am sorry, Damien."

With infinite gentleness, Damien grazed her cheek with his knuckles. "Let's cry truce, Rie. In truth I've as many regrets as you about what took place in Brighton. But it is

218

not the past that prompted me to follow you here. It is of the future that I wish to speak."

Even as she registered the information that fate had had nothing to do with his unexpected appearance, Ariane's stomach plummeted to her toes like a deadweight. What future could he possibly propose to her? He was in such a mellow mood . . . Could he still be seeing himself in the role of her guardian? Perhaps he would suggest she imitate him and seek out the joys of holy matrimony . . .

"I have my future planned," she cried quickly before he could crush her by suggesting that she live intimately with another man. "I shall live at the Willows with Colin and Mary. I shan't ever marry. I know I wouldn't care for matrimony. I am too headstrong." She looked away, imperceptibly straightening her shoulders as she did so. "But allow me to congratulate you on your future, my lord." Her voice, she was proud to note, was steady. "I am certain Miss Ashton will make you a model marchioness."

Damien did not reply at once, but leaned back upon the step. Because he did not release her hand, Ariane was forced either to lie full-length beside him or to turn and face him. She chose the latter course. He was, she saw, gazing abstractly into the middle distance.

"Will Cecily make me a model wife, do you think?" he mused lazily after a moment.

"Well! Of all the nonsensical questions to ask," Ariane gasped, indignation sparking in her eyes. "Of course I cannot say."

As if she'd not spoken, he continued half-wonderingly, "She cannot ride . . ."

"She cannot ride at all?" Ariane was astonished into echoing.

Again he did not seem to hear her. "And she fears water to such an extent she will not even venture into a rowboat on the lake there." Damien shrugged. "She hates any form of travel. Even this trip to Bath has been a trial to her."

Suddenly Damien looked up at Ariane. Unprepared, she caught her breath at the warmth of the gleam in his eye. "And, I do not imagine, though I cannot say for certain, that Cecily would tremble if I touched her. I have not

219

touched her, you understand—I have never had the least inclination to do so—but if I had, I imagine she'd have frozen like a block of ice."

At his words an anger such as Ariane had never known swept her. His plans for her future were clearer now. She was not a block of ice, they both knew that well enough. Though he would marry Cecily to please his family, he intended to take her for his mistress.

"You scoundrel!" She lashed out vigorously at his chest. "You, you rake," she spat, redoubling her efforts in her fury. "How convenient for you. Miss Ashton for your wife and me for your mistress! Well, I am sorry to disappoint you, my lord, but I have no intention of accepting such an offer."

Incredibly, infuriatingly, oh, she did want to kill him! Damien gave a great shout of laughter, his amusement rendering him helpless against the blows she rained freely upon his shoulders as well as his broad chest.

At last, though weak from laughing, he caught her hands, pulling Ariane around so that she must face his dancing eyes directly. "You would make the worst of mistresses, sweeting."

Perversely, Ariane was insulted. "Whatever do you mean?" she demanded.

To her intense irritation, Damien laughed again, but with her hands held fast, she was powerless to resist him when he not ungently pulled her down so that she lay half across his chest, her face only inches from his. "Because, my little firebrand"—he smiled a smile of aching sweetness—"you are far too inclined to jealousy."

She ignored the warmth of his breath on her cheek. "I am not!"

"You are." His fine mouth curved. "You've been positively green since you were told that I was betrothed. Erroneously."

Ariane's mouth opened, but no sound emerged for several seconds, and when she did find her voice at last, it sounded oddly raspy. "What do you mean?"

"I mean, my sweet, that sometime this afternoon, it is my brother, Lionel, who will announce his engagement to

Cecily. You've not met Lionel, but he is much more the gentleman than I, which is likely why Cecily has been enamored of him since they were in leading strings together.'' Damien smiled indulgently into Ariane's wide green eyes. "Did I neglect to tell you that the count was misinformed as to which of the de Villars had an understanding with Miss Ashton?"

Ariane's eyes flashed. "You know very well you did," she cried, trying to twist away.

Her efforts only had the effect of making Damien's gaze smolder. "You are having a pronounced effect upon me, my dear." His grin flashed, devilish and irresistible. "And unless you wish to consummate our marriage here and now, I suggest you make an effort to be still."

Despite herself Ariane's pulse quickened. Then, realizing suddenly exactly what it was he'd said, she looked up startled.

"At last you listen." He smiled so that her heart turned over.

Unable to resist the temptation her soft, open lips presented, he kissed her, pulling her close against him so that she was achingly aware how her breasts pressed against his firm chest.

Damien pulled back only when Ariane was breathless, her cheeks were flushed, and her heart hammered painfully. "You will marry me?" he demanded gruffly.

Ariane searched his black eyes a long minute before answering, and then it was not to say yes.

"You are certain you want me for a wife, my lord?" Though her voice was husky, it was plain that she was deadly serious. "I've no dowry to speak of, and I behave like no marchioness I've heard tell of, as you well know. Your family must certainly object to me on every count."

"They could never object to your beauty, my love." Damien laughed softly when Ariane's eyes flashed with warning. "You are temptingly easy to tease, I'm afraid." He grinned and kissed her nose. "But I shall be serious, and as you've asked, I shall reveal to you that my family has long despaired of my ever marrying anyone. I have had many women, it is true, but not one of them interested me for long. They all lacked something—generally spirit. But if they had spirit, then they lacked intelligence. Or if they possessed intelligence, then they lacked passion. Do you understand, my love? You are the woman I have been waiting for, and my family is, for I have already told them about you, so delighted with the news that I wish to marry that they do not give a fig for your dowry. Now, what is your answer?''

Ariane laughed at him, a gurgling sound of pure joy. "I say yes, my lord."

She'd scarcely finished answering before she was once more lost in his embrace. It was some little time before they came up for air, but when they did, she moved away a fraction. "Why did you not tell me about Cecily and Lionel before, you beast?''

Damien seemed more interested in nuzzling her ear than in answering, but Ariane would not be distracted, pushing on his chest until Damien admitted defeat with a sigh. "In the first place, you would scarcely speak to me at all, and in the second, I was somewhat distracted with the matter of keeping you safe, despite your best efforts to put yourself in danger. Do you realize that this is the first time since I met you that I've had nothing more serious to address than your sweet lips?''

Thus reminded, Damien once again claimed Ariane's lips. "I think you had best marry me forthwith, little witch," he confided huskily after several minutes. "You enchant me so, I cannot be certain of my control. And I have no intention of leaving you as I did in Brighton.''

"Is that why you left?''

"You needn't look so radiant at the thought that I was forced to turn tail and run, but I suppose in the interest of truth I should gratify your vanity and tell you it is why I left so abruptly, and why I remained away so long. Maccauley had requested my presence in London, but there was nothing urgent in his summons.'' A corner of Damien's mouth drew down in a wry grimace. "And then, when I returned, you were wearing that deliciously flimsy costume of Triens'. I very nearly called him out over it.''

"You were jealous!'' Ariane laughed, absurdly pleased.

"But you needn't have been. The count interested himself in me only for the insubstantial reason that I am young. I realize that now."

"Foolish infant," Damien chided indulgently. "I grant that it was your youth and considerable beauty that first attracted him, but once he came to know you, he was helpless. I had not expected him to fall in love with you, you know, though I can't say I would not have used you in the same way had I known. He was that dangerous. Can you understand, Rie?"

Ariane nodded. "Yes. I have thought a great deal about it all, and I have come to accept what you did. It is true that I could not have been friendly with him had I known everything. But, my love, you must accept that I did care for him and even that I can understand why he worked as a spy."

"Will it help, compassionate child, if I tell you that he is being sent back to France in exchange for a man of ours?"

"Oh, yes, Damien! It does, indeed. He did not seem so cruel as Sir Henry, and I thought he did not deserve the same fate. Thank you for telling me."

Damien smiled. "Having secured your hand in marriage, I can afford to be generous." After kissing her nose lightly, Damien rose, lifting Ariane up after him. "Come along, my love. Let's tell your brother that I have proposed just as he told me I could."

"Colin knew?"

Damien laughed into her stunned eyes. "You must not look so very put out, love. I swore him to secrecy until I could return from London."

Little wonder that Colin had been so adamant that she attend this party, Ariane thought, smiling, as they returned to the festivities, where they were met by a barrage of congratulations. Colin, it seemed, had not been able to wait for their return to apprise everyone that he knew what their absence portended.

Toby's was the most exuberant response, for he jumped up and down, exclaiming, "I knew it! I knew it!" when he saw them approaching hand in hand.

"Well, I did not, you sly puss," Lady Grantham cried,

rushing to kiss Ariane's cheek. "Sir Randall has explained the whole to me. What a pair you two are!"

Dora claimed she had long suspected there was something havey-cavey about Ariane's relations with the marquess. "No one could feel as strongly about a mere cousin as you did, Rie!"

Mr. Huntsleigh came, too, kissing Ariane's hand and saying he had guessed long since that something deep ran between the two, a belief that Mary allowed she had shared.

That so many had known or suspected prompted Ariane to remark she was the only one who seemed not to have known what was afoot.

"Only because you're too stubborn to admit what is as plain as the nose on your face, sister mine!"

Colin was given a rude punch, but everyone, Crissie included, had a laugh at Ariane's expense.

To Ariane's relief, Damien's family greeted the news with as much pleasure as he had said they would. Lady Bandbrooke actually thanked her for "settling the boy at last."

Lionel, to whom she finally was presented, gave her a heartfelt kiss on the cheek, saying, "So you are the vixen Cecily maintains is such a perfect match for my outrageous brother!" Cecily, who had come to offer her congratulations, blushed at being quoted, but smiled shyly as Lionel continued his greeting. "I can see for myself what brought you to the scamp's notice, Miss Bennington, you're the beauty he said you were. Our father, by the by, sends his regrets. He did want very much to travel down from Suffolk to meet firsthand the girl who 'pulled the greatest trick imaginable.' Those are his words, my dear. He is predisposed to treat you as a veritable treasure for the magic you've worked on this rascal, and in his name, I welcome you into the de Villars family."

It seemed to Damien, at least, an appropriate time for another kiss, and certainly Ariane did not object, though half the garden party looked on clapping and shouting as he took her in his arms.